CROW

THE RIVER BEND SERIES

TJ MAKKAI

This book is a work of fiction. The characters, events and storyline are drawn from the author's imagination and are not to be construed as real. Any resemblance to actual persons, living or dead, businesses, companies, or events is entirely coincidental.

For information contact:

info@makkaibooks.com
makkaibooks.com

Editing: Starr Waddell with Quiethouse Editing
Cover: Jason Van Winkle
Formatting: Bad Doggie Designs
Website: Scott Oine with LittleBox Social

ISBN: 9781735477831

I dedicate this book to my favorite library patron
My Mom
Grace

CROWS

*Black birds known for their intelligence and
adaptability, and for their loud, harsh "caw."*

—Live Science Website

CROW

verb

1. *To make the loud shrill sound characteristic of a
   cock*
2. *To utter a sound expressive of pleasure*
3. *Exult,   Gloat.   Brag,   Boast*

noun

1. *Any of various large glossy black birds related to
   the jays*

—Merriam-Webster Dictionary

CHAPTER ONE

Seventy-two hours ago, I had proudly walked across a stage in my cap and gown, and accepted my college diploma, full of accomplishment and with a slight hangover. What I could not have known at the time was that graduating from college pales in comparison to surviving attempted murder, finding the true meaning of family, and owning up to your past decisions. And maybe finding love for yourself and others.

It was now Tuesday afternoon, and again, I was slightly hungover.

Debby—my red Ford Escort, who I'd named after Debby Boone, the 1970s singer—and I rattled north on Interstate 90, which was dotted with farmland and exits to small towns. I was aiming for River Bend, on the Wisconsin side of the

Mississippi River, to stay with my aunt Ellen Grace—we called her EG—for the summer.

I would be playing caretaker and chauffeur for her because, at the age of forty-three, she was battling cancer and needed weekly chemo treatments throughout the summer. Her prognosis was good, but the doctors had said it would get worse before it got better.

I glanced at the gas gauge. Oh, god, no. I'd been too distracted to notice it was almost on E.

I turned off the air-conditioning to save gas and calculated how far I was from a gas station, my stomach knotting up. My phone rang a second later, startling me, and I grabbed it to see who was calling. Mom.

"Hey, Mom, I can't talk right now, I'm driving."

"Oh, Claudia, I thought you would be there already. I wanted to see how EG is," she said.

I rolled my eyes. "I already told you, I got a late start this morning. I'll be there in thirty minutes."

"Ok, honey, let me know when you get there."

"Talk to you later." I hung up, feeling guilty.

My parents didn't know about the court date I'd had this morning, and I'd lied to them about why I wouldn't be able to leave for River Bend the morning after the graduation ceremony.

I had the best parents ever. They gave me everything a girl could want. Not in the spoiled, I-have-everything type of way but in the way of love, support, guidance, and just being there whenever I needed them. I tended to tell them everything, but I just did not want to hear the mocking when I told them about my court date. My younger brother, Connor, would be relentless (as would I if it were reversed). Plus, I was blaming this court date on my boyfriend, Jackson.

Several weeks ago, I had pulled in sideways on the side of the road so Jackson could pee. I was sure it looked like I was screaming at the tree line when the police car pulled up.

The officer asked if I had been drinking, eyeing me warily.

I could not tell him my boyfriend had had to pee so badly that I'd pulled over, and he'd hopped out of the rolling car to pee behind a tall bush and that I had been yelling for him to hurry up.

"I think we'd better do a Breathalyzer to be sure," the officer said.

I gave him a little smile, but my throat felt like it was going to totally close up. "W-well, ok."

After administering the Breathalyzer, he narrowed his eyes and stared at me for an uncomfortable minute, probably surprised by the result. "You've blown under the limit, but I have to give you a summons to court so you can pay your other fines."

"I don't understand. I don't have any speeding tickets. I rarely drive while here at school," I said, feeling smug since I had beaten the Breathalyzer. Dealing with smart-mouth college kids must suck for police officers.

"Miss, only the first twelve violations showed up on my computer, but there are even more than that. You owe nine hundred and forty dollars, and from what I see, with this funny parking job and all those tickets, you should go to driving school again and learn how to park and feed parking meters. Here is the summons to see the judge on Tuesday, May twenty-second." Backlit by his headlights, the officer held out the piece of paper with a smirk and walked back to his car.

As I looked down at the summons, everything started to come together. I had been letting Jackson use my car all year long and had not realized what he'd meant when he kept saying "Meters don't count."

I only had one option: get back in my car and drive away. Jackson would not come out of the bushes while the cop was still there. If he'd heard any part of the conversation and knew what was good for him, he would be running down the alley and across the field and not show up at my place tonight. He would know to show up with the money and flowers tomorrow, right?

I realized on the way home that I had to go to court and beg for mercy. I didn't think I should pay the fines, and I knew Jackson did not have the money. Students with fines were allowed to participate in the graduation ceremony, but my college would not mail diplomas to anyone who had fines outstanding with the school or the city.

Jackson kept saying he would pay the fines, but while he was quick with talk of money and lots of apologies, cold hard cash never materialized.

I had enough to cover the fines, but I had a job with a publishing company lined up for September and would have to put a deposit down on an apartment in Chicago soon. While I cared for EG this summer, my income would be nil but so would my expenses.

This morning, I had gone into court prepared to show the judge that I had rarely driven and had, instead, taken the bus because parking was hard to find. Well, legal parking was hard to find.

Looking around the courtroom as I sat down, I thought, Why isn't Jackson here to support me?

I soon grew bored waiting for my name to be called and twiddled my thumbs. I need him now more than ever. I thought he would always stand by me.

I had once been accused of stealing a term

paper and threatened with expulsion. Jackson had come to my rescue by figuring out that two printing jobs had been mixed up and I hadn't noticed when I assembled the project in the binder. He helped me prepare my statement and get backup material, and he even got a second professor to make a statement for me.

Things had been going so well that I had suggested we live together this fall. We balanced each other with our wants and needs, and I thought living together was the natural next step.

He had encouraged me to take the job in Chicago despite the salary not being great. No one but me knew how poor the salary really was.

I had encouraged him to find a kitchen apprenticeship for a semester and join a band so he could work on his music. And if nothing happened with his music by the end of the fall semester, then he could finish his degree, and his résumé would still look good because of the apprenticeship.

Although he would only be there temporarily, it would give me time to find a job that paid a living wage.

"Claudia Middleton," the court clerk said loudly, jolting me out of my thoughts.

As I walked to the front, I regretted the goodbye margaritas with my roommates last night. I didn't know one could go from bored to ridiculously shit-stopping nervous in under three seconds.

Judge Lobal confirmed my identity and reviewed my case within nine seconds. He paused, which put me in a panic so I started talking.

"Good morning. Yes, sir. The fines. Nine hundred and forty dollars. Belong to my car. But not to me. Someone else was driving my car. Yes, the fines are on my car. I have a campus bus card. I was in class during the ticket times. Here's a signed statement from the bus driver confirming my attendance on the bus during those days." The people in the courtroom laughed at that. "I just ask to pay. I mean, pay monthly. I mean, wish you'd set up payment plan." Oh, help me.

From high up on the bench, the judge peered over his bifocals and waved his hand. "Miss?"

"Yes," I squeaked out between breaths.

"You wish to pay the fines?"

"Yes. No. I mean to say I just need a payment plan. I have a job, but it doesn't start until September . . . I'll be caring for my EG this summer. And I'm unclear whether the other person involved will have the money before I do."

Something flickered on the judge's face. "Miss Claudia Middleton, would you be the niece of Ellen Grace Graham—the author?"

"How do you . . . ah, um." Get it together before you say or do something really dumb. "Yes, sir. That is me. Claudia. Miss Claudia Middleton."

Hell's bells, that was stunning. What is happening to me? It's just parking tickets. What if this was something more serious? I'd be a complete horror show opposed to an annoying nitwit. Focus. I need to focus.

Judge Lobal looked at me pointedly. "I understand that a fine of this size is a challenge for a college graduate with a delayed employment. Will you accept a reduced fine of one hundred fifty dollars and one hundred forty hours of community service?"

"Ugh," I muttered.

"There is a senior living center in River Bend that could use volunteers. You are to report to Judge Konrad in River Bend within two weeks. Report to her your temporary address, registration of volunteering, and every two weeks, your accumulated volunteer hours. Once the fine is paid and the community service hours are completed, her office will notify me and this case will be closed. Failure to comply with any of these rules will result in the original fine of nine hundred forty dollars, plus three hundred twenty-five dollars for court fees and the hassle. Your diploma will be held until we hear from Judge Konrad."

Judge Lobal banged down the gavel. "Court dismissed for lunch until one thirty." He stood up, and his brown eyes hit mine with a look I have never seen before.

He quickly went through the door, and the crowd murmured behind me, unhappy about the two-and-a-half-hour break until their cases could be heard.

I stood there, breathing slowly, sweat running down my back despite the freezing temperature in the room.

The court officer tapped me on the shoulder. "You're dismissed. You can go."

I wandered out to my car, which was loaded down with everything I owned.

Jackson stood beside it, looking like a lost puppy, holding a vase of flowers. "How did it go?"

"Well, they dropped the fine to one fifty and gave me a hundred and forty hours of community service."

Jackson smiled and bounced on his toes. I almost thought that he wanted to keep the flowers for himself.

"That's great, babe. Let me pay you now. Do you want to go back in and pay? Why do you look so pale? Was it Mad-Dog Judge Lobal on the stand today?"

"It was him. Although I don't know about any Mad-Dog in his name."

"It's from—"

"I don't care where it's from. I still have to do the community service, not you! How does that make sense? I can't take care of EG, find a summer job, and do the community service. I didn't really even get a chance to explain. I did a lot of talking, but Lobal connected me to EG and put this all into motion, dismissed the court, and gave me a weird look on his way out."

"Maybe he's a big fan of EG and her books and got sidetracked when her name was mentioned." He smiled and held out the flowers. "Here take these. I also made you and EG some soup. That's why I didn't make it to court. I was late, and I wasn't sure if I could come in after the doors closed. Some of the soups are still warm. You can freeze them when you get to EG's."

What Jackson lacked in timelines and the ability to plug meters, he definitely made up for in his cooking.

CHAPTER TWO

I snapped back to reality when the car radio started playing George Harrison's "Got My Mind Set on You." He might have been rock royalty, but I didn't think there was a worse song. Not even Starship's "We Built This City."

My mother had introduced me to '70s music, but my dad had given me my love of '80s music. We didn't always agree on who the best rock groups were, but we did agree that some of the music still held up over thirty years later. My dad can provide a lyric from an '80s song for any occasion, and because of that, "Back on the Chain Gang" by the Pretenders rattled around in my mind until my thoughts wandered back again to *How am I going to tell Mom and Dad I got community service? Oh, god, please let me make it to a gas station.*

This morning, I had dressed nicely and fixed my hair to look respectable for court, but now, with the windows down, I looked like a frizzy blonde mutt who'd had its head stuck out the car window for the last hour. Jackson's flowers were being shredded by the wind in the passenger seat.

Up ahead, the Welcome to River Bend sign heralded the city limits, greeting me as it had all passersby for generations. A feeling of warmth flooded me. *Some great memories here.*

River Bend was a typical small Midwestern town, on the Mississippi River, surrounded by farms and home to Jameson College. I thought about the Fourth of July parades I'd attended, which had ranged from dismal to epic, depending on the weather. At least five scarecrows were always in the parade. Scarecrows were everywhere in River Bend. EG was to blame for that because of her first story.

EG was a tremendous writer even in the beginning. *The Scarecrow* had started as an award-winning short story when EG was in high school. In college, she developed it into a novel at just twenty-one years old. Before that, her first paying writing job was at the age of nineteen working for a small publishing house that printed magazines for women living in rural communities and farms. That was the start of EG's successful publishing career.

The book made her and the town famous. River Bend would have gone unnoticed if it hadn't been for EG. The locals took such pride in the book becoming a national best seller, they decided to embrace the scarecrow theme.

Bronze statues had been erected through the town, and scarecrow Christmas ornaments were sold year-round, as well as scarecrow window displays in shops that sold tacky scarecrow T-shirts and bumper stickers.

EG went on to write many successful mysteries, and one was even considered for a movie. That first story, though, was the one that brought fame to River Bend. It also brought hundreds, maybe thousands, of scarecrows.

What a legacy, I thought. Scarecrows.

My prayers to the gas gauge held up. *Almost.* I did make it to the gas station. Just not to the gas pump. I rolled into the lot on fumes, and my car stopped eight feet from the pump.

What am I supposed to do now?

Feeling humiliated, I got out of the car and stood there, dripping in sweat. It was past hot, and the humidity was beyond anything people should have to deal with. My perfectly highlighted blonde hair went from windblown to being plastered on my face.

Cars beeped at me as they maneuvered around my car. *I know I'm blocking traffic. Do you think the beeping is going to suddenly move my car?*

To add insult to injury, a big white splotch plopped down on the roof of my car. I looked up, shielding my eyes, and saw a crow flying past. *That was close.*

Another car honked its horn, pushing me to think. *It will be ok. It really can't get worse than this.*

Then, I got hit in the head with a ball. A deflated white football.

"Who has *white* balls?" I mumbled and picked it up.

"A lot of men do," said a guy standing by a pickup truck at the pump.

"What?" I finally got the joke, and heat rose in my cheeks. "Oh."

Again, I thought this couldn't get worse, but then, Sheriff Thomas Dalton came over.

He gave me a look of pity as if I were a damsel in distress. "Hey, push the car while I pop it into neutral," he said, motioning at White Ball Pickup Truck Dude.

Sheriff Dalton hopped into my car, and the two men maneuvered it to the pump. I was nervous the sheriff would rub against Debby and get dirt on his crisp clean uniform or some oil would drip on his boots. Never a wrinkle or spot would be found on him. I have only met him a handful of times, but I have a feeling he is one man that can work the iron and ironing board and he would not subject his wife to do it.

"Good to see you, Claudia. How is EG doing?" the sheriff asked.

I was thankful for the subject change. "She's fine. Treatments started last week, but she seems to handling it well. She told me you won the campaign for sheriff last year. Youngest sheriff in the state! It's a bit late, but congratulations."

His mouth twisted up in a little smile, and he got out of the car. "I appreciate that."

White Ball Dude stepped away from my car, and Sheriff Dalton bent down and looked through the back window at all my possessions.

"Do you have money for gas?" he said as he straightened back up.

I nodded, hoping to be spared any more embarrassment, but White Ball Dude sidled up and pulled a plastic Subway sandwich bag off the back of my sweaty leg.

Sheriff Dalton waved and said, "Ok, then. Sorry about the ball hitting you. Give my best to EG. Tell her if she needs anything to give me a call." As he strolled back to the squad car, he yelled, "I also have a broken hockey stick if you want it now."

Thank god, White Ball Dude responded before I had to figure out whether he was talking to me or not.

CHAPTER THREE

I pulled into EG's driveway and sighed with relief, remembering my past visits. The house was a simple white two-story with a black steepled roof and a screened-in front porch. Some years, EG planted flowers, but the yard was still charming when she didn't.

I wished I could have planned to stay longer, into the fall, which was the best time of the year in River Bend. Three maple trees in her yard showed the full range of the fall color spectrum. New England in October had nothing on River Bend. That little town showed off the best of Wisconsin, and EG's house could have been on the cover of the very magazine she used to write for.

I had always felt comfortable and at ease here, not bored, which might have been the case with most small towns, though I had never really explored the town itself. My visits had always centered on EG and the gatherings at her house. On the occasional weekend home from college, I spent one night with EG and continued on in the morning to St. Paul, MN, where my parents and younger brother, Connor, lived.

EG and my mom, Katie Lyn, who is seven years older, were born and raised in River Bend. My mom had attended college here and met my dad, and they stayed for a few years while trying to start a family. Once they had me, they immediately moved to St Paul.

Mom was always surprised that EG had returned to River Bend after attending college in Minneapolis. EG had traveled the world but always returned to River Bend. In her midtwenties after she married, they bought the house she currently lives in. She tragically lost her husband a year after their wedding but still chose to remain in River Bend.

I got out of my car and stood with my hands on my hips, looking at the house. Excitement welled up in me. I had missed EG, and we'd all been worried since her diagnosis.

I walked to the screened-in porch, which was a second living area with a comfortable sofa and several chairs. Guests usually preferred that couch to the guest bed upstairs.

I knocked on the front door. No answer came, so I knocked again. Still no answer. Trying the knob, I found the door unlocked and poked my head in.

"EG? Are you home?"

The living room was empty, and the lights were off. *Is she napping or upstairs writing?*

The cross breeze pushed my hair across my cheek, but the heat was ever present in the house. EG had never had central heating and air installed and even refused a window air-conditioning unit. She said she'd rather listen to the hum of the fan and the song of crickets. That might have been great for the fall, but I would have rather listened to a jackhammer than have to survive this sweltering heat all summer.

I quietly closed the door behind me. I heard news radio playing from the kitchen. EG is the only person I know who has an AM/FM radio in her kitchen. It's the old-school type of radio with an antenna and no capability to listen to any type of streaming service. It said something about a fisherman finding some bones before it switched back to the farm report. Meandering through the living room, I ran my hand along book spines on the bookshelf that took up one whole wall. Its shelves were filled with knickknacks and several hundred books. A picture frame my brother made at summer camp years ago stood there with a picture of EG and me from the road trip we took to pick up Connor from that very camp several hours north. I was probably thirteen or fourteen years old at the time. Our shirts and faces were covered in blueberry and cherry pie stains.

It had been her idea to stop at the roadside stand and eat while sitting in the back of her Jeep with our legs dangling out. A stray cat had walked under the Jeep, and its tail had flicked across EG's leg. She was so startled she managed to knock the pies out of both of our hands, and they landed all over us.

We laughed so hard tears streaked down our checks. Only EG would think to capture the moment.

The frame was next to a wooden beaded necklace given to her by some Indigenous women from somewhere in South America, where she had gone on a mission trip for several months after her husband died. On the trip, she helped cultivate farmland in developing areas. By working hard days and sleeping from exhaustion, she somehow learned to move forward. EG learned if these women in the poorest areas of the world can live and raise children without modern medicine and only the basic items to survive, she could live and maybe one day thrive.

In the dining room, between the living room and kitchen, an epic dining table sat empty. It was long and curvy but not an oval nor a rectangle and had a natural live-cut edge. Ten people could sit comfortably around it, in chairs of mixed styles. Its odd shape lent itself to simple intimacy or open family. It was such a statement piece its function was understated by the beauty of its artful presence.

I ran my hand along its smooth surface, memories of EG's amazing book club dinners coming back to me. The guest list was rarely the same, and to be invited to one was a treat. EG had a gift of bringing together the right mix of people.

My first year of college, I had attended a dinner with two high school students; EG's dentist; Phil (who owns the local hardware store); a real estate agent; and EG's next-door neighbor, Jorge. Three years later, we still all emailed each other. Those five hours of that one night brought about some of my best running relationships although we had not been in the same room since then.

I smiled, hoping EG might feel up to hosting a book club dinner this summer.

I walked into the kitchen to get a drink to replace some of the water I'd lost from sweating so much. EG sat on a barstool at the kitchen island, staring out the window, with a mug in her hands. Her face was bathed in the natural light streaming in from outside. She'd always had a natural beauty and wore very little makeup. Through the years, her floppy, wavy reddish-blonde hair had fluctuated between short bobs to long locks cascading down her back. Now, she had it just above her shoulders and had a habit of tucking it behind her ears. I had seen pictures of her and my mom when they'd been in their twenties, and they still looked the same twenty years later.

"There you are. I figured you might be writing" I said.

She didn't move or respond.

"EG?"

Still no response.

I walked over and put my hand on her arm. "EG?"

She jumped, the contents of her mug sloshing onto the island's countertop. "Oh!" She brought a hand to her chest, wide-eyed. "Claudia. You scared me."

I gave her a minute to calm down and asked, "Why are you so jumpy? Are you ok?"

She snapped of the radio. "It's nothing. I'm fine. Just lost in thought."

I eyed her warily but didn't want to press.

She turned on the barstool, then stood and hugged me for a long time. With EG, it was either a hug or just a hey. The hey also meant you were loved and welcomed just like an old friend. The more casual the greeting, the more you were like family. "Hey" meant just come in and help yourself to whatever you need, you are loved and trusted here. You wanted the hug or hey but nothing in-between.

"You made it. Great to have you here." She had a long pause and seemed to refocus her attention away from what had captured her attention on the radio a minute ago. "Let's get this summer started. Skip your unpacking until tomorrow. Right now, shall we walk along the river, checkout the jazz trio concert in the town square, or are you up for a mystery movie marathon?"

I smiled and did not hesitate. "I'll get the popcorn started. I always love a good mystery."

CHAPTER FOUR

When I woke up at EG's house the next morning, there was a stillness I hadn't felt in a long time. I had been living with two college girls, after all. The sweet hum of a fan—instead of an air-conditioner's noise—created a quiet calm.

I sat up in bed and ran my fingers through my matted-down hair, and I grabbed a pair of socks. I always had socks on. I hated cold feet. I didn't understand flip-flops—cold feet and needing an unnatural effort to keep them on while walking. Socks and shoes was the only way to live.

I looked around the room and could feel love. EG had had my mom bring stuff from our house in St. Paul that would make me feel more comfortable here. Across the bed was the blanket I'd made in school, and there were frames with photos from family vacations and the real winner was the wall with two posters. I am not sure whose I idea it was—my mom's or EG's—they both have the same fun twisted sense of humor. Growing up, I always thought they were one person but just born years apart. One or both of them managed to find a poster with the '80s rock band Def Leppard, and the second poster was of the Jonas brothers. My musical taste range plastered on the wall.

My mind wandered back to present day and this summer and how anxious I had been the past few days, which was most likely due to the court date. Then a realization hit me. *School is over. Really over.*

Apart from caring for EG, finding a summer job, and completing the community service hours, I didn't have any obligations. When I am done working a shift; the rest of the day will be mine. *No more studying. No more exams.* I buried my head in my hands.

For the past four years, I'd felt unsettled. There was always something more that I could/should be doing for a class project, another chapter I should read, or a midterm to rewrite. An ongoing hum in my head kept me trolling along as if I should never be idle.

And now . . . School is done. No more homework. I can be idle. I can be idle! I am going to have to process that.

I had been worried about exams and excited about the commencement ceremony, and I hadn't realized what that all meant.

Some quiet time might be nice before moving to Chicago.

The sun streamed through the window and lit up the bed like a meditative candle.

I took a deep breath and whispered, "I can be idle." I tried soaking it in but felt like a doofus.

I headed downstairs for some tea. I was not a tea drinker but EG was a tea drinker, and so I was until I could find a Starbucks.

There has to be one in River Bend. It's a college town. But how am I going to afford daily Starbucks on a volunteer's paycheck?

I tapped my fingers mindlessly as I ate my cereal and drank tea. The stillness was getting annoying. EG must have been out of the house for one of her early morning walks because the teakettle was already warm when I'd turned it on.

We'd had a great night last night until I mentioned my whole court experience. I had not expected her to be so defensive and pointed when I told her the story. Of all the people I'd told, I thought she would laugh it off.

I thought it was maybe nerves about chemo, but she had a strange reaction to my courtroom story, especially when I mentioned the judge. EG was used to being recognized, but she was usually cordial and found it amusing when strangers pointed her out. Her reaction was anything but amused. She asked if I had to report back to Judge Lobal. I confirmed I had to submit everything here, and my case would be closed. She explained she knew Larry Lobal from her college days, and she was not a fan of his. She had gone quickly to bed after that.

We had several hours before I had to drive her to chemo in Rochester. I looked up the address to the nursing home and headed out. EG's car was blocking mine in the drive, and I could not find her keys to move it. *I guess that means I am walking. Oh, joy. Not!* I had finally gotten a text this morning from Jackson. Our goodbye had been jaded because I'd been cranky about the community service hours. We did not talk about his plans for the fall. Did he get a cooking apprenticeship? He had talked about opening a restaurant one day.

I left a note for EG. Why couldn't she take her phone with her when she walked like most people? I dug through my two duffel bags and finally found the least wrinkled shirt I had. It was technically not a job interview since I was assigned community service.

I headed for the nursing home and hoped I looked good enough. Halfway up the hill, I realized I had to check in with Judge Konrad. *Crap! Do I turn around and find the courthouse or continue to the nursing home?* With the heat and humidity rising so early, the easy option was to continue up the hill. I could scout out my route from the top of the hill to the courthouse and maybe find a Starbucks.

Reaching the top of the hill, I was not sure I was in the right spot because Chambray Senior Center looked like a resort and not a nursing home. Multiple one-story buildings, which looked like apartments, surrounded a four-story administration building that looked like a clubhouse rather than a sterile hospital. I could only imagine the view from the top of the administration building.

Walking up to the clubhouse was the best part. Lilac bushes in bloom masked any stale septic smell that I had been expecting. A water fountain stood in the center of the circular drive, adorned with a bronze scarecrow and crow to make it unique to River Bend.

At 8:00 a.m., the cool air-conditioning in the reception area was already a relief. Again, my expectations of a plain, sterile institutional senior center were stifled. The reception area had a homey but modern country club feel to it. Tall windows let the natural light in, and vibrant artwork hung on the walls. Past the reception desk was a sitting area that looked inviting. Several residents were watching the morning news and reading newspapers.

At the reception desk, a young woman with purple streaks in her blonde hair and a nose ring gave me the stare down.

"I need to complete some volunteer hours. Who can I speak with?" I asked.

"If you don't have an appointment with Mrs. Baron or papers, I suggest you see her secretary. Down the hall, first desk on the right," she said. I just stood there. No appointment. No papers. No answer.

She finally offered up "Are you looking for summer work?"

"I said I'm here to volunteer."

"Oh, I'm sorry. Most students know the drill before coming here to get their credits fulfilled. So you don't have papers?"

I'd like to pull that nose ring out! Is this my interview? If I got past this snotty receptionist, I'd get to pass Go and collect my $200. Was there a hidden camera and someone watching and judging how much attitude I could take before I lost it? I was a volunteer. Shouldn't everyone have been excited to see me?

"Papers?" I said weakly.

"Yes, the course credit papers from your dean or court papers from Judge Konrad." She smiled.

That little tart knew I was here for community service and was pushing me.

There was no denying it now.

"I am supposed to see Judge Konrad but didn't realize she would send me out with *papers or forms*."

She smiled again. She had clearly known from the start I was not here for college credit. I imagined her job wasn't exciting, so she was amusing herself with my volunteer status.

She must have seen a *help me, I am pitiful* look on my face because she shifted in her seat, smiled, and finally said, "My roommate works in Judge Konrad's office. There is no court in session today, but the judge has an open-door policy for situations like this. Go to the courthouse and look for signs to the Registers Office, and they will direct you to the judge's office. Jenna will be out front and will have your file ready to hand to the judge. When you speak to the judge, don't say too much. She hates chatty kids. Accept the papers she signs and walk out of her office and hand the file back to Jenna, and she will email me a copy." With more mercy, she picked up the phone to Cheryl, who I assumed was Mrs. Baron's secretary, and got me an appointment at 7:30 a.m. on Friday.

"Seven thirty a.m.?" I said rather quickly.

"Would you rather walk back up here with papers this afternoon in the heat and hope for whatever appointments remain for next week?"

"No, thank you. I appreciate it." Pressing my

luck, I asked, "Is there any place to get a good cup of coffee?"

She laughed. "I understand your passion for caffeine and admire your devotion to it even in this heat. In town, all the coffee shops have a different brew so you will have to figure out what you like. No Starbucks or any other big chain. Thanks to the college kids, most cafés open early and stay open late. If you're desperate, walk down and see Cheryl. She will have a cup ready for you, but keep walking. Cheryl is great but real chatty, and you could get stuck there for an hour. The door at the end of the hall does not have an alarm on it during the day, and you can exit the building and head out towards the path downhill to the town square and courthouse. It is steep but it has no stairs like the last hill you walked up."

She picked up the phone again and dialed a number. "Cheryl, it's Kay again. I need a coffee to go for Claudia. She'll be running past in thirty seconds. No, no, she's in a hurry, just have it ready to go, black is fine. Thanks."

"How did you know I walked? Does everybody in this town walk?" I said.

She rolled her eyes at me and turned to talk to a resident who walked in. "Oh, hello, Roger, what can I do for you?"

Before he could answer, they turned their attention to the newscast playing on the TV in the corner.

"A local fisherman found bones in the Mississippi River, and they don't appear to be from an animal . . ." The same story that had broken yesterday afternoon. This small town may have some excitement after all. I wondered if EG knew anything about this.

I walked down the hall, noticing my shirt had sweat spots everywhere. If I was going to make it to the judge's office and home in time to drive EG to chemo, I needed to hurry.

I snatched the coffee from Cheryl's desk and kept moving. I was running not only because I didn't want to get engaged in a conversation with Cheryl, but I was also hoping to be out of the building before the stale and antiseptic hospital smell hit me.

The back gardens were as beautiful as the front drive, but here, more residents were out socializing. Letting the coffee settle me in, I took a moment to enjoy the view. I could see all five church steeples, the town square, the courthouse, the river, and the freeway.

I found the path rather quickly because, of course, it was marked with a bronze scarecrow holding a directional sign to the town square and Jameson College. On the way down the path, I passed a biker, two moms with strollers, and a guy who looked familiar. It was White Balls Dude, carrying a pom-pom.

Hmmm, a pom-pom?

He smiled at me, and thankfully, he kept running, because what would I have said to a guy running with a pom-pom?

Thanks to Kay, the rest of the morning went smoothly. It took me several minutes of no success in finding the judge's chambers before I remembered Kay had said to go to the Registers Office first.

The lady in the Registers Office, Carol, had to walk me to the office since everyone seemed to miss the hallway, and she seemed to enjoy her unofficial role as courthouse tour guide.

Gotta love small towns.

Jenna seemed to be expecting me and had my papers ready to go. Judge Konrad was all business. She reviewed the material from Judge Lobal, confirmed my temporary living arrangements, signed the papers, and confirmed that I would report my volunteer hours every two weeks. I just smiled and nodded.

As I walked out, Jenna was waiting for me and quickly scanned my papers and handed me the originals.

I headed back towards EG's house. In the courthouse parking lot, Judge Konrad stepped out the back side of the building and lit a cigarette.

She saw me looking and seemed to want to

say something, but I smiled and waved my papers, changing my route as if I was heading back to the senior center. Within minutes, I had a text confirmation of my Friday 7:30 a.m. appointment with Mrs. Baron, so no more extra walking was needed that morning.

CHAPTER FIVE

I didn't know why I was nervous during the ride to EG's chemo treatment. My mom had gone with her to the first one and had given me the play-by-play as to what to expect. My mom proclaimed she would be there for any of the doctor visits and anything more than just the chemo treatment and I should consider myself just the chauffeur this summer. I was hurt at first thinking my mom thought I could not handle it but then I realized how closed those two are and it must painful for my mom to watch EG go through something like this. They are both so nurturing. My roommate in college, Mia, once had the flu. I went into full nurse mode that bordered on obnoxious. I made the other roommates move out for three days, I cleaned every surface, contacted all her professors to deliver the note from the college nurse and stocked up the pantry with her favorites of Tang and beef Ramen noodles. EG sent me $20.00 so I could stop at 7-11 and get her her favorite drink ,wild cherry Slupree, each day. Mia was either so grateful or delusional from the fever she said 'thanks mom' twice. I took that as a compliment. My mother taught me well.

It was a simple ride between River Bend and Rochester. As we left the woods and hills of River Bend and crossed the river into Minnesota, the land smoothed out and farmland anchored both sides of the highway.

We usually had an easy time talking, but today, she was unusually quiet. She was always so strong, and nothing seemed to rattle her. I never would have thought that a chemo treatment would have made her stiff and distant.

I looked over at her staring out the window. Her standard wardrobe included jeans and a T-shirt and no shoes or socks when at home, a simple look that she made look hip. Today, she had on jeans, a white T-shirt, and penny loafers. Lying in her lap was a light gray shawl. She'd always had a fear of being cold inside buildings especially during the summer. If she went to the movie theater in July, she dressed like she was going skiing.

"Are you nervous? Did the doc say if it will

hurt?" I asked.

EG seemed to snap out of deep thought. "I'm not nervous. It's simple stage one, and this is routine. I am only forty-three and in otherwise good health. I may not even lose any hair. Sorry I've been quiet. I was thinking about some things and how to lay it all out."

"Are you mulling a new story around, even on the way to chemo? You know you can take a break from writing."

"It's not a new story but the real story that needs to be told." I drew my brows together. "Are you going to write a documentary?"

"Something like that. Why don't you park over there, and we can get you some coffee before we go for treatment."

I understood the conversation was over and did as she'd asked. After grabbing some coffee, we went into the hospital and found the treatment room.

It was not what I had expected. In a large sunny room, patients sat in chairs resembling those found in nail salons but without the massage rollers. Half the chairs had their own TVs.

Some patients were alone, and others had someone with them. A low murmur filled the air, but it wasn't morbidly quiet. On one wall, a huge bookcase held a large selection of magazines and homemade quilts and blankets that had been made by former patients. The room was a cross between an upgraded waiting room and a high-end salon. A nurse recognized EG, and a nurse technician found one of EG's books on the bookshelf and had her sign it before returning it to the shelf. I was curious if it would be there next week because I could see a few people eyeing it. The treatment room had a take-one-leave-one library. I would be curious if her signed book would ever be returned here after the next person read it. Then true to EG's generous nature, she said she would call her book agent and see if the publisher could send more books from their catalog and help fill the bookshelves with a variety of authors.

The eighty-minute session went fast, and EG said she felt good and was told the effects of the treatment would be like a slow wave sneaking up on her.

She wanted to visit her friend Dr. Ellen Touras, a psychologist who had an office two blocks away in another part of the hospital. EG walked fast and was in good spirits, so I didn't argue about this side trip. The office was on the second floor, and she insisted we walk up the stairs.

Still walking and we are not in River Bend!

In the office waiting room, a few women and one man worked the phones, and several patients were waiting to be called.

A doctor was in the front room talking with

one of the receptionists, and when she looked up at us, a smile lit her face. She came around and gave EG a hug.

EG broke the hug and gestured towards me. "Ellen, this is Claudia."

"So pleased to meet you, Claudia. EG has told me so much about you. She said you have a job with Colton Publishing. Ah, so you are following your aunt's footsteps into the same profession? Are you going to put River Bend on the map again?"

"Nice to meet you too, Dr. Touras. I am not a writer or in the publishing industry," I said, giving her my standard answer. I wasn't sure why I never explained that I was in Human Resources, but then the reason hit me. *I don't need too many questions until I figure it all out.*

She shook her head, her brows knitting together. "Please call me Ellen. Did you get a chance to meet Pastor Theo?"

"What?" EG said sharply.

"I just got to town yesterday, and I haven't met many people," I said.

Ellen smiled, clearly not recognizing EG's alarm. "Pastor Theo lives in St. Paul, but he's here in the building today. Unfortunately, most of his visits here are to visit terribly sick patients. I thought I could boost his trip so I mentioned EG's chemo treatment. I was hoping we could all go for coffee. How long has it been since we have all been together? If you tell me it was high school, I will die."

"If you see him, tell him we're sorry we missed him, but we must be going. Sorry we couldn't stay longer." EG grabbed my arm and pulled me towards the door.

Ellen followed us. "EG, you look good after treatment. I thought it would be fun to catch up, and I'd like to know what everyone in River Bend is saying about the bones they found."

"Maybe next time, Ellen," EG said and closed the door behind us.

We walked straight to the stairs, and finally, she let go of my arm.

I stopped at the bottom of the stairs. "Is she talking about the Pastor Theo I know?"

EG stopped and turned sharply towards me. "What do you mean? You know Pastor Theo?"

"Not really, but Mom didn't like the senior pastor at our church, and when it was his turn to give the sermon, we would sometimes drive to South St. Paul and listen to Pastor Theo. I never knew that you knew him. So is he from River Bend as well?"

"Yes, he is," EG said softly.

This was not the time to ask about our abrupt exit, so I followed her to the car in silence. The drive home was as quiet as the drive to the hospital. I thought she would be tired after the treatment, but instead of sleeping, EG stared out the window. She seemed more rattled than tired.

I pondered what it was like for EG to face this alone. She had a group of close friends and was close with my mom, but that was not the same as having someone at home with her. She had been married many years ago, but her husband, Duncan, was killed in an automobile accident just after their wedding. Jackson's greatest skill might be his cooking, but I had him to help me get through situations.

CHAPTER SIX

We exited off the freeway early and enjoyed the country roads that led into River Bend.

We rolled into EG's driveway, and a car pulled up and parked on the curb, under a large maple tree. Mayor Eugene stepped out of his car, wearing creased khaki pants, a short-sleeve plaid shirt, and sensible shoes. He was easy to recognize because I'd met him and his father, Carl, several times when I'd visited before.

A member of the Phillip family had always been mayor, but something was strange about that family. Mayor Carl had retired, but he had been a towering figure, politically, physically, and always seen as a leader in the community his whole life. EG told me he had been great in academics and sports in high school, excelled at Jameson College. After graduation, he'd served four years in the army before returning to River Bend. He was elected mayor at the age of thirty-two. The town loved him, and no one ever had really had a chance at campaigning against him, and there was no need or want to push him out of office. The women adored him, and the men wanted to be in his company.

When Carl had retired, Eugene assumed the role of mayor, and no one was sure what had happened with him. EG once told me he was very much like his paternal grandfather, Erwin, another former mayor. He was always teetering on manhood but couldn't take the last step.

It seemed the good genes and common sense had skipped some generations. Unfortunately, this was the era of the missing link. Eugene is the type of guy that can enter a room full and people and have no one notice him for an hour. Hopefully in another decade, the next Phillip would bring some personality to the job. Eugene and Rhonda's son, at the age of fourteen, is already showing talent in the classroom and on the basketball court.

Eugene raced up to EG's car door and tried helping her out.

She brushed him off like a fly. "Eugene, I'm fine."

Everyone loves EG and she loves everyone, but do not coddle or underestimate her. That is her line in the sand. After her husband died and she was ready to finally move forward, she kept getting pulled down by folks who seemed just to want give her pity and leave her in her sorrow for good. She worked hard to let people see she had healed and could thrive even when alone. She began teaching a writing course at the college and hosted a book club for high school kids. She started the Art Now of River Bend. For a small monthly fee, locals could rent artwork that has been created by the students from the college and high school art departments. The art pieces were rotated out every several months, bringing exposure to the students and something fresh into people's homes. EG had said, with each initial step into the community, she was met with pity and had had to fight for people to see her for her and not as someone who was half of a broken couple.

"It is my second treatment. I can manage on my own."

"Yes, of course, Ms. Graham. My dad, Mayor Carl—"

"I know who your dad is. You can call him Dad, Mayor, or Carl. You are or were all mayors. We get it," EG said.

"He sent me over to check on you and to say you two need to talk. He would've come himself, but his knee is bothering him, and the doctor told him to stay off it for a few days. He was hoping I could convince you to come over tomorrow if you are up for it."

She stepped from the car and away from Eugene. "I don't think I have anything for him at this time, but if something comes up, I will give him a call. I also suggest you move your car. The crows are bad this year. They sit in that tree you parked under, and they will decorate your car pretty quickly."

"Yes, of course, I will move the car directly. If you need anything, please let me know. I know you have Claudia here, but I'm here too."

He stood there like a dog waiting for the command to fetch or sit. He seemed to be trying to determine if the conversation was over. EG nodded and moved towards the house.

"Did you hear about the bones? Crazy! Crazy for something like that to be found here in River Bend," he said.

I don't think EG seemed to be interested in any more conversation because she continued to the porch and ignored Eugene.

But hell, I was curious as to what he knew. "What about bones? Where were they found?"

"Hello, Ms. Claudia. So nice to have you in River Bend this summer. Your aunt must be so happy."

I could have sworn he'd practiced these lines. I'd bet he had a book called *Things Mayors Should Say*, and he and Rhonda practiced nightly. It was not so much what he said, but the singsong tone and how he seemed to be mentally checking off the list of proper things to say from chapter one of this imaginary book. He now seemed to have a slight bounce in posture. "The bones were found in the Mississippi River. Sheriff Dalton is not saying much. He's claiming it's because of the police investigation."

"Don't you have some authority to see the report?"

The screen door shut, and EG watched us from inside the porch.

Eugene—*sorry, Mayor Eugene*—looked a little jilted and the bouncing stopped as I questioned his authority. Stumbling for words, he replied, "Yes, but right now, it's a matter of jurisdiction. They are trying to pinpoint the exact location in the river to determine if it was on the Wisconsin or Minnesota side. From the initial looks of what was found, it seems as if the bones were in the river a long time. The FBI might get involved."

"Still, don't you get the reports?"

He didn't like my response. Not because I questioned his authority again but because he didn't know his role of authority.

He started to back step toward his car to retreat, and with a little fumbling, he said, "As the sheriff said, this is an ongoing investigation so I can't say much. I probably already said too much.

Tell your aunt to call my father."

"What's that in your hand?"

He returned to where I was standing. "Oh, this is a casserole. My wife organized a meal program with some of the ladies in the community while EG is in treatment, and I am the pick-up and delivery man."

"That's sweet, but, Mayor, we are fine. EG is not an invalid. I am here to assist with meals. Please tell the folks we appreciate the thought, but no thank you."

Eugene stared wide-eyed at me. "But—"

From inside the porch, EG yelled, "That's right, Mayor. Listen to Claudia."

"But—"

"Ants covered the dish Rhonda left last week when I was out of town. If you don't stop this Meal-on-Wheels program she cooked up, I will have you pay for the extra pest control. Give the meals to people who can't cook and have no support. You must know that half the ladies in this town don't know how to cook, and not everything should be turned into a casserole!" EG opened the door to the house and went inside.

Eugene flinched a little. "Make sure she returns that last Tupperware dish when she meets with my dad."

CHAPTER SEVEN

The rest of the afternoon was a lazy day of unpacking, doing the washing, and fixing a light dinner for me and EG. The heat was breaking for a bit, and it definitely helped when the sun set. The local news did not have any more information about the bones. They rehashed the jurisdiction battle and promised an interview with the fisherman who pulled the bones out of the water.

After dinner, EG went upstairs to the second bedroom, which was her at-home writing studio. She also had a condo in Chicago she used as an away-from-home writing studio. She said the change of scenery helped her concentrate on writing.

I told her I was going to explore the town. Four blocks from EG's house, I found Main Street.

Within the first few minutes, I discovered one café and only one coffee place. Not sure what Kay had been referring to when she implied there were lots to choose from.

Across the street, two twentysomething women, laughing and looking primped-up for a fun night out, were headed away from the main square. I thought maybe they were headed to a friend's house, but I remembered that Jameson College was a few blocks away. For lack of anything better to do, I followed them.

To my surprise, I found the Jameson College epicenter. Within a five-block radius, there were six bars, four coffee shops, a tattoo parlor, yoga studio, paint-your-own-pottery studio, a closed-down tanning salon/movie rental place, an apparently thriving travel agent, an art supply store, a bike shop, and two hair salons.

I think I just found my salvation for the summer.

It was fairly quiet since it was a Wednesday in a small town and no college classes were in session. I loved going to different towns and scoping out the local places. I was surprised that I had never explored this part of River Bend.

What did this college campus have to offer? I wondered if it was closed to the public and encased with a stone facade ensconced in ivy, but I was delighted to find a beautiful open campus comprising old stone buildings and a few structures influenced by Frank Lloyd Wright, a native to the state. The campus boundary lines blended easily into the community.

The college bars were typical. Some were sports themed, one was trying to be an Irish pub, one might have been a dance club, and the others were good ol' drinking bars. I found one kinda amusing and somewhat odd because it was a bar called BAR.

"Hey, Paper Girl, that bar doesn't open early in the summer."

I turned. It was Kay, the receptionist from the Chambray Senior Center, who was talking to me. Her roommate, Jenna, stood beside her. They had heavy makeup on and wore simple but well-planned outfits, looking like they were headed out to scout for men.

"I figured that much. I was just going for a walk to look for all the coffee shops you talked about."

"If you want, you can join us for a drink at the Draw Bar, and we will give you the rundown on the restaurants and stuff to do in this town."

"Thanks, I appreciate that, but I don't have my purse."

Kay waved a hand. "Don't worry about the cash. Plus, it's summertime, so you probably won't get carded. Most bars don't care since the college kids are gone and the underage drinkers won't return until fall. It will be my treat if you offer up the story about your community service." One corner of her mouth turned up in a grin.

I cocked my head. "What do you mean?"

"Really, don't count us as fools. You had to see Judge Konrad, and with the number of volunteer hours you need to fulfill, it seems to add up to a good story."

Jenna added, "Plus, we haven't received your full record from Judge Lobal's office yet."

I loved her honesty. I shrugged and accepted their offer. It was better than waiting for Jackson's call at EG's while she worked.

We walked into Draw Bar, and I was surprised at how busy it was. Not wall-to-wall screaming kids, but all the tables were full and the bar only had one barstool open. Several people were waiting for drinks from the one bartender on duty. The TVs were showing the Milwaukee Brewers and Minnesota Twins game. Each play had people cheering and booing.

I shook my head and laughed to myself. *Border towns, gotta love it.*

"It's going to take forever to get a drink. Let's go somewhere else," Jenna said.

I snatched a twenty-dollar bill from Kay's hand. "Why don't you guys grab the table that just opened up, and I will get us a pitcher."

I saw an easy opportunity to get our drinks

fast and marched up to the bar, thinking I could score a few points with my new friends. The bartender was no other than the white-balls-pickup-truck-pom-pom-carrying dude.

I squeezed into the open spot at the bar. A woman was trying to get the bartender's attention and failing, but I had an advantage. "Hey, Mr. White Balls, what do I have to do to get a pitcher of beer around here?" I said as he walked past.

"What?" he yelled back.

"Mr. White Balls!" I yelled again as the baseball game cut to a commercial and the song ended on the jukebox.

Half of the people at the bar turned to look at me.

Can I have any dignity in this town?

With my face growing warm, I smiled at them and turned back to the bartender. He grabbed the $20 from me and handed me a pitcher of light beer.

I glared at him. "So you assume, as a woman, I will order light beer?"

"No, as a bartender, I noticed you are here with Kay and Jenna, two regular patrons who happen to prefer light beer. *And* it's the Wednesday special."

"Oh," I mumbled.

He leaned in as he handed back the change, and I couldn't help but notice his blue eyes and clean-shaven face.

I expected him to apologize for being so curt, but instead, he whispered, "In all fairness, I should tell you that they are pink. So, please, call me Mr. Pink Balls."

My face grew hot again, and I grabbed the change and quickly threw down a tip. I did a sharp turn to exit from my embarrassment with as much dignity as possible and wobbled my way back to the table.

I filled Jenna and Kay in on the parking ticket fiasco and Mr. White—no, Mr. *Pink* Balls. They were funny and keen observers, and if they'd let me, I might make them my summer friends.

A little while later, I felt a nudge on my arm and shook my head to clear it.

"What have you heard? Has EG given you any stories, or does she not believe the legend of the Gray Lady?" Kay asked.

I'd been watching Mr. Pink Balls working the bar and hadn't heard a word of Jenna and Kay's conversation. "What are you talking about?"

"Chambray Senior Center is haunted," Jenna said.

I narrowed my eyes at her. "How can that be? It doesn't look that old."

Kay leaned in closer. "Rumor or legend has it that, during the 1800s, women climbed up the hill to watch for their husbands and sons to return from the Civil War. They watched the river for boats and the track for trains returning soldiers home. It is said that one lady who was engaged to be married still waits for her love. She is stuck there in grief because the love of her life returned to town but he went into the arms of another woman. Even though he returned to River Bend alive, her love was unrequited, and she hung herself from a tree. When strange things occur, people believe it's the Gray Lady reaching out for love."

"You guys don't believe that, do you?"

Jenna shrugged. "What else could explain all the things that happen? Plus, it makes for a good story."

Kay nodded. "Initially, I had my doubts, but after working there for two years and talking to the residents, I now tend to believe. Some things just can't be explained. Some residents have experienced lights and appliances turning on randomly, pockets of cold air sweeping past them, and small items being in a different spot than they remembered placing them."

Jenna and Kay went on to debate the merits of the legend, and my eyes wondered back to the bar.

Kay nudged my arm again. "You keep glancing at Mr. Pink Balls, but he doesn't date bar girls so your efforts will be wasted, and you said you have a boyfriend."

"I know I have a boyfriend—soon to be my live-in boyfriend. It's interesting to watch him work. He seems to know everyone and can handle the busy place by himself."

Jenna laughed. "Yeah, that's his specialty—drinks and guys in bars."

I didn't know why I was disappointed to find out he was gay. I had Jackson, so why should it matter?

I left after an hour. It was clear those two were out to find a man and were there for the long haul. While I walked home, Jackson called. He always had good timing.

"Hey, babe," I said.

"Hey, guess what? I found a few apartments to check out."

"That's great. Send me the links so I can see what you're looking at."

"But why, don't you trust me? After all, I picked you. I think I can find us a place to live."

"I know, but you're only going to be there until December. Aren't you going back to finish up your degree? I'll still be living there and paying rent when you're gone. I don't want to be in a place like a cabin at summer camp—something good enough for a while but not for long-term living."

"Ouch, that hurts, but I get your point. I'll send you the listings. I gotta go, the guys are waiting. Have fun in Bends," he said before hanging up.

CHAPTER EIGHT

On Thursday morning, I thought I'd gotten up early, but again, EG was up and off on one of her walks when I went to say good morning.

One last day of freedom before I start at the senior center, I thought, deciding to find the café Kay had suggested for coffee and pastries.

Jackson had sent me the listings at 5:30 a.m. this morning. The apartments were ok, but I wasn't sure about the neighborhoods.

The air was comfortably warm outside, but the temperature would quickly rise again. I meandered over to Peach's Café. Sitting there and finally having a goood cup of coffee and scrumptious pastries put me in a blank state of bliss.

My phone rang, snapping me out of it. I

didn't recognize the number, but it appeared to be local. It was EG on someone else's phone, asking me to pick her up from a strip mall seven blocks away. I ran home to get the car, and when I got to the strip mall, she was sitting on the patio furniture on display outside the local hardware/home goods store with her feet up, chatting with Phil, the owner. They were eating donuts and having tea. The scene was confusing. They were laughing and appeared to be having fun.

"EG, are you ok? Phil, is she ok, what's going on?" I said, my words nearly tumbling out on top of one another.

Phil waved off my worry and came closer to give me a big hug. "She's fine. We didn't mean to put you in a panic. I would have driven her home, but my car is blocked by the delivery truck."

"Relax! I'm fine. It's just"—EG pointed to a box on the sidewalk—"this box is too awkward to carry. See how big it is? It has nothing to do with my being sick. I just asked you pick me up. If you are going to be high anxiety all summer, I will trade you for your mother."

I slowed my breathing, trying to calm my heart rate. Sweat ran down my forehead. "I'm here to help you. Please take advantage of it."

Phil laughed and gestured towards me. "I must agree, EG. Take advantage of Claudia." He turned to me and said, "It is nice to have you in town this summer, but after that last book you recommended to me, you need to be penalized." He laughed as he put the package in the back seat, then turned and cleaned up their impromptu breakfast.

"What are you talking about? You said you finished it. You've stopped reading other books after two chapters, so the fact that you finished it means you liked it. And don't give me any crap about the female lead having seven husbands just because you think a person should only be married once."

Phil crossed his arms. "That's only the start of it. Do you remember—"

EG held up a hand. "This is probably not the time for a book club meeting," she said in a raised voice.

With that declaration, we said our goodbyes and got into the car.

As I pulled out of the parking lot, EG said, "You're not here to be my ambulance driver or nurse. You are here to drive me to and from the Mayo Clinic for my treatments—remember there is a difference between ambulance and Debby. I am well enough to ride shotgun in Debby your Escort and not lying down in ambulance. This summer is for us to talk and enjoy each other's company."

"We always talk."

"I know, but I have some things to tell you,"

EG said quietly.

I slammed on the brake to avoid hitting a squirrel, and the box in the back seat slid forward and hit the back of my seat.

"What was so important for you to get this morning?"

"I got you a coffee maker."

"What?"

"I know you must have your coffee. I figured if I haven't converted you to tea yet, it probably will never happen. It's the least I could do."

"Thank you, I appreciate it, but you didn't have to do that. I found great coffee this morning, but thinking about it now, I probably can't afford to go out daily. How were you able to get in the store? It's not even seven thirty yet."

"Phil saw me through the window during my morning walk and waved me over. His wife had just brought over fresh donut holes for the staff, and he invited me share a few with him. Everyone is all eager to talk about those damn bones. While I was there, I told him I need a coffee maker for you, and he pulled one from the shelf for me. I see you were at Peach's Café when I called."

"How did you know?"

"That place has some of the best pastries, but they overdo it with the powdered sugar."

I knew better than to look down at my shirt. I was sure powdered sugar was everywhere, plus, probably sweat stains from walking to the café and then running home to get the car. I was just proud my hands didn't have jam on them.

"When we get home, I'm going to rest and maybe write a little, and then I can take you to the diner with the best soup for lunch. What are your plans for the morning?" EG said.

"I'm hoping to connect with Jackson and review our housing options for this fall. I'm getting anxious since we don't have a place."

"We? You never said anything about living together."

"It's just for a semester. Jackson decided to take an apprenticeship this fall and will go back and graduate in the spring."

When we got home, I brought in the coffee maker and inspected its beauty.

I need to focus on the apartment search.

After making coffee, I took a seat on the patio with a fresh cup and called Jackson.

"Jackson, thanks for the listings. How many places are you going to see today?"

"Slow down there. I hope to check out some places tomorrow. I'm going with PK and Dane to see a band tonight. Michael is bartending at this place and heard the band may need a bass player to fill in for a bit. I want to check them out and see if they're my type of band."

"So you don't have any appointments set

up? You can't just show up. We're running out of time."

"How's your aunt? Are you stressing her out too? Because I don't think that's a good idea."

"She's fine. Tired but fine. She's had only two treatments so far. I'm good too. Thanks for asking." I hoped he'd catch my sarcastic tone. "I'm worried about the fall."

"Take it easy. I'm doing all the work while you're up there. I will figure it out. How was the soup I made?"

"I put it in the freezer. I decided to ration it out over the summer. Thank you for doing the apartment search," I said, my voice squeaking.

I wondered if I could manage my volunteer schedule, the chemo rides, and a trip to Chicago next week. It would be another week before I could start looking for a part-time summer job. Then again, putting off employment was beginning to be my specialty.

CHAPTER NINE

EG decided to be lazy by avoiding the kitchen and diverted all talk about the bones found in the river, so she sent me to the Blue Daisy Diner for salads and the chef's famous mac and cheese. I went to grab the car keys, but she pointed out the diner was just six blocks from the house and that it was easier to walk. She wrapped her arm around me and walked me to the door and told me it was ok for me to roll my eyes at her suggestion but still insisted that I walk.

When I ordered, the cashier asked if it was for EG. Apparently, besides being the local celebrity author, she was also known for her love of the Thursday mac and cheese special. She gave me twice the amount of mac and cheese than I ordered and did not charge extra.

EG had instructed me to go to Aaron's Diner for pie after I went to the Blue Daisy, but I couldn't find it. I tried searching for it on my phone, but nothing came up. I went back to the Blue Daisy to ask where I could find Aaron's, wondering if it was tacky to ask one diner about another diner.

Oops.

The cashier said there was no Aaron's Diner in town.

The gentleman at the counter overheard and said, "Young miss, I bet EG is talking about Aaron Rhoimly. If you're going to pick up some pie, talk to Aaron at BAR. Find Aaron and tell him that I said EG better not get the last one. We got a Rotary Club meeting tomorrow, and it would be a shame if there's no pie for us. BAR's between the village square and college loop on Main Street. If it's not open, try the back door. I'm not sure of the summer hours. I saw him working in there before I got here."

Happy to know where I was going, I walked towards Main Street, laughing at the name BAR. Last night, when I was wandering around, I thought BAR was a sign to signal to the college kids this was where one should come and order drinks, and to know it was really called BAR's Bar seemed even more pathetic.

When I got there, the front door was unlocked and music was playing, but no one was around. I wasn't sure if the place was open for business, but I heard some noise in back.

It was fairly dark inside, and my eyes had to adjust after coming in from the bright sunlight.

I was pleasantly surprised once I was able to focus—it was open, airy, and comfortable. It seemed to be a cross between a flannel-wearing man's cabin and a sporty hipster's loft. An odd combination but it worked.

The front area had a mix of booths and tall tables and the bar was farther down the right hand wall. The wall leading to the bar was composed of baseball bats lying horizontally in a brick pattern, some broken, some covered in what appeared to be blood, and others that looked brand-new. Another wall was a collage of sports equipment, some of them broken and some looked brand-new, but like a cool art mosaic, it blended together nicely. There was everything from lacrosse sticks, tennis rackets, cricket bats, basketballs, lots of tennis balls, and even a few pom-poms.

"Hello. What are you doing? Stalking me?" said a voice behind me.

I let out a little yelp and turned around. It was Mr. Pink Balls. Again, he was wearing cargo shorts and a well-ironed dark-blue tennis shirt that made his blue eyes pop.

"I have been in this town for forty-eight hours, and you seem to be tracking me," I said.

"I didn't mean to scare you. I'll save that for the Gray Lady at Chambray. But it appears you are stalking me. Considering this place is mine, I will recite a favorite grade school quote: *I was here first.*"

"What a sharp comeback. You win a lot of fights with that one? Can you please tell me where I can find Aaron?"

He stood back and leaned on the back bar with his arms crossed, rubbing his freshly shaved chin, like a professor looking down to his students. He eyed me up and down as if he was evaluating so he could label me friend or foe. He didn't say anything for a minute and, finally, seemed to decide I was at least worth questioning.

"That depends on what you're here for. Are you looking for a job, collecting a debt, paying up an old debt, or just general stalking?"

I was evaluating my options to answer his interrogation and decided at this point just to be direct but he cut me off before. "The answers are maybe, no, no, and no."

"What do you mean *no*? Am I not stalk worthy?"

"Is that what you got out of that conversation?"

I laughed. "Yes, and pie. Does *pie* get me closer to meeting Aaron?"

"Who sent you?" His arms were still crossed and his body not moving.

"EG," I said.

"No."

Wow, saying her name at the Blue Daisy gets me extra mac and cheese, and here, it gets me shut down.

"But the guy at the Blue Daisy said this was the place to find Aaron."

That seemed to spark real interest in him. He stood up straight. "What guy? What did he look like, and who heard?"

"I don't know his name, but he was probably late sixties, had a heavy gut, and seemed to be the type to wear suspenders every day. No one else heard except the cashier. Wow, you paranoid? I assumed I was picking up pie, not narcotics. Oh, and he said something about a meeting with the sheriff here tomorrow."

"That's Duane. You tell EG if she wants her pie, she should come for herself and not send in decoys."

"What are you talking about? She's too tired from chemo. Give her a break. I'm no decoy, just her niece."

He relaxed his shoulders and dropped his arms. "Oh shit, I forgot. I didn't realize she started treatment already. She knows better than to keep this quiet. I don't want every person over the age of forty in here begging for pie. She gets only one this time since I need some for the Rotary Club tomorrow. Come and follow me."

Walking past the bar and his office to the cooler, I tried to figure out why I was nervous. I glanced in the office and saw the white deflated football sitting on his desk. I hoped he was going to hand me a pie and not some heroin.

"What's with the covert operation? Please tell me about the pie and why the secrecy."

"Don't be scared, but yes, this is a covert operation. Come in the cooler with me, and you can have your choice." He smiled.

Damn, those blue eyes can melt a person.

I followed him in and was only a foot away from him. Despite it being forty degrees in the walk-in refrigerator, I was warm.

I selected a blueberry pie over the apple and peach pies. My face felt flushed when his hand touched mine as he handed it to me.

My teeth weren't rattling, but I still bumbled when I said, "So it is just pie. There must be a story."

"Let me get you a beer, and I'll give you the pie story."

"Thanks, but I can't. I've got a boyfriend."

"Good for you, but I just got some new promotional beers and need to get a second opinion about whether I should put any of them on tap this fall. I thought you could taste some and give me your opinion."

Oops. Now, my face really grew hot. "Ok,

you got me there. I still have to leave. I've got cold pie and what once was a crisp salad and hot mac and cheese that I need to get back to EG's." I headed towards the back door.

"I understand. By the way, if I ever were to ask you out for a date, you'll know it and it will not be for a beer at my bar."

I turned back towards him and smiled. "So you're Aaron."

"Yes, I'm Aaron."

"One more question. Are they still pink?"

As the door closed behind me, he laughed and yelled, "Of course."

CHAPTER TEN

Friday morning, I had my first cup of coffee while EG had her tea. She was dressed in jeans, a plain light-blue T-shirt, and was barefoot. I would have looked scruffy and unkept in that outfit, but she pulled it off, looking hip and artistic.

The afternoon before, we'd devoured all the mac and cheese, salad, and most of the pie. I was happy EG had had an appetite after her latest chemo treatment. I hadn't been sure what to expect and neither had she.

"I forgot to ask last night. What's the story with the pie? I could only get one."

EG laughed. "Aaron was probably fishing to find out if I was hosting a book club dinner and angling to get invited. I normally get one pie, but if I'm hosting a special guest dinner or a book club dinner, I can manage to get two and maybe three if Aaron is invited."

EG stared at me as if she was waiting for me to respond.

"Oh, sorry. I was thinking about that dinner you hosted three years ago. So anyway, yesterday, I took a tour through town looking for Aaron's Diner only to be told by Duane at the Blue Daisy to go to BAR's Bar."

"Crap, Duane knows there's pie in town? Thankfully, we got ours before the boys got their hands on it. I should have told you more before I sent you out, but I thought you knew."

"I had pie here before, but I thought you baked it."

"Now, that is funny. I can cook but I cannot bake. There is a big difference. Anyway, Aaron's grandmother, Ms. Clara, used to own Peach's Café and had the most amazing pies. Peach was her specialty, but she did mighty fine with all the others. Clara moved to St. Paul, to live with her sister Maria and to be near to her daughter Lesley. Her other daughter, Clara, took over the café.

"There is no way for me to make this story short, so stay with me, Claudia—it might be long, but it explains the pie custom. Aaron's brother, Charles, wanted to open a bar in town but his liquor license was denied, as it usually is on the first try. He smarted off to the town council, which didn't help his case. At the following meeting, the town council had their holiday potluck.

"Charles had convinced Aaron to speak on his behalf and for his grandmother Clara to bring pies. Everyone was so excited to see Clara and her pies, and the liquor license was approved that night in Aaron's name. Poor Aaron. Anytime he's been gone for several days or a car with a Minnesota license plate lingers outside his loft, people go sniffing around for pie. He has even bartered pies for repairs on his truck with Jorge."

"How is it decided who gets pies? Does Aaron or Clara decide? Are you blackmailing him? God, I love small towns."

EG laughed. She had such an easy laugh. "It's nothing like that. I was a loyal customer at Peach's Café, and when I publish a new book, all my Twin Cities book signings are held at Cedar's Book Store, which is owned by Aaron and Charles's mother, Lesley. For some reason, Clara associates us with the success of her daughter's bookstore and cafe and always makes sure I get a pie or two."

"I've been to some of your book signings there, but I didn't know the River Bend connection. Why didn't you say something? Who is *us*?"

"I assumed you knew. You and your mom are regulars at the bookstore. She has probably done more for the success of the bookstore and cafe than I have with my meager book signings she's helped with the launch of the cafe."

"You're always assuming I know things. I knew she had helped opening the cafe, but I did not know the River Bend connection. I best be off for my first day. I'm meeting Mrs. Baron at seven thirty. What days do we go to the clinic next week? I need to coordinate my schedule and maybe a trip to Chicago to apartment hunt."

"Tuesday, I have treatment and, Thursday, an appointment with my doctor here in town. We should be back by eleven each day. Are you going to see Jackson?"

"Despite Jackson's newfound ability to get up early, he has not found us a place yet. He sounded optimistic this morning, but I don't think he'll find something on his own. I'll set up some places to look at next Tuesday and Wednesday. Should I have Mom come Tuesday afternoon? You were so tired after your last treatment."

"Katie Lyn doesn't need to come. Don't call her. I was tired but not immobile." She paused and had an earnest look on her face "Honey, I say this with love. If you want you can go in my bathroom and use my hair cream. It will help with the frizz."

"You are the best," I said and kissed her on the cheek before darting into her bathroom.

On my way to Chambray, I picked up some pastries. When I arrived, I walked through the lobby, once again covered in powdered sugar. I dropped the pastries off to a grateful Kay since she'd helped me navigate town and Judge Konrad's office.

Mrs. Baron did not have me cleaning bedpans or playing bingo with the old people. She seemed offended when I used the word *bedpan* and, I think, had second thoughts about giving me valet and shopping duties.

Today and most days, my duties would include collecting grocery lists, delivering dry cleaning and laundry, and picking up maintenance requests.

She explained the facility was divided into three areas. The center building, where we had our meeting, housed the administrative offices, the café—"Do not call it a cafeteria"—and the physical therapy center. The four-story building housed the residents—"Do not call them patients"—who needed assisted living care, and the fifty cottages—"Do not call them apartments"—were for residents fifty-five and over with no special needs. They could have someone clean their cottage once a week for an extra fee.

Mrs. Baron was polite and easy to follow, but at the end, I felt like I should stand, salute, and say, "Yes, sir."

I wanted to ask about the legend of the Gray Lady but figured this was not the time or place for rumors.

She partnered me with Meredith, who was to train me for the next six hours.

During the walk to the first cottage, Meredith said, "The residents who do their own cleaning are subject to an extra inspection to make sure there are no pests. We have a serious ant problem on the hill, and we don't want a mice problem."

With a mocking tone that sounded like Mrs. Baron, Meredith continued. "I tell all the Chambray associates it is their responsibility to look after the welfare of the residents and the facility." She continued in her regular voice. "Just don't let them catch you snooping. Some will think you're stealing, and others will think you're being rude by double-checking their cleaning. Most residents don't know you're looking for ants and mice, and those who do appreciate our efforts."

After Meredith had given me the tour, she figured I could handle my own assignment, and gave me a golf cart. Before she left, she said, "Only take one box of supplies at a time. You don't want food sitting on the cart too long while you're in another cottage. We have plenty of time to get everything done as long as you keep moving."

I picked up a box of supplies from the food pantry and drove to the cottage that belonged to a resident named Abigail.

She looked up from her book when I

entered. "Oh, come on in." She was dressed in workout clothes, her brown hair pulled back in a simple ponytail.

I was surprised by how young she was. Everything had been a surprise when it came to Chambray Senior Center—the lack of a clinical hospital smell, the beautiful grounds, no bedpan duty, and now, such young residents.

"Hi, Abigail, I'm Claudia. It's nice to meet you."

"Well, now, are you EG's niece?"

EG was the one who usually got recognized by strangers, so I was taken aback and didn't respond.

Abigail must have seen a look of surprise on my face. "I heard you were coming to town, and your resemblance is remarkable." Her manner of speaking was clear and direct, with a mixture of talking to me and talking down to me. "Dear, it is a small town. We know when people are coming and going."

When I still didn't respond, she followed my gaze. An entire wall had been turned into a giant bookshelf. Half the books seemed to be nonfiction, books on classical music, Renaissance art, and world history. The other half was everything from Oprah's Book Club to the *New York Times* best seller list for the last three years.

"I am the unofficial library for the folks here.

Since the town has a wonderful library, Chambray Center did not add one," she said.

"I see you love reading, but do you need eight copies of the same book?"

She smiled. "I would think you'd be touched, considering that's your aunt's book."

Once again, I wasn't sure if she was talking to me or down to me.

"Why only her first book? The one that made River Bend famous. What about her other works?"

"I do have several of the others, but nothing compared to the first book. Please don't tell EG I said that, but I have a feeling she knows. Those extra books are for the tour. If you could assist me and hide seven of those in the drawer, that would be great."

"Hide?"

"Yes, when prospective residents tour Chambray, I let Stuart—he's in charge of sales—use my cottage as part of the tour. The prospective residents see the scarecrows in town and here on the grounds and get excited when they realize they could live in the town made famous by EG's book. When they come through, I screen them to see if they are a good fit for our community. If I don't like them, I offer them a signed copy of the book, and Stuart understands what this means. After he accepted that loudmouthed, complaint-ridden Wendy, who has been nothing but trouble since moving in, Stuart likes to have a second opinion. I'm not sure if he has more complaints from Wendy or about Wendy from us. I figure the goodbye gift of an autographed book should make their denied application a little easier to handle."

"And you feel less responsible." *Damn, I gotta stop with the smart-aleck remarks. It's my first day here.* "Sorry, that was rude of me."

Abigail waved a hand at me. "That's fine, but don't share this information. This routine serves Chambray and the town very well. Tell EG we probably have enough books to get us through September."

"What does EG have to gain by giving away books?"

She gave me a sharp look and put her book down. "She is part of this town and knows we should take care of everyone that comes here. She is one bookend, and I am the other bookend."

"Bookend?"

"Yes, I consider us two bookends, two sturdy objects with lots of stories between us. I am the front, and she is the end. It is always about the books and the stories they tell, but if there are no bookends holding them in place, who knows what would happen to those stories. They could disappear forever, or the wrong person could read the wrong book," she said calmly.

I wasn't sure I knew what she meant, but I

knew the conversation was over and went to put away the food.

Abigail held up a finger. "Oh, Claudia, the new grocery list is on the kitchen counter. Add butter and fresh blueberries to it. When you turn it in to the main kitchen, make sure you give David those muffins next to the oven. It's the only way he'll give me fresh blueberries this time of year. I don't want to have to go to the store just for fresh berries. I'd say you could have some, but I see you were already at Peach's this morning."

I wrapped up in the kitchen and headed for the door. "It was a pleasure meeting you, Abigail. You gave me a lot to think about. Is there anything I should know about the other residents?"

With a lighthearted laugh, she said, "Don't be silly. We don't all have an agenda here. We just do things to make life on the hill comfortable."

"Ok, well, see you later." I opened the door but closed it again. "Oh, what do you make of the bones story?"

"I'm sure it's nothing. Probably a dog burial. I haven't heard more. I've been out of town."

"They said it's actually human bones."

She seemed to tense up, but politely said, "I'm sure it will turn out to be nothing. Please say hi to EG for me."

I knew the conversation was over and left her cottage.

The rest of the day went smoothly, and I figured I could handle visiting cottages for the summer.

On the way back to EG's house, I thought about the routine we had if she was recognized in public when she visited me at school or when I met her in Chicago. If she got recognized, she had to buy me a book, but if they recognized her and asked for a selfie, I had to buy her a book. If they asked me to be in the picture, we gave $10.00 to charity.

I took my shoes off at the front door and heard EG clanging around in the kitchen. She brightened as I walked in.

I plopped a stack of magazines on the kitchen counter, smiling. "I'm not sure what the protocol is for when *I* get recognized so I bought us these."

She laughed and hugged me. "I love it. Any good stories from the hill people? Who recognized you?"

"Hill people? Is that what you call the old folks at Chambray? I met your *bookend*, Abigail. She implied there was some story between you two."

"What is that bitty doing these days?"

"She is not an old bitty."

"I didn't say *old*, just bitty. It's more polite than the alternative. I give her signed copies of my book to hand out to prospective residents."

"Yeah, she told me about their little routine to ward off annoying people, but it was more than that."

EG stood there for a moment. "Well, no, not much more. We went to the same schools here. We are among the few who remain in town. Like your mom, most River Bend kids leave and very few return. She seems to think we have some strange bond. High school was over twenty years ago. She needs to let some things alone."

"She didn't seem old enough for a senior living center."

"Technically, the fifty-five-plus age requirement is a suggestion, but her family developed the center so she assumed a cottage when it was built, thinking she would move in much later. Then her husband suddenly passed away a few years ago. She's only a year or two older than I am, but sometimes, she acts like she's the old town matriarch trying to make the folks in town her little minions."

"So her little bookend story is BS, or is there really some stuff between the two of you?"

She paused and let out a quiet breath. "Bookend, my ass! I don't know what she knows or what she thinks I know!"

CHAPTER ELEVEN

The next two days of volunteering flew past. I tried logging ten hours each day, but Sunday afternoon was a challenge. There wasn't much to do, and the weather was too nice to be working.

I left at 3:00 p.m. and went home. EG was in her office, deep in thought, and I didn't want to disturb her. I quietly backed away from her door and tiptoed down the stairs.

The nice weather was calling to me, so I grabbed EG's book *The Scarecrow* and headed for the town square. Several businesses surrounded the square, and beside a gazebo and children's play area were great chairs for relaxing or watching band concerts in the summer.

Norman Rockwell, here we are, I thought as I sat in one of the chairs. The early summer heat was beginning to let up slightly, and heavy rain was forecasted for the week's end.

There weren't many people around so some teenagers had free rein of the gazebo to perform skateboarding tricks without complaints from pedestrians.

I took off my shoes and was completely comfortable with my left foot buried in the grass and my right leg tucked under me. I was in my happy place—outside with a book for leisure, not a class lecture, and without distraction from roommates. The hum in my head that had never let me be idle finally started to disappear, and I breathed a sigh of relief.

I can't believe it, I'm actually being idle.

I read the first and last pages in each chapter of EG's book to help me recall the story. I'd read it in seventh grade, thinking I would find information about the big family secret I had discovered. The secret should have thrown me into a spiral and created more questions, but it gave me great comfort and answered questions I didn't know I had.

The book, I had discovered, had nothing to do with me.

It was a tale of a pathetic baseball team that had not won a game in ten years. EG had written a good mix of romance, bullies in the classroom, and an underdog hero.

The climax of the story happened at the last game of another losing season. It was 1-0 going in to the bottom of the ninth inning. River Bend was losing, but there was hope. There were two outs and one kid on base.

Everyone in the stands let out a deep sigh as Earl, an awkward junior who'd never played sports before, walked up to bat. He had not had a hit all season, and the only reason he was on the team was so they had enough players.

Earl had always felt invisible, and his good grades and debate team skills earned him no respect from his classmates, especially girls. He figured this might be an opportunity for someone to notice him. On this pathetic team, there was only one way to go—up. Earl wanted to be part of a real sports team and catch the attention of a girl. Any girl.

He knew the expectations were low, but he didn't care. They should thank him, he thought, because without him, there would be no team.

Earl walked to home plate. The other team was in their dugout, packing up as if the game was over. That made Earl mad. As he wiped his nose on his sleeve, the anger grew. He hated being counted out before he'd even come to the plate.

Standing there, watching that other team, he knew this was his moment.

When the first pitch came, he swung,

missed, and actually fell to the ground.

Everyone laughed except for the catcher, and that was probably because Earl had knocked into him as he'd fallen. It was clear the pitcher was not taking him seriously now.

Earl was done. He was done with all the laughing and everyone underestimating him.

He took his stance again and knew this was his moment *again*.

The pitch was perfect, and Earl knew a second before everyone else that he had a hit. It was not just a hit but a home run.

The ball flew high and fast, and it took everyone a moment to realize what was happening. The runner on first had barely left the base as Earl approached. In the dugout, his team stood frozen in awe.

Then something went wrong. As the ball was about to fly over the outfield fence to the farmland beyond, it hit a crow and came straight down into the center fielder's glove. The crow was knocked down on the other side of the fence. The center fielder didn't even realize he'd caught the ball because he was busy plucking feathers out of his hair.

For those five seconds, Earl had believed he was going to be the hero. He'd seen everything in his life change. He'd seen respect, admiration, and more importantly, acceptance from his teammates.

He'd had it all until that damn crow.

That damn crow!

As usual, River Bend wrapped up the season with another winless record. Earl did gain five minutes of notoriety as the story spread through school, but he did not get much more respect.

He spent the summer, fall, and winter making scarecrows and placing them all over town. He did this at night and in secret, not wanting to be known as the creepy scarecrow kid. He put enough of them out there to scare the birds but not so many for anyone to become suspicious. He had enough problems and nicknames already.

Earl also spent those months lifting weights and studying baseball, determined to graduate with respect, which he'd only obtain through baseball. His good grades and nice but shy personality were not going to do it.

No one was more excited for the baseball season to start. At the first game, Earl was fourth to bat. He was hoping for his second moment in the spotlight.

He saw the pitch, took a deep breath, and swung. "Oh my god, oh my god, oh my god." He had a hit.

Safe on first base, he was the last to realize the bat had broken and part of it had hit the pitcher, giving him a cut and a bruise under his eye. The pitcher was removed from the game.

Earl didn't get another hit that day because he was too nervous every time he stepped up to the plate. He wanted to prove himself but had never thought he would harm others.

With his one hit, Earl's team ended up winning their first game in eleven years. That day, his team credited their win to the fact the other team had to put in their backup pitcher.

Earl's role in the win was later recognized as the catalyst for their first winning season.

I was startled out of my thoughts when I heard someone say, "Today, they are yellow."

When I looked up, Aaron was standing there, pointing to a tennis ball by my chair. I hadn't realized it had landed there.

Tossing it back to him, I said, "Is that all you got? Good pie and colorful balls?"

He grinned. "What else do I need?"

"EG told me the story about how people in town are nutty for your grandma's pies, but you have to explain the balls."

"It's all from the book you got there. Or, at least, that's what I've been told. I haven't ever read it."

"It is a story about the lonesome underdog who wants respect and a losing baseball team. And of course scarecrows."

"Those damn scarecrows give me the creeps. Sorry, no offense to EG."

"I think she would agree with you."

Aaron sat in the seat next to me. "The balls . . . Well, that's because I volunteered to clean up sports equipment tossed from vehicles along the freeway or left somewhere by visiting teams. The town doesn't want to waste resources picking the stuff up."

"That seems a bit unfair to you."

"I don't mind. I love running, and it keeps me out there longer. I'm helping the community and staying on the sheriff's good side. Anytime I have trouble with college kids, he and his officers are quick to help."

"So what's up with all the discarded equipment, and what's with the pom-poms and white footballs?"

Aaron smiled.

Damn, he's got a great smile.

"Years ago, on the anniversary of the her first book, EG wrote a short story about a broken bat being buried under home plate and that the town has never had a losing baseball season since. Nobody was sure if the story was nonfiction or not, but this time of year, busloads of kids heading to sports camps or competitions leave stuff behind for good luck. And the white football is actually a rugby ball."

"I get it now," I said.

"I didn't intend to have a sports-themed bar,

but then again, I never thought I would have my own bar."

"But you have two bars, right?"

"I just have BAR. The other night you saw me, I was helping my friend Jim. During the summer when the Jameson kids leave, most bars don't open every day. So I had some time to help Jim out when he needed to leave for a few hours.

"I have to ask—BAR? There were no other options left to name a bar, or were you trying to dumb it down for the Jameson College students?"

"Well, aren't you a little high on yourself for a college graduate? Come with me to BAR now, and if you can figure it out in thirty minutes, I will give you a whole pie; otherwise you have to do the highway run this week."

"I have a boyfriend," I blurted out.

"I don't. Plus, you already told me that. I also have brown hair, blue eyes, and my taxes are up-to-date. But who cares, I was placing a bet and not asking you on a date."

My cheeks grew hot. "I don't know why I said that. Maybe another time. I should get back to EG's."

He nodded, and we said our goodbyes.

I couldn't help but feel sorry for him. My roommates and I had had a hard time finding boyfriends in our small college town. I could not imagine how many options there were for a gay man in a town of this size. I should have taken him up on his bet because pie sounded good.

But why does it sound so dirty?

CHAPTER TWELVE

When I got home, I slipped on my pj's and went downstairs. EG was on the couch with enough popcorn to get us through two movies. I knew before she said anything it was going to be a night of Hitchcock thrillers—her latest kick. Last summer, it had been science fiction movies (I stayed away). I was happy to be here for the Hitchcock classics. I couldn't imagine if she'd gone with foreign films or documentaries. We could've had our first fight.

Monday morning before my 8:00 a.m. shift, I stopped by Abigail's cottage. She seemed a little surprised to see me but was welcoming. The cottage was brightly lit with the natural sunlight and it smelled like apple pie but I didn't see any and the oven was cool to the touch.

"Who has you doing rotations so early? Is it Mrs. Baron? I know it can't be Chef David as you have no pantry food with you."

"No, just me. I brought some fresh strawberries. You make amazing muffins with frozen blueberries so I'm curious what you can do with fresh strawberries. David said the fresh blueberries would be another month. If you need anything that David is not willing to supply from the main kitchen, I can get it from the store for you."

Abigail smiled. "That is sweet of you. I can take myself to the store, but I like using the services offered here at Chambray. David is being cheap. He may not get any more muffins until I get some fresh berries from *him*."

"I think he has a thing for you. He got a sparkle in his eyes when we went over your requisition list."

"Don't be silly, David is like that about all the ladies. Come back after your shift, and I will have scones ready for you. And tell David to stop ordering that pathetic thing he calls orange juice and get the real stuff."

"Will do. This morning the staff could not stop talking about that fisherman. What are the rumors with the residents about the bones found in the river?"

"To be honest, I'm not in the know. I don't mix with most of the senior residents. Since Mayor Carl has not been around much because of his knee, my line of information has been cut off. He hasn't been mayor for three terms now, but the sheriff and most everyone else confides in him more than Eugene. I'm surprised your aunt hasn't provided you with the details."

"She hasn't heard any more than anyone else."

With nothing more to learn, I said goodbye to Abigail and started my rounds.

After my shift, I returned to EG's to find her talking with the sheriff, some of her old notebooks and her laptop were on the dining room table. He was tall and a good-looking guy, and a uniform usually has me hooked, but not with him. Maybe because I have always known him to be married he never crossed into my space of "older men that I could date." I loved a guy in uniform, but the visible gun made me nervous regardless if he was on the right side of the law. They seemed to be having a lengthy discussion but stopped talking when I came in.

"Good to see you again, Claudia," Sheriff Dalton said.

"Yes, nice to see you too. Thanks again for your help the other day at the gas station."

"Don't worry about it. It happens all the

time."

"It does not. No one else has my luck, but thank you for making me feel better. What's going on here?"

"I stopped by to pick EG's brain. With all the research she's done for her books, I think she knows more about detective work than I do."

"Does this mean there's more information about the bones found in the river?"

"Well, since I shared it with EG, I guess I can tell you as well. The bones are from a human male believed to be forty to sixty years old. They have been in the river for twenty to thirty years."

"That's amazing. How can you tell?"

"I'm not sure. That's all the information I got. The medical examiner from Kirkasaw County, down south a couple of miles, is handling the investigation and made the determination. I'm only getting the information on an as-needed basis officially. My buddy down there said he would send me the report when he has a copy and his boss is gone for the day. From what I gather, the body was in a canvas sack of some sort and was weighted down with cinder blocks and rocks. The guy who found it said his anchor snapped off his boat, and he went back with his brother in his brother's boat to try to retrieve it. They were trolling the bottom of the riverbed and pulled up the old guy. What a surprise! Can you imagine that? They said they didn't know what they had until they reached the shore. They thought it was trash getting caught up by the dam."

"That's crazy!" I said.

"Tell us about it. EG and I were in high school around the time this happened. EG is my first stop, and then I'm going to head up the hill to see Abigail. She used to be the town historian and worked at the library. We figured I could get her to help me pull articles from the town archives or old newspapers. See if we can come up with any unusual stories from the time period. No missing person from then matches the age of anyone listed in the county." The sheriff was speaking to me but looking at EG.

I didn't know what to make of it, but it was weird. Shivers ran through my body.

"That's not a bad idea. I saw her a couple of hours ago. I bet she's still in her cottage. By the way, you can put that mug of tea down. EG has a coffeepot now."

EG grimaced. "How dare you rat me out. People expect tea from me, and it's easy. Don't change expectations."

"That's ok, EG. I'll keep your secret," Sheriff Dalton said and stood to leave.

A car door slammed, and a moment later, Mayor Eugene was walking up to the screened-in porch with dishes in his hand.

Without getting up, EG yelled, "I told you to stop with the food delivery."

Eugene stood outside the screened-in porch, dressed in his summer uniform of well-pressed khaki pants and a new-looking short-sleeve plaid shirt with the fold marks from the packaging visible. He looked exasperated. "Well, the ladies keep bringing stuff."

"You eat it," EG yelled.

"I tried, but it's just me, Rhonda, and sometimes, my father. I don't want to tell Ms. Robin no."

Sheriff Dalton glanced toward EG with a hopeful look.

She looked down at the table and sighed. "What's in the dishes?"

"Well, Ms. Robin made her chicken cacciatore and Ms. Faye made her tuna surprise."

After a hushed conversation with the sheriff, EG directed me to get the chicken cacciatore and declined the tuna surprise. I told Eugene to stop coming over with food and sent him on his way. He looked like a dog who got his tail slapped for peeing on the carpet.

Sheriff Dalton took the chicken cacciatore and promised to return the pan to the mayor himself. He gave EG a hug and me a wave, and he left.

"What were you able to tell the sheriff before

I got here?"

"My third book was about a body discovered in the spring after a harsh winter. I had to do a lot of research about bones, decay, and body identification. He has always been a good resource for me, but this time, he came to me for some reason. He was asking questions like it was an interrogation."

"I thought it was odd—when he was telling me the story, he seemed to be looking to you. Trying to gauge your reaction. Do you remember anything from that time period? I should ask my mom. She has a sharp memory. I guess you all would remember if someone you knew went missing back then."

"We all remember a lot from that time period. I think you and I should talk it all through. Give me a few days, and we can walk through it. I just need a little more time."

EG's phone rang, but after glancing at the caller ID, she declined to answer it.

"Who are you ignoring?" I asked.

"Just an old friend."

"Too many suitors?" I laughed.

She ignored me. "We have chicken potpie and berry tarts for dinner."

"You've been busy while I was gone, and I don't even see a dirty dish in the kitchen."

"I wish I could take credit for it all, but

Aaron stopped by. He knows the ladies in town were trying to put us on a meal plan and what that means. Last year, he broke his arm, and he was inundated with food. He ended up back in the hospital with food poisoning from Heidi's green-bean-and-meat-surprise casserole."

"Why would he think we want his food?"

"Don't knock it until you try it."

CHAPTER THIRTEEN

Early that evening as we were cleaning up, EG got another phone call. I could only hear her side of the conversation.

"Hello, Abigail," she said.

. . .

"Yes, I talked to Thomas."

. . .

"You worked at the library and were the town historian. It's only natural for me to send him to you. I really don't know anything!"

. . .

"We don't need to get together."

. . .

"You what? You called Theo. What for?"

. . .

"I don't think we need to get together."

. . .

"Go ahead. I can't stop you from having this mini reunion, but that doesn't mean I will be there."

EG hung up and stood there, staring at nothing for a moment. Quietly, she said, "I'm going out. I shouldn't be gone long."

As she was getting her shoes on, we heard a car pull up.

She looked towards the door. "If that's Eugene with another meal, I am going to get my gun and shoot him."

"You have a gun?"

"Yes, there is a gun club out on Highway 25. I always go to them with questions when I'm writing a book. I started target shooting as a hobby. I don't keep it for protection. There is no need for that in this town. I hardly lock my door. And no, I don't expect you to shoot anyone." She looked out the door. "No, don't shoot this man."

EG walked out to greet whoever was there. Only muffled conversation made its way to where I was drying the last of the dishes in the kitchen.

Loudly enough to reach my ears, EG said, "I'm going out for a while. See you later."

My curiosity was piqued, and I hurried to put a plate into the cabinet so I could see who had stopped by. I startled a bit when the screen door opened, not expecting the visitor to come inside after EG had left. *Who would be coming by to see me?*

"Claudia?" a male voice said.

Jackson? Jackson! Oh my god.

I dropped the dish towel and rushed to him, throwing myself in his arms. "Oh my god, what are you doing here?"

He held me but pulled back a little so he could look into my eyes. "You left a cranky note, and I didn't like it. Plus, I don't need to go to Chicago," he said, a proud smile on his face, and kissed me. His kiss was deep and hungry for more.

My heart nearly burst from happiness. "What do you mean? You found a place? How? Where? How much is it a month? Do you have pictures?"

"Not now. I will tell you about it later. I'm assuming EG won't be gone long." He grabbed my hand, and we headed upstairs.

We were still lying in my bed an hour later when I realized EG had not come home yet.

What if something happened to her? My stomach lurched at the thought. I sprung out of bed. "We're going for a walk, Jackson, get up."

"It's eight o'clock on a Monday night. What are you so worried about? Is EG that sick? She looked great."

"The chemo has really not hit her yet, but she is tired or distracted. Like she has something on her mind. I can't figure it out. Get dressed and help me find her."

"Can't you call her?"

"She didn't take her phone. And stop playing games and tell me about our place in Chicago."

"Just a second," he said and pulled on his shoes. "I need to go out to my car." Not saying anything more, he went downstairs.

I came down a minute later, and Jackson returned from the car with some flowers.

"They're for EG," he said, rattling his keys in his hand. "Why don't we drive around? We'll cover more ground."

"She may be on a trail or by the river. We'll be able to cover more ground if we walk." *Did I really suggest walking?* "If she's fine, we can say we're out for a walk and not look like paranoid babysitters. I would rather not frighten her. If we need the car, one of us can run back here and get it."

"Sure, whatever I can do for you. You should have told me more about her," Jackson said.

I wandered around the first floor, looking for my shoes and phone. "You're not listening. She's not that sick, but she's been irritated and seems very distracted these days." I stopped and looked at him shoving leftover chicken potpie in his mouth. "What are you doing?"

He shrugged, smiling. I couldn't do

anything but sigh.

"Let's go," I said after I'd located my phone and gotten my shoes on.

EG's neighbor Jorge was working in his garage but had not seen her, so we headed to the town square. There was no sign of her there either.

Probably best to look on the trail near the river, I thought.

Sure enough, as we arrived, EG was coming off the river path. Nearby on a park bench, Mayor Carl Phillip and Abigail were in a heated discussion.

Even from a distance, anyone could have known it was them. Abigail was sitting up straight wearing a perfectly coordinated summer outfit and her hair was in an elegant twist.

With his 6'5" skinny frame, collared short-sleeve button-down shirt, pressed khakis, and walking cane, Carl couldn't be confused with anybody else—even his son. Eugene was the mirror image of his father except Carl towered at least a foot over him, and now the cane had become his sidekick.

Jackson and I stood off where we couldn't be seen and watched the scene unfold. EG saw those two on the bench and turned sharply away. She appeared to be headed in the direction of her house.

Carl and Abigail seemed to be getting

nowhere in their conversation, and we started to leave, but Sheriff Dalton came walking out of the woods. He seemed to be carrying something small in his hand, and his uniform pants were dirty from the knees down.

I waved, but I didn't think he saw us. He had a fixed look on his face and walked directly to his squad car and left without acknowledging his surroundings.

"He seems to be transfixed on whatever's in his hand and getting out of here," I whispered.

"I bet he tripped and was embarrassed. Or maybe he found a clue to an unsolved case and is rushing the evidence back to the station."

"I don't know him well, but he seemed more robotic than human—out of character for him."

"Not everyone has to have an outspoken demeanor to be normal," Jackson said.

I shook my head, fighting myself to not roll my eyes. "Perhaps. Do you want to walk for a bit before we head back to EG's?"

"Sure," he said, taking my hand.

No matter how much I pressed him as we walked, he would not give me the details of the apartment and was being coy. He said the rent was great and I would approve—I just had to trust him, and he would tell me all once everything was confirmed.

Forty minutes later, we found EG sitting on

the porch, talking to my mom on the phone. I said hi to my mom, and she said they would see me this weekend, which was a nice surprise. I gave the phone back to EG.

Inside, Jackson plopped down on the couch in front of the TV, and I took a shower to cool down.

As I was coming down the stairs, EG was saying, "Of course, you can stay here. I appreciate the flowers." She turned to me. "Oh, there you are, Claudia. Ok, well, I'm off to bed, you two. We don't have to leave for the Mayo Clinic until ten, so sleep in since it's your day off. And, Jackson, there are some tarts in the refrigerator if you want something sweet."

"Thank you. You are so kind." Jackson stood to give EG a hug, and he headed into the kitchen.

I waited until he was done eating before I declared myself exhausted.

"What are you talking about? It's only nine thirty. I thought we could explore the town some more."

"I have been working since I got here."

He followed me upstairs, obviously thinking exhausted was code for I want more sex. He was disappointed when he realized it wasn't.

CHAPTER FOURTEEN

I fell asleep fast and hard but woke at 2:00 a.m. and had to use the bathroom. I spent the rest of the night tossing and turning. Two people sleeping in a double bed without air-conditioning and someone's snoring habit makes for an early morning.

Since we were up so early, I took Jackson to Peach's Café. At 7:00 a.m., the place was packed.

We ordered our breakfast and coffee at the counter and watched Aaron and Jan, his aunt and owner of the café, argue over what appeared to be a broken broom. We couldn't hear the discussion, but it appeared to be a friendly disagreement. He grabbed the broom and his breakfast sandwich, then turned and almost ran into us.

I jumped a foot back, bumping into Jackson to avoid getting hit with a broken broom. "Hi again," I said. "Aaron, this is Jackson. Jackson, this is Aaron."

The boys nodded and both grunted hello to each other. Jackson turned around and took a couple steps and looked around the cafe. Aaron leaned into and said, "So this is the boyfriend I heard so much about."

My face went pink and I nodded and move the conversation back to the scene we just watched "What was that all about? A family squabble?"

Shouting so Jan could hear, he said, "Apparently, some people think a broken broom belongs in my bar with all the other broken hockey sticks."

"Learn your sports," she shouted back, looking at us and waving to the corner seats. "Why don't you three take a seat on the sofa, and I'll bring your coffees over when everything is ready."

Glancing around, I saw something I hadn't noticed before. In the back corner on the other side of the small one-step wooden stage, there was a cozy living room set with the personality of a hippie chic with a Goodwill budget. It all looked too heavy to move and had probably been in that spot for decades.

An oversized mint-green velvet couch was covered with clean linens, which was odd since none of the tables had any tablecloths on them. Across from the couch were an orange corduroy love seat and an enormous royal-blue chair, which looked like a throne fit for a king, and in the middle of it all, a laminated table held a lamp with no discernible style. While all this should have shouted tacky and weird, it gave a warm, comfortable feel.

Jackson stepped back to join me and Aaron. "Shall we?" I asked, gesturing to the sitting area.

The men nodded, and we made our way over. Jackson took giants steps to claim the throne as his chair. Since the couch was covered with laundry, that left the love seat for Aaron and me.

"Ah, King, what finds you here in River Bend?" Aaron asked.

His joke seemed to be lost on Jackson. "I came to see Claudia and check on EG."

I turned to talk to Aaron, feeling awkward as if I was on top of him. I forced myself to relax and swallowed the lump in my throat. "Seriously, what's up with the broomstick?"

"My aunt was trying to convince me that Quidditch is a sport; therefore, the broken broom has a right to hang in my bar." He shouted for everyone to hear, "Harry Potter be damned!"

Jan approached with two coffees, a latte, and two breakfast sandwiches. "That's right. All sports, real or imagined, should be represented. You are a good man, Aaron. Keep it that way." She smirked and tousled his hair.

Doing his best Jan impression, Aaron said,

"Keep it that way. Keep it that way. Keep it that way." He took a deep breath and continued in his normal voice. "Aunt Jan, how about I don't complain about the powdered sugar and you don't decorate my bar."

Jan laughed and left us to our breakfast.

I turned back to Jackson. "Aaron has a sports bar and takes broken equipment and hangs it from the walls. It's kinda cool."

"Oh," Jackson said as he picked up his breakfast sandwich.

I looked at Aaron again. "A broomstick. That has to be the weirdest piece of equipment you have?"

He laughed, dropping his head to run his fingers through his hair. "One would think so, but no, not at all. It comes close, but it's not at the top of the list." His face was more serious when he looked back up at me. "I saw EG last night down by the river. I waved but barely got a half a smile from her. I doubled back around to make sure everything was ok, but she was already headed away from the river. Is everything ok?"

I shrugged. "We were there but didn't see you."

"I was running. I saw Mayor Carl too, hobbling to his car. He seemed very stoic. Abigail looked like she was solving the country's financial problems. There was an odd vibe all around the river last night. I had stopped at EG's house earlier in the day and didn't want to keep bothering her. I figured you were there, so she would be ok. Is she?"

"Yes, we are there for EG," Jackson said.

He'd brought flowers and asked how she was doing, so now he was acting like a caregiver? *Really? That's ballsy!* I was beginning to rethink a lot of things.

I pushed it out of my mind for the time being. "She's fine. Just, sometimes, I find her lost in her own mind. I don't know about any odd vibe, but we also saw Sheriff Dalton walking out of the woods by himself."

"That's funny because when I turned onto the river path, I saw Jean, his wife, leaving the area but not the sheriff. She seemed to be in a trance. Like I said, odd vibe."

Aaron finished his sandwich in four bites, grabbed his coffee, and got up. "Sorry, I gotta go. I have early deliveries this morning. Nice meeting you, Jackson. See you later."

"See ya. Thanks for dinner last night," I said.

With that, he was gone.

Jackson glared at me. "You had dinner with him last night?"

"No, you idiot. He is the one who brought over the chicken potpie and tarts. By the way, you could have been nicer."

"What do you mean? He didn't make that

meal for me. I didn't even know until now that he brought it over."

"He cooked it for EG. I meant—you showed no interest in the guy."

"What, why should I? You got a thing for him that I should know about?"

"Don't be ridiculous. I was talking about his bar, and you had the interest of a peanut."

"It's a sports bar. I have seen hundreds of sports bars. What's the big deal?"

I stood up, frustrated with the conversation. "You don't get it. Let's go. I want to clean up the house before we head to the Mayo Clinic. Wipe that powdered sugar off your face."

"What powdered sugar?" he mumbled as I was halfway out the door.

We walked back to EG's without speaking and found her in the kitchen reading the paper, finishing her breakfast. I started to go upstairs to clean but stopped when I heard Jackson and EG talking.

"The neighborhood where your loft is— what's it like? Is it a safe area?" Jackson must have heard me pause on the steps because he shouted, "No clues about our place, so keep going up those steps."

After cleaning upstairs, I started on the downstairs bathroom. EG stomped in, yelling, "You are here to drive me to my chemo appointments. You are not to clean the house. Now say goodbye to Jackson, and we can head out early."

I turned to find Jackson standing there with his duffel bag.

"I'll see you later," he said.

"What, you're not even staying twenty-four hours?"

"I'm going back to Milwaukee for the night, before I head to Chicago." He turned to EG and said, "I hope today is an easy day for you. Thanks for the advice on the Chicago neighborhoods. I may call you if this place doesn't work."

He gave me a hug and kiss and left me standing there with rubber gloves on, holding a rag, and a stunned look on my face. I was more surprised at his sudden departure than his sudden arrival yesterday.

I didn't bother to tell him about the powdered sugar on his sleeve.

CHAPTER FIFTEEN

We had a simple trip to Rochester, and while EG had her treatment, I taught two nurses how to track their teenage daughters on social media, how to track the girls' phones, and how to know who they are communicating with. When we were leaving, another nurse asked if I knew how to track her husband's movements. I didn't have an answer for her but wished her well.

When we got back to EG's house, we were surprised to find Sheriff Dalton standing in the living room.

EG looked at him, wide-eyed. "Tommy, what are you doing here?"

"I was returning the casserole dish. I knocked and no one answered, so I walked around, and as usual, your back door was unlocked. I told you to be more careful."

"I told you to take it back to Eugene. He created this meal delivery mess. Let him return the pans to the rightful owners."

"Right, well, if you get more food, don't hesitate to call me. Jean is with her sisters in Milwaukee for a few days, and I'm left to cook for myself until she gets back." He said his goodbyes and was gone.

"That was odd, or do you always have men in your house?" I asked.

"I don't understand it," she said, shaking her head. "Thomas is usually not that intrusive. He could have left the dish on the patio or delivered it directly to Eugene."

"How about I pick us up an early dinner at the Blue Daisy. And since I won't have to go to Chicago this week, I'll start cooking for us tomorrow."

"Stay away from the Blue Daisy on Tuesdays. The part-time cook is on duty on Tuesday and Wednesday nights. Head out Route 29 for two miles. Just before the freeway is a diner. Get two meatloaf dinners. And don't roll your eyes about meatloaf until you try it from Towne's K&B Restaurant. But before you go, could you move some boxes in my office?"

"Sure, let me call Chambray and see if I can pick up extra hours since I'm not making the trip."

After I called and picked up an extra eight-hour shift, I headed out for dinner. Halfway there, I realized I had forgotten to move the boxes for EG.

When I came back home, she was napping on the porch. I ate some of my meatloaf but decided EG did not know everything about food in this town. Meatloaf was meatloaf, and there was no making it great. I ate the last of the chicken potpie instead and left for the grocery store.

At the store, I meandered down the aisles, not knowing what I was going to make during the week. I stopped when I saw Kay talking with a man in a pinstripe suit and wingtips. He was only a few years older than her, but with her nose ring and purple-streaked hair, they seemed to be mismatched. She was laughing and reaching out to touch his arm as he talked.

Is she flirting with him?

She pointed to the wine aisle and took her phone out as he walked away.

I ambled up next to her. "Is he your type?"

"Oh god, yes. You have to figure he's wound up so tight that he'll explode, and I hope to be there. Hey, do you know how to make anything? I don't have a great phone signal in the store. I was hoping to Google something while Edward is buying wine."

"If you're trying a domestic thing, try the engagement chicken recipe. It's a roasted chicken with lemon. It's said once you make it for a man, you will be engaged within six months. It's a whole chicken and—"

"I don't want to marry the man. I want to—"

"Yeah, yeah, I get it. Ok. Just go with tacos. Ground beef and—"

"I know how to make tacos. That's a great idea. Thanks." She turned on her heels and said, "Edward, save the wine for another time. I think it's a margarita night."

I decided, although EG and I could not marry each other, I would still make engagement chicken dinner for us. With the shopping cart full of stuff I mostly knew how to make, I headed back to the house.

By the time I got back, she had eaten half her meatloaf and was watching the news.

"Any update on the bones?" I asked.

"Not more than we already knew. I called Eugene, and he has nothing new to report."

"I thought you would have better luck getting information from the sheriff."

She paused before she spoke. "I was thinking the same thing, but something about the way he was here this afternoon irked me. I called Eugene and told him exactly what to say to the Kirkasaw County investigator to get him to share the information. If he doesn't fumble it up and gets the report, he said he would bring it over here. I'm sure his father has some information as well."

"I loaded us up on food for the week. I'm working early tomorrow, but I have sandwich stuff here for you and I thought I could roast us a chicken for dinner. Tell me what boxes you need moved, and I can do that for you."

"That's odd, I thought you moved them because I found the box I was looking for while you were at the store. Everything is good now."

"What's in the box?"

"Old newspaper clippings and such. What are your plans for the night? It's only seven thirty."

"This town might be finally getting to me. I was thinking of going for a walk. Want to join me?"

"No, no, go ahead. I'm going to grab a book and read in bed for a bit." She came over, gave me a kiss on the head, and headed to her bedroom.

I walked along the river trail and found it peaceful and beautiful. A couple of families were putting stuff in their cars and wrapping up their day along the river. One fisherman was trolling along looking for a spot to cast his pole. I saw a couple of high school kids wander away from the river towards the woods. One was smoking, and the other appeared to be trying to smoke for the first time. I heard coughing and saw puffs of smoke.

Are people ever going to stop smoking?

Farther down the trail, Aaron ran towards me, out on his nightly run. He ran past and said, "You might want to turn around on the path before you get smothered." And with that he was off.

I didn't know what he meant until three minutes later when I was attacked by hundreds of mosquitos. I finally figured out why the families had left quickly and the kids had gone to hide in the pine trees away from the river. Eight p.m. was happy hour for these little buggers, and I was fresh bait. I turned and started running.

Aaron yelled from a distance, "You should get better running shoes."

I had no patience or quick wit for a snappy comeback so I ran back to EG's.

After showering off my six-minute run for my life/mosquito apocalypse, I called Jackson, but Mia, one of my roommates, answered.

"What's up, Mia? Why are you answering Jackson's phone? Where are you?"

"It's good to hear from you. We're at the apartment. Jackson came by looking for some clothes he said he left here. He was in the bathroom. Here he is now. Bye."

"Hey," Jackson said.

"What clothes are you looking for? You know I took everything I own from that apartment when I left last week."

"Just my favorite Toad-Hammer Band

sweatshirt. I didn't think to ask when I saw you, and I was just driving by, so I thought I would ask Mia or Sherrie. Hey, I think that place I found in Chicago is not going to work out. Will you ask your aunt about the neighborhood just north of Wrigley Field?"

"Why won't it work out? Aren't you going to see it?"

"I don't think I'm making the trip. The band I wanted to watch canceled."

"But what about the apartment? Will you go look at it? I picked up extra hours, so I can't come down this week. Aww, dammit!" I said, scratching the plethora of mosquito bites on my legs.

"Is something wrong?"

"I was walking by the river again and didn't heed Aaron's warning about not going through the marshy area and got attacked by bugs."

"You were with Aaron again? Should I be worried?"

"No, you don't understand. I was walking by myself, and he was running and shot me a warning but I didn't listen. Plus, I'm not his type. You are."

"Huh, ok, well, I gotta go. I'll talk to you later," Jackson said.

"Why do you have to go? You have no clothes at that apartment. Just wave goodbye to Mia and Sherrie so we can talk some more. I barely saw you before you left."

"I don't want to be rude to the girls here. Be sure to ask EG about that neighborhood. I'll call you tomorrow."

I ended the call with Jackson and tried ice on my bug bites. It helped for a short time, and I found an old bottle of pink stuff that was supposed to stop the itching. It was so old, more lotion was crusted around the rim than what was left in the bottle. It must have worked, because I was asleep in fifteen minutes.

CHAPTER SIXTEEN

The next morning, EG was up having breakfast when I rolled downstairs. Morning light was streaming through the open windows. I could hear Jorge's lawn mower and could smell the fresh-cut grass. I inhaled and stretched. Summer mornings were awesome.

EG was listening to the radio, and she looked good, and chemo did not seem to be drastically affecting her. "Maybe I can teach you some yoga this summer, and you can begin to love every morning. You're cooking dinner tonight, right? Do you have enough food for more guests?"

Thinking she was preparing for a book club dinner, I was delighted, but then realized I had not read a book. "I should have enough, and I will think about the yoga thing. It never really appealed to me," I said.

"Yoga will help in ways you could have never imaged." And then EG smiled, almost wickedly. "I have a surprise guest for you."

She wouldn't tell me any more, so I made my way to Chambray. My morning shift had me rattled. I'd spooked myself because of the silly stories Kay had told me about the Gray Lady.

I delivered pantry items to Abigail's apartment while she was not home, and it was the first time I had gone into a cottage when no one was present. I felt like someone was watching me.

After I used my master key, I placed it and my daily duty sheet on the kitchen table as I put away the pantry items.

Some of the items were missing, and I realized I only had one of two boxes from the pantry. I grabbed my key and looked at the list before I left to make sure only one box was missing. When I returned to the cottage, the list was flipped on its backside. I wasn't sure why I'd notice such a thing, but I also couldn't imagine how or why it had gotten turned over.

Am I beginning to believe in the legacy of the Gray Lady?

The afternoon hours were dreadfully boring. Several offices were getting new carpet, and I had to move furniture and files. Files that have been around for decades. I spent most of the time in search of tissues because I could not stop sneezing from all the dust. I was looking forward to going to EG's and relaxing but realized I had to shower and get ready for dinner.

I was still sneezing and blowing my nose during the walk home. My eyes were blurry, and my head was in a fog from the allergy medicine that Kay had given me—although I wasn't sure it was actually for allergies because my head was tingling. I walked up to the house, not noticing the canary-yellow VW Bug parked outside. Inside, my roommate Sherrie was sitting on the couch, talking with EG.

"Ahh," I squealed and dived bomb and gave her a hug while she was still curled up on the couch. "What are you doing here? I love it. How did you get up here?"

"I drove up. The little yellow Bug made it here with no problems. Can you believe it? The car is at 199,992 miles. Eight more and it rolls to two hundred thousand." Sherrie's eyes were wide with excitement.

"This is a great surprise, but why?"

EG looked at Sherrie. "She called to see how I was doing, and I thought you could use some girl time together so I made the suggestion she come up here."

They'd met when EG had come to pick me up for a weekend trip to Chicago. Like many people, Sherrie had fallen in love with her, and EG had taken an instant liking to Sherrie. She had gotten one of the rare invitations to a book club dinner last year.

EG turned to me. "Oh my, you should probably shower and change." I looked at my clothes. "That's terrific, not only did I encounter the Gray Lady today, but with all the dust on me, I'm channeling her look."

I explained my encounter in the cottage, and they rolled their eyes.

"Go shower, and hopefully, the steam will help clear your nose and head. Hurry up, we have one more guest coming for dinner," EG said.

With a knock on the door, we turned. Aaron stood on the porch, holding a pie and a loaf of bread. He wore a light-blue button-down shirt with the sleeves rolled up, and like every guy in their midtwenties, he was wearing cargo shorts. But apparently, he knew how to clean his shorts opposed to the college guys I knew who wore them so often they turned from a shade of khaki to a shade of dirt. It was a casual but smart look on him, and the shirt highlighted his eyes.

EG introduced Sherrie and Aaron and started directing us. She sent me up to shower and get rid of the dusty clothes, and Aaron was sent into the kitchen. On my way up, I heard EG talking quietly to Sherrie about tomorrow. I didn't pay close attention, hoping Sherrie would tell me later.

I was down the stairs fifteen minutes later with wet hair, fresh makeup, and clean clothes, feeling almost human again. It probably had to do more with the "allergy" pill Kay had given me than the shower, but at least I could talk without snot dripping out of my nose.

Sherrie was lost in a haze of giggles as she talked to Aaron. She flashed me a look and mouthed *he's so cute* behind his back when he wasn't looking. They had managed to set the table and were now making a salad.

"You guys can slow down on the chopping. The chicken will take a while," I said.

Aaron grinned at me. "Actually, it's already in the oven. I stopped by an hour ago to pick up the potpie pan, and EG invited me to dinner. I told her I couldn't because I have a commitment later. But you know EG being EG, that conversation ended up with me roasting chicken and being sent out to get some pie. I came back here to find a new guest has been added to our group."

The shower had cleared my sinuses enough for me to catch the juicy flavors coming from the oven. "It smells delicious," I said.

EG went to the stereo and turned on some music. "Claudia, why don't you get some wine from the basement?"

We declared that since EG wasn't

drinking—it wouldn't have mixed well with her chemo—we would abstain as well. I grabbed some sparkling water, and when only Sherrie was looking, I pulled my earlobe. It was our code for when we were in bars and had to signal to our friends that a guy was gay and just not into you. Rubbing the top of your nose was the signal the guy had a girlfriend.

"I don't believe you on this one," she whispered.

As dinner was wrapping up, Aaron said, "Well, this has been fun."

"It has been fun," EG said with a smile, raising her glass. "I'm so glad you all came."

Sherrie and I nodded, clinking our glasses with hers. EG eyed Aaron until he finally joined in.

He laughed and shook his head. "I'm going to check out a band tonight. They're hoping to get a monthly gig at my bar this fall. Would you all want to come along and give me your opinion?"

EG clapped her hands together. "That's a great idea. Sherrie, Claudia, you should go." She mouthed *tomorrow* to Sherrie, and with that, she practically threw us out the door.

Everyone loved EG and felt connected to her, but I could not help but wonder what was going on between her and Sherrie. I gave up hope that Sherrie would tell me. She was a fierce and loyal friend, but once she was told to keep a secret, there was not much anyone could do to get her to spill the beans.

We stepped outside, and I started walking towards the town square.

"Where are you going? We have to drive," Aaron asked.

"Where is the band playing?"

"In La Crosse. You think any decent band could draw a crowd in this town on a Wednesday night when Jameson College is out of session for the summer? Are you guys up for the forty-minute drive?"

"Of course." Sherrie giggled and hopped in the front seat of Aaron's truck.

I was going for the back seat when Aaron said, "You'll have to ride up front since I've got construction supplies in back."

"Ok," I said, sliding in beside Sherrie.

The truck was old but well cared for inside and out. There were tools and two buckets with stuff in them in the back seat, and the front seat had a rip across it, but I could tell it was well maintained.

Maybe my thinking was warped by all the guys I knew from high school and college. I always expected an old bag of fast food lying on the floor, and a minimum of three empty soda bottles tossed in the back.

Aaron noticed the once-over I gave the

truck. "It was my grandfather's. I bought it from him before I went into the army. He could keep any engine going for decades but didn't care about the interior so much."

We drove the entire forty minutes with Sherrie doing most of the talking. It was nervous talk with no straight line of conversation. She was talking just to talk. She had no shot with Aaron, so I didn't know where this nervous behavior was coming from.

La Crosse was another town on the Wisconsin side of the Mississippi River. The bar was a block from the river with a large patio that had an outdoor bar, a stage, and lights strung across wooden trellises.

When we went outside to the patio, Aaron spotted the owner, Paul. After Aaron introduced us, Paul took us to a tall corner table with a reserved sign on it and said he would send a pitcher of beer over. The crowd was a mix of baseball teams, regulars, and a large group that seemed to be there for the band.

Beer helped calm Sherrie down. She finally stopped talking a mile a minute and caught the eye of a baseball player. He came over, and those two hit the dance floor.

Aaron and I sat at the table in uncomfortable silence for a few minutes. I was sitting on my hands, swinging my legs under the barstool, and taking nervous gulps of cheap beer. Aaron had his fingers wrapped around the plastic beer cup, holding on for dear life or maybe hoping a conversation would pour out of it.

"I thought she would not stop talking," he said.

Beer gushed out of my nose. After our laughter died down, I said, "I don't know what's gotten into her. She is not normally that chatty. I guess it takes a cute guy and dancing to stop her from talking."

"Maybe it will get you to start talking," Aaron said as he grabbed my hand and led me to the dance floor.

The song ended, and a new one began—a slow song, of course.

"Maybe next time," I said, walking off the dance floor.

"Not so fast." He grabbed my arm and pulled me close.

"What are you doing?"

"Dancing. I hope."

"I have—"

"Yes, I know you have a boyfriend. You mention it every time I see you, *and* I met him. This is just a dance."

"I guess it doesn't matter."

"What doesn't matter?"

"W-well, uh-um, because you play for the

other team?"

"What do you mean? You think I'm gay?" He stopped dancing.

We stood there for a few beats. He grabbed me again and started dancing.

"What made you think that?"

"Well, one of the many times I blurted out I have a boyfriend, you said you did not. The first night I saw you bartending, Kay mentioned something about you being into bar boys, and what straight guy would name a sports bar BAR? Oh, and what straight guy would use that much hair gel?"

"Interesting. Yes, I said I did not have a boyfriend. I was just mocking you. Bar boys? Not sure what Kay meant, but yeah, I don't flirt with her or Jenna. They're not my type, and I pay attention to the guys who spend money in my bar. It makes for good business sense. BAR is the name of my bar because those are my initials. My full name is Bart Aaron Rhoimly—B-A-R. As far as the hair gel, I don't have an argument because I don't know what you mean." He removed his hand from my back and ran his fingers through his hair.

We slowly moved in step with each other as the music continued. "So you're not gay. I guess I'd better tell Sherrie she was right."

"Oh, please don't do that. I mean, she's nice and cute, but I can't handle the talking."

"Don't worry. With a few beers, she'll mellow. Where is she anyway?"

"Over there," Aaron said. He shook his head and mumbled, "Hot hell." He turned me, and we watched her at the bar doing tequila shots with her new baseball buddy and his friends.

The music picked up, and we walked back to our table.

Sherrie came back to the table with shots for us. "I got something for you guys," she said, smiling.

I quickly learned she had done more than one shot herself.

"But you guys have to do the shot. I got him to buy these for us," she said, slurring slightly.

"No, thank you," we said in unison.

She picked up the shots and headed back to her new friends, downing one of them as she strolled back over to the bar.

The bar owner came back, and he and Aaron talked shop for a bit. As he left, Sherrie staggered over and declared it was time to leave.

"Why, did you get his number?"

"Yup, I got that he is a dick," she said, hiccupping.

"How did you figure that out?" Aaron said.

"He's, he's ma-mmmarried. We were going to walk towards the river and got to the" —*hiccup*— "door, and I saw his ring finger had a tan line. I told him I had to pee so here we am." She hiccupped again.

I looked at Aaron. "Sorry, do you mind if we go now?"

"Sounds like a good idea. I heard enough of the band and some us of had enough of the bar." He gently took a hold of Sherrie's arm and guided her to the back stairs of the patio. When we got to the car, he said, "Sherrie should have the window seat in case she gets sick."

I nodded, and we all climbed in.

"All you men suck," she said, looking at Aaron. "Well, I don't know about your team, but you probably understand."

"Actually, Aaron is not."

He jabbed me in the ribs, and I kept his secret from drunk Sherrie.

"Actually, Aaron is not going to contradict you," I said, smiling.

CHAPTER SEVENTEEN

As we rolled into River Bend, Sherrie was sleeping with her head pressed against the window.

Aaron looked at her. "Are you in a hurry to get home?"

"I have no reason to run home, but I don't think Sherrie needs any more to drink."

"We're not going to a bar. Just trust me," he said.

We wound up in the parking lot near the riverbank. Aaron parked, hopped out, and motioned for me to follow him out of the truck from the driver's side.

Whispering so I wouldn't wake Sherrie, I said, "I don't want to get eaten alive by mosquitos."

"They're not that bad now. They come out after dusk for about an hour and then fade away.

Follow me. Put some of this spray on, and you'll be fine."

The air was slightly cool because of the light breeze. People sat in beach chairs by the river, and about half a dozen boats floated on the water. I followed him to the bed of the pickup. He put a blanket down and folded up some beach towels for pillows and stretched out.

"What the hell is this?" I said.

"I know, you have a boyfriend. No shit. You told me several times. You see the other cars here. Nothing is going to happen. Just lie down."

I don't know why, but I did as he said.

"Tonight, there's supposed to be an amazing meteorite shower. Look up and watch."

"This is pretty cool. Good thing you're not gay because this move would be wasted on a guy."

"Thanks? I appreciate the feedback. I will note it in my dating log." He laughed.

We lay quietly side by side looking at the sky, one pointing out streaks of light for the other.

After a few minutes, I broke the silence with giggles. "How long did it take you to come up with the name BAR?"

"My brother, Chuck, wanted to open a bar—"

"EG told me a bit about what happened. But not about how you chose the name."

"Ok, well, my family pressured me into

putting my name on the liquor license. They didn't think I had a plan for the future since I had just got done with my stint in the army, but then again, they didn't ask if I had a plan. I went to support my brother, and one thing led to the next, and my name is on the license, which is fine since Chuck took off at the first sign of any real work needing to be done."

"So you kept at it? Running the bar?"

"I realized I could make decent money while developing my other project. I'm surprised you don't know this already. It's pretty easy making money with a bar in a college town once you figure out a few things."

"Like what?" I asked.

"Hire the right people and do things to keep them honest and know when to stay open and when to close."

"So that's why you're closed now. No college kids to feed your pockets."

"Over the summer when most of the students are gone, we rotate who stays open. It's a win-win for everyone. All the bar owners get time off, and I can work on other projects."

"What other projects?"

"Just some other things I'm working on. The bar gives me an opportunity to build some savings and explore my interests."

We fell quiet again. He sat up and reached

back into a plastic bin and pulled out another blanket and offered it to me. I draped the blanket over my legs and eased back into stargazing.

"Can I tell you a secret?" he asked.

I looked over at him. "Sure."

"The name BAR was a mistake."

"What do you mean, a mistake? It's your place."

"That night when I agreed to put everything in my name, I was nervous and flustered. When it came time for the paperwork, I messed up. This town still does some things with pen and paper. I was in a hurry, and the line that read Establishment, I read it as a question of what type of business so I wrote in pen BAR. I didn't realize my mistake in time and had to submit it before the meeting started. I figured I could change it later. As they read the application, I didn't think it was a big deal, but then Jean, Sheriff Dalton's wife, read the application out loud and declared it such a cute idea. Her words, not mine. To quote her, 'Oh my, Bart Aaron Rhoimly, B-A-R. Ladies and gentlemen, we must declare this approved, this fine young man must open BAR.' I did not want to do anything to jeopardize the approval process, so I went with it."

"Your secret is safe with me."

"That lady Jean has her hand in everything. Opening night, I invited about fifty people. She was

144

there with Thomas. I can't prove it, but I swear, she took my dollar."

"You're upset about a dollar?"

"I know it sounds corny, but after the hard work of getting everything ready, I was excited, and I bought a special frame for the first dollar I ever made. Chuck's army buddy Todd ordered the first drink. Everything was going to be complimentary that night, but he insisted on paying and said it was a bad omen to give away the first drink. The money was on the bar one minute, and the next minute it was gone. There was so much going on. People brought food, and of course, we had pie on the bar so it could have gotten tossed around, but I swear, I saw her nick it."

"I don't know what to say to that."

"There's not much to say. I thought since I was telling secrets, I would share that too."

Our attention turned to the sky, and we fell silent until I started giggling again.

"I have to ask, what's with Bart? Your parents not happy when you were born? Bart."

"*The Simpsons* had been on TV for a while, and somehow, they thought the name was going to be the hot new name. After a few years and luckily before school started, they started calling me Aaron."

I started rhyming everything I could with Bart and finally broke out in a fit of laughter. Aaron joined in with more rhymes and even told me a song his brother had made up about his name. The song was in the tune of "Barbara Ann" from the Beach Boys. He sang it once but refused to repeat it based on his boyhood ego still being fragile. I couldn't help just repeating *Bar Bar Bart Aaron* to the music from the Beach Boys. I made a mental note to get the full lyrics if I ever met Chuck.

With both of us cry-laughing, we didn't hear the truck door open, but we did hear "Where the hell am I?"

"Hey, Sherrie, we're back here looking at the meteorite shower. Join us," I said.

She walked to the end of the truck and slid her butt across the tailgate, then leaned against the side of the truck and reached for a blanket.

"How long was I out?"

"Don't use that blanket. That belongs to Rita. Here, use this, it's clean," he said, handing her a towel. "You haven't been out long. We've only been here twenty minutes. Do you want some water?"

We nodded, and he tossed both of us a bottle.

"Thanks. Look, there's the creepy guy from the gas station this afternoon," Sherrie said.

"What guy?" Aaron and I said in unison, and we turned to see Eugene walking along the trail.

"I was getting gas and talking on the phone with my mom. I told her I came here because EG called and wanted to talk. That old guy heard me say EG's name and hobbled around the pump and started to babble something about EG. I couldn't understand the point he was trying to make. Oh, wait, I don't think that's the same guy. The old guy had a cane, but they are dressed alike. Who the hell wears pleated pants these days?"

"You probably saw his dad. I thought you called EG?" I said.

"What difference does it make?"

"You two have been whispering behind my back. What's up?"

Aaron held his hand up. "Here comes Eugene."

We turned our attention to the parking lot and saw Eugene—sorry, Mayor Eugene—walking up in huff and swatting away bugs.

"Mayor, what brings you out tonight? Watching the show in the sky?" I said.

"Good evening, Aaron, Claudia, Miss." He nodded to each of us and continued. "I am looking for my father. He was in a sour mood this afternoon and never came over for dinner. My wife, Rhonda, said he never called. I walked over to his house and the car is there so I'm assuming he's out walking, but I'm not sure how far he can get with his bad knee. It's not like him to be gone at this hour on a

Wednesday. I can't imagine where he's gone."

"Have you checked the bars? That's where I would be," Sherrie said.

Eugene looked askance at her. "What?"

"Eu—Mayor Eugene—this is my friend Sherrie. Sherrie, this is the town's mayor," I said.

Aaron picked up his phone and dialed a number. "Hey, Jim, what's up this evening?"

. . .

"Really?"

. . .

"Yeah, the Yankees suck. The Brewers will get them next time. Anything else exciting?"

. . .

"Really?"

. . .

"Interesting. Keep me updated. I got another month or so before I open up again full-time. Give me a call if you need help." He ended the call and looked at Eugene. "Your old man is up at Draw Bar. Just sitting in the corner drinking."

"Why did you do that? I don't want people thinking he is missing or lost."

"Calm down. Did you hear me say his name? Jim thinks I was checking if he needed help. Draw Bar is one of three places open tonight. Anything happening in this town will be up for full discussion by anyone and everyone that walks in there. Do you not understand this town we live in?

148

He told me about the crowd that's there for the game and mentioned a few guys in the bar. He thought it was unusual for your dad to be there by himself. Just say thank you and move on."

I stifled a laugh. Aaron just schooled Eugene on his own town.

The mayor hung his head, shaking it. "Guess I better get out there and get him."

After Eugene left to retrieve his dad, Aaron said, "I think we should call it a night. What about you ladies?"

Sherrie and I agreed, and we piled into the truck again.

When Aaron pulled into the driveway, we were surprised to find the lights on in the living room and kitchen. Inside, EG was sitting on the sofa with her legs folded under her and a cup of tea in her hand. The TV was on, but the volume was low.

"I guess we're not the only night owls tonight," I said, coming around to the other side of the couch. When I saw her face, I stopped dead in my tracks. "What's wrong, EG?"

She brought her focus to us and motioned for the two of us to sit. "I went to bed early and woke to the sound of someone throwing rocks at the house."

"What! Did they break anything? Did you walk around?" Sherrie asked.

"Do you want me to call Sheriff?" I asked.

Calmly, with an even tone and a shrug, EG said, "Sit down, you two. Everything is fine. It's probably some high school kids getting restless early in the summer. I think it was rocks or pebbles. As long as it wasn't eggs or bricks, I'm ok. I stayed up and see if any neighbors would stop over if they had the same thing happen."

"Well, was it a neighborhood thing, or were you being harassed?" I asked.

"No one stopped over tonight, but I'll ask in the morning. I'm not worried. Besides, Jorge came home ten minutes ago, so if anything else happens, he will be all over it." She smiled, but it seemed forced. "How was your night?"

I let it go for now. "Goo—"

Sherrie jumped in. "It was interesting. The band was great. Men suck. Meteors rock. And Aaron is not gay. That pretty much sums up our night."

"Of course, he's not gay. How did you girls miss that one?"

"I misunderstood something Kay said. I'm going to walk around outside to make sure it's safe," I said.

"Sit down, Claudia. Nothing is going to happen. Actually, let's all go to bed now," EG said. She got up and turned off all but one of the lights.

"Fine, but only because I'm sleeping on the sofa tonight. I'm going to make sure the doors are locked, and I'm leaving the porch light on," I said.

Sherrie held up a hand in protest. "No, I'll sleep on the sofa. That was the plan."

"You go pass out on my bed, and I'll take the sofa."

She wouldn't let it go. "I didn't drink that much tonight. I was more tired than drunk, and with all this activity, I'm not sure I can sleep anyways."

CHAPTER EIGHTEEN

The morning was a delight. For once, there were no volunteer hours on the hill, no drive to chemo, and no drive to Chicago to apartment search. Although the latter was still bothering me. Jackson's lack of urgency was edging my nerves, but to be honest, no one knew how critical finding the right apartment was for me and my budget.

EG and Sherrie were having tea and coffee when I came downstairs, and I suggested a walk to show Sherrie the town.

I got such strange looks from both of them that I stopped midsentence and sat down like a child who'd gotten hushed.

EG patted the table. "I want to talk to you, and figure we can have breakfast here."

"Sure, everything ok? Are you feeling ok?

You look a little pale."

"I told you last night, I did not drink that much. I was really, really tired," Sherrie said.

"That's great, but I was talking to EG. You know our gal with chemo, not the one with tequila breath."

"Yes, I'm fine. Just tired. There's a quiche on the stove, and Sherrie cut up some fruit."

"Oh, look, here comes that little weirdo again," Sherrie said, gesturing to the front door.

Eugene was on the porch, about to knock. He was again in a plaid short-sleeve shirt and pressed pleated khaki pants. I dared not look at what color his socks were, but the docksider shoes were spotless.

"If you have food, go away, otherwise you may come in," EG shouted.

"Thank you, EG. No food today, but I have a report from the medical examiner's office," he said, holding up a manila envelope.

Sherrie jumped up and grabbed it. "Oh, is this about the bones found in the river?"

Eugene tried pulling the envelope away, but Sherrie had more willpower and towered over him by a foot.

"It's ok. I'm Sherrie—Claudia's friend. I'm studying criminal behavior. I know how to read these things."

"Eug—Mayor Eugene—this is Sherrie. You

met last night," I said.

Sherrie ignored us and pulled the papers from the envelope. She started to read the report.

Should I have told Eugene that Sherrie was a liberal arts major, or let it go? Ah, I let her have some fun with it.

EG smiled and turned to Eugene. "Anything interesting in the report?"

He seemed unsure of where to turn his attention, and he finally spoke to EG with one eye on Sherrie. "It's a preliminary report. The medical examiner determined the bones were from a man with Eastern European descent. Cause of death at this stage in the investigation is undetermined. Age at the time of death has been narrowed down to fifty to sixty years old. Everything has been sent to an FBI lab for further testing and identification."

"How could they determine cause of death after all these years?" I asked.

EG was standing, but rested one hand on the table to steady herself. "Probably a crack or hole in the skull."

Eugene shrugged. "Actually, I didn't read the whole report. Somebody gave it to my father. He was carrying it around last night as he went for a walk and fell asleep holding it. After I found him at Draw Bar, I drove him home, and he did not speak a word. I waited to leave his house until he was sleeping, and as he was falling asleep, he mumbled the words 'It's him. EG.'

"I went back this morning. He's still sleeping. I think he mixed pain pills with some Scotch last night, which is very unlike him. I took this report because I figured he would bring it here himself sometime today, and I didn't want him on his bad knee again."

"Why here?" I asked.

"He made several copies. He had one with EG's name and one labeled Teddy."

Eugene stopped talking and awkwardly swooped down to catch a falling EG.

We had been so focused on Eugene, we hadn't noticed EG bracing herself, trying to maintain an upright position. Her arm must have weakened as she was trying to grab the table, but she slouched and pushed a glass off the top. We all jumped when the glass shattered on the floor. I grabbed her and tried to have her sit at the table.

She waved us off, but after a moment, she said, "Can you help me to the couch?"

"Are you ok? What can I do for you?" I said, and my hands trembled.

"I'm just feeling faint."

"We'll take you to the hospital," I said in my most commanding voice.

"My car is out front, or should we call 9-1-1?" Eugene asked.

"I'll drive. My car is in the driveway. We can

156

hit the big two hundred thousandth mile on the way there!" Sherrie said.

With a sideways glance at Sherrie, EG said, "No, no, just let me rest. Too much going on."

Sherrie brought EG some water and started cleaning up the broken glass. I sat with EG on the sofa and tried figuring out what was best. EG gave me the name of her doctor, so I called and left a message, hoping she'd call back soon.

Eugene excused himself, muttering something about all these sick people around him.

We let EG rest on the sofa. Sherrie went upstairs to shower, and I went to the porch to call Jackson.

"Hey, I'm glad you called," he said.

"It has been crazy here. I wish you were here today."

"Yeah, me too. I would love to ask your aunt more questions about Chicago."

"Well, that won't be happening." I explained everything in reverse order. Starting with EG nearly fainting, the rock throwing, the bar in La Crosse and Sherrie meeting a married guy, Sherrie's surprise visit, the dust whirlpool of moving boxes at Chambray, and the slight possibility that I now believe in ghosts.

"So she's not up to talking about Chicago."

"No, no, she is not. I have to go, Jackson," I said in a flat voice.

"What's wrong?"

"I don't understand you. I just explained that she nearly fainted, and I think I'm in the beginning of a weird science fiction book. All this odd stuff going on, and EG, my rock, is beginning to shake."

"I know. I figured I could take her mind off her illness. You know me—Mr. Cheerful. Who kept you going during your cheating scandal? Who solved your money issues about moving to Chicago when I agreed that we live together? Who brought you flowers and soup for your court date? I am the guy to solve problems. You said that's what you like about me. Your knight in shining armor."

"I guess you're right. Just a lot going on here. Why don't I talk to you later."

I ended the call, and Sherrie came out to the porch, freshly dressed and carrying a cup of coffee for me. She had an inquiring look on her face.

"What?" I asked.

"I don't mean to eavesdrop, but why didn't you mention Aaron to Jackson?"

"Sure I did."

"No, you didn't. You talked about everything else except Aaron."

"I mentioned the road trip to La Crosse."

"You left out that Aaron was the reason we went, and you definitely did not mention the smooth move of the meteor shower on the river. Do you like him?"

"No, well, yes, I think he's nice, but I have a boyfriend."

"I know you have a boyfriend, but I asked if you like Aaron."

"No. I didn't even think there was a reason to like him. I only found out twelve hours ago that he's straight."

"But now that you know, what do you think?"

"Don't you hear me? I have a boyfriend."

"Why do you always say you have a boyfriend and never mention his name?"

"I do? I never noticed."

"Well."

"Well, what?"

"Do you like him?"

"Again, I have a boyfri—Jackson. Is this about you? You can go for Aaron, but I can tell you that your first impression was a bit much. Go slow and ease up on the talking."

"Noooo, he is cute but not my type. I was hoping you liked him."

"Why?"

"Because it would make telling you this easier."

"What, why?"

"I don't have great news. And I am not one hundred percent sure, but I can't not tell you. I think Jackson has no interest in finding a place in Chicago and—"

My heart was pounding. "What?"

"I don't know for sure, but I think he wants you to ask EG if you guys could crash at her place in Chicago and—"

"He would not do that. We talked about this for months. What makes you say that?" My arms were locked straight, fists in a ball, and I actually stomped my feet like a child.

"Well, I think he's—I don't have any proof of this either—but I think he, um, he maybe—"

"Spit it out!"

The house phone rang in my hand. Any other time, I would have chucked it off the porched, but the caller ID showed it was EG's doctor.

I answered and tried to focus on what the doctor was saying while giving Sherrie the stink eye. The doctor said to let her rest and make sure she drinks some water or better yet Gatorade or fruit juice of some kind. She said EG had an appointment today, but the doctor volunteered to come to the house instead.

I ended the call and was ready to resume my conversation with Sherrie, but someone knocked on the screen door.

Perfectly dressed in white jeans and a pink blouse with her perfect brown hair, Abigail was easy to recognize.

"Abigail, is that you?" I asked.

"Ah, yes, I came to see EG. Is she around this morning?"

"It's not a good time. I can have her call you later."

"I can wait if she's out for a walk."

"No, she's not out for a walk, but it is still best if we have her call you. Is there anything I can help you with?"

"It's important that I talk to EG as soon as possible."

"I will have her call you. See you later this week. I think I'm on shopping rotations so I will stop by your place on Friday."

She finally relented and turned away from the house.

As she was leaving, the phone rang again.

"For the love of god, who could this be now?"

Sherrie grabbed the phone and spoke in Spanish, then hung up five seconds later. The phone rang again, and again, she answered, speaking Spanish. That conversation lasted ten seconds.

"What was that about?" I asked.

"It was some old guy. Babbling and asking for EG. I thought it would be funnier speaking Spanish instead of just hanging up."

"Confusing an old guy is mean."

"I think it was the creepy guy from the gas station. The old mayor dude," Sherrie said.

"The mayor is not creepy. He is actually on the cool side of things for an old dude, but his son is riding the sliding scale of weirdness. What makes you think it was him?"

"I think it was his voice, and he said something about Eugene."

"Ok, I guess we can have EG call him later. Let me check on her, and I'll get some of that Ensure drink they have at chemo and fresh orange juice. The doc mentioned something about it."

"You stay here with EG, and I'll go to the store. I'm assuming it's close, I mean I can't have my car turn over to two hundred thousand miles on the way to the Piggly Wiggly to buy Ensure. While that is endearing, it sure is not sexy, and I'm sure EG would understand that."

"It's four blocks from here, and it's probably easier if you walk." *Did I really suggest walking in this heat?* "Let's go in, and I'll get you some cash."

We turned to walk into the house and heard knocking on the door. "Now what!" we said in unison.

A woman stood there, wearing a spring floral blouse with a matching sweater draped over her shoulders with coordinating pants and holding some books. It took me a second to recognize her. Jean had the appearance of always trying to be on point with fashion but seems to be one step short. It was not a bad look, but her wardrobe always reminded me of the pictures online with the high-priced designer look and the copycat budget look, and people were supposed to guess which was the more expensive outfit.

But her style was the third look that should in the "Find the differences" section of kids magazines., and while looking similar in shape and color, one would find more differences and it was not always for the better.

"Hi, girls, I'm Jean Jan. Thomas's—Sheriff Dalton's—wife. Most people call me Jean, but with two Jeans living here, I just want people to know I'm not Jean-Linda. I have some books for EG."

We walked back through the porch and headed outside to talk with Jean.

"Yes, we have met. I'm Claudia, EG's niece, and this is my friend Sherrie."

"Of course, good you see you again. That's right, you're taking care of EG this summer." Jean turned to Sherrie and extended her hand. "Hello, nice to meet you, Sherrie. I was going to leave these books on the porch. Is everything ok? You gals seem rattled."

"Sorry about that greeting. We've had a lot going on here the last twelve hours," I said.

"Oh my, is there anything that my Thomas can do?"

"I don't know, but some kids were throwing rocks at the house last night."

"Really? Show me what happened, and I'll tell him." She walked towards the side of the house, and I don't know why, but we just followed her like little schoolgirls.

We walked around the house in silence with Jean leading the way. Sherrie and I kept looking at each other, shrugging our shoulders and hoping we didn't disturb EG, who hopefully was still resting inside.

"Well, girls. I have learned a thing or two being married to a sheriff for all these years. I love reading all the crime reports. That's between us, ok? I don't and especially my Thomas would not want people to know I read all the reports."

"Yes, ma'am," we said together.

We continued our walk around the house in silence.

"I don't think someone was throwing rocks," Jean said.

I caught up to her. "EG definitely heard something."

"Oh, I agree with that, but I don't see any rocks near the house, and if kids had been throwing something, I don't think they would come clean it up. The screen on the door to the porch is pushed in, and the bushes near the windows are missing some flowers. I think someone was trying to get in

164

or at least get EG's attention. If I recall, the doorbell isn't working, so someone was probably eager to talk to her. I don't think it was an attempted burglary. It would be fairly easy to pop the hook off the screen door or break one of the rear windows. Does EG have any jilted lovers?" She said that last line with a slight laugh.

"I will have to ask her, but I don't think so. I'll have her call your husband later today. Thanks for the books," I said.

Everyone said their goodbyes, but before she was gone, I turned and said, "Jean, you know EG, and she would not want a big deal made of this."

Jean smiled. "Yes, dear. Thomas will have the patrol car cruise the street on a regular basis, and he will tell the patrol officers there was some crazy driving reported in the area the last few nights. The secret is safe with me."

"Thank you, very kind."

"I told you girls, I read crime reports and know a thing or two about handling officers." She smiled again. "Maybe someone was throwing rocks at the crows perched up in these trees. It's odd, of all the trees on this street, the crows found this one to nest in. Let EG know that I can have the town put a bronzed scarecrow in her yard. Good day, girls."

On our way back to the porch, I whispered to Sherrie, "I don't know if that last part was supposed to be funny, bitchy, self-promoting, or just odd."

Sherrie didn't say anything but shivered and pushed me through the door to escape the current scene. Before we made it inside the house, the phone rang again. This time, we just rolled our eyes, but before I could finish saying let it go to voicemail, Sherrie answered.

"No, she is not available. May I take a message?"

. . .

"No, this is not Claudia. What can I do for you?"

. . .

"Does she have your number, Pastor?"

. . .

"Ok, let me get a pen."

Sherrie finished up that conversation, and I went to check on EG. She was sitting on the couch, and her color was coming back. She was wrapped in a blanket despite the warmth of the house.

"Are you ok? You gave us a scare. Stay where you are. Sherrie is going to run to the store, and I'll clean up breakfast."

"What was all the noise outside? You ladies having a party or discussing anything important out there?" EG said, looking at Sherrie.

I answered. "Just a lot of people looking for you. Sherrie, take my wallet. There is some cash in there. Go right one block and then left for three, and you'll find Green's Grocery Store."

"Ok, text me if you want me to pick up anything else. I'll be back shortly."

Sherrie left, and I nibbled on some of the food while I told EG about Abigail and Jean stopping by, the phone call from someone who could have been Mayor Carl—and that she would probably have to explain the weird message-taking from Sherrie—and that one more person had called, but I wasn't sure who. Sherrie had even been polite to that person and had taken a message with a phone number. As I went to grab the phone message, I told EG about Jean's observation that she found no rocks near the house.

"That's odd. I know I heard some ticking and not necessarily someone knocking. Give me the message," EG said, holding her hand out.

When she read the message, she visibly tensed up and then gave me a forced smile. "So you and Sherrie weren't discussing anything big? I thought I heard you raise your voices."

She was obviously trying to change the subject, but I let it go. And I was not about to tell her about Jackson's effort to schmooze his way into her Chicago apartment. "We were just getting tired of the interruptions. Why do I have the feeling you and Sherrie have some secret about me?"

"No secret, darling, but we need to talk.

Why don't you finish cleaning up, and when Sherrie gets back, we can start then."

A little rattled, I said, "Start what? Are you breaking up with me? Because I don't think by law you can break up with a family member."

"Oh, you and your sense of humor. Clean up, shower, get dressed, and then we can all talk."

I texted Sherrie not to let on about Jackson to EG or do anything to rattle her.

CHAPTER NINETEEN

Thirty minutes later, I was sitting with EG and Sherrie in the family room. I was dressed and had finally eaten breakfast but had an unsettled feeling in my stomach. I kept fidgeting with my bracelet and was trying hard not to bite my nails. *I am a college graduate. I need to start being professional, and that starts with a good manicure or at least nails that are not chewed up like a five-year-olds.* I looked at both of them and blurted out, "Ok, you two, what's up? You have been giving each other funny looks for the past twenty-four hours."

EG cleared her throat and looked at Sherrie, who nodded, then back at me. "Claudia, I wanted to talk to you about some things while you are here this summer. Sherrie called to check on me, and while we were talking, I figured you could use some support."

I stopped fidgeting and murmured, "Support?"

"Maybe that's not the best word," EG said, wringing her hands.

"Come on, you're a writer. How are you at a loss for words? Are you really, really sick? More than you've let on?"

"No, no. I thought it was time you knew some things. We—your mother, father and I—have talked and we agreed you should know everything now. Sherrie doesn't know what I'm going to say but thought it would be good for you to have someone to talk to about this."

"You're scaring me. Plus, *you* have been the person I always talk to." I turned to Sherrie and said, "Sorry, no offense."

Sherrie shrugged. "None taken. Don't worry. Let me know if you want me to step out for a bit so you can have some privacy."

"Maybe that's a good idea. Can you give us some time? There is always an afternoon matinee playing, or there are some cute stores to walk through around the square but they close at five." EG reached out, squeezed Sherrie's hand, and softly said, "Thank you."

Sherrie hugged me quickly, and she whispered, "Good luck."

After Sherrie left, I sat on the couch beside

EG. The windows were open, a soft breeze coming through, and the room had a gray look instead of the usual soft shadows from the sunlight. The clouds must have been casting strange shadows.

Rain is probably on its way, I thought. Suddenly, I was still. Fidgeting was gone, stomach has stopped turning, and my mind was still. I was open to hear whatever she had to tell me. There was never fear with EG. She was always the calm in the storm and voice of reason. If there was chaos you always wanted EG there to wrap her arms around everyone and make it right.

EG was sitting straight back with her legs crossed at the ankles, holding a cup of tea. She was looking at me and past me at the same time. *Is she leading me into chaos now?*

With an even, calm voice, she said, "First, don't worry, no one is dying. I love you, and we all love you. I thought it was time that you knew everything about our family. Your mom and dad offered to drive here tonight, but I asked them to wait and come tomorrow. I hope to give you the whole story or as much of it as you want."

"Ok, I think I understand but . . ."

Taking a deep breath, EG put down the tea mug and reached out to touch my hand. "It's time, in more ways than one, for you to know everything."

"Family? Mom, Dad. Wait, before you start," I said.

I had thought about this moment for years. Played it over in my head lots of times, but I never dwelled upon it because I had no reason to worry. Stillness held me in one place, but I began to sweat everywhere—under arms, feet, hands, and even behind my ears.

"No, I have to tell you everything." She smiled, and tears filled her eyes.

Tears started to roll down my cheeks, and I was sniffling. I grabbed tissues and passed some to EG.

"I have to tell you . . ." EG paused and took a deep breath.

In that moment, I knew for sure before she said it. I slowly whispered, "It *is* you."

"What? How? Let me talk." She looked at me as if she was trying to understand what I said or what I understood. "Claudia, let me tell you what I have to say."

Looking at EG with her face full of love and fear, I struggled to make my voice break through the tears. "Stop, it's ok. I know. I think I know. Well, until now, I didn't know it was *our* story. I just put that together. Actually, sometimes while growing up, I hoped it was you."

Looking aghast, she held herself frozen. Rain was hitting the window, and the breeze picked up. I noticed the shredded tissues in EG's lap.

"How? What do you know?"

"I've known for sure since middle school. Well, at least I was pretty positive without scientific proof."

EG looked at me. I guess she was waiting for an answer. Or maybe not so much an answer but approval or acceptance or even forgiveness.

"It's ok. I love you. I obviously don't know everything."

We reached out and hugged, holding each other and crying until lightning cracked through the window. It was late afternoon but looked well past midnight. The rain was coming down nonstop. We pulled apart to grab more tissues.

"You ok?" she asked.

"Yeah, I'm fine," I said, wiping my eyes.

"You must have questions, and I would like to tell you what happened."

"You would think I'd be more prepared with a list of questions after all these years. I had just made peace with it because everything I had was good. There are reasons for everything. I was weirdly comforted by knowing I was in on the secret."

"How? I'm sorry, should I answer your questions before you tell me how you figured it out?"

"I overheard you and Mom, I mean—"

"It's ok. Katie Lyn will always be your

mom."

"I always thought it was funny that the story of my birth was kinda off or different. I don't know why the story was always off a bit. I know my brother's story of being born in the snowstorm—yada yada yada. We all know it was epic, blah blah blah. But when anyone asked if I had a great story, Mom got a little weird and said I had a peaceful entry into the world. You know Mom can make a story out of anything, but with that, she was always a bit short-winded and would give me an extra smile or hug. Then, the summer before seventh grade, I heard you and Mom talking. I couldn't hear everything. You and Mom didn't know I was in the house. I had been at Beth's, and we decided to go swimming. I came back to the house to get my stuff. You were sitting in the backyard, and I was in the kitchen. I left, never grabbing my swim stuff."

"You are something special," EG said. "You should probably call your parents. They are both home now. We can go into the whole story of how I came to be pregnant and how Katie Lyn and Matthew raised you as their own."

CHAPTER TWENTY

After I hung up with my parents, I felt so much love. When I called, they answered on the first ring. My mom said hello with a shaky voice, and I could tell my father was there. We spoke for only a few minutes, and I told them I was ok and I loved them. I had the need to keep repeating the words *Mom* and *Dad*. It was as much for them as it was for me.

EG was right again. No matter what the story is, Katie Lyn and Matthew will always be Mom and Dad. I almost asked them to drive up here tonight, but I realized I wanted to hear the whole story and have a moment to myself. We were family no matter what I learned. They told me how much I meant to them and that they were proud of me. I figured I would maybe tell them later that I have known for over ten years. I figured it didn't matter when I had learned the truth.

I found EG at the kitchen table with some cheese, crackers, and hot tea.

"Shouldn't you be having more than a snack? A couple of hours ago, we were ready to drive you to the hospital."

"I'm fine. I think that dizzy spell was more from nerves than the chemo. I figured we could have something light to eat now, and here comes Sherrie."

I looked through the window and saw Sherrie jump from a car and dash through the rain. The driver hopped out too and headed for the porch.

How does she do it? She's here for twenty-four hours, and she already has a cute guy, a really cute guy, driving her home.

Sherrie came in through the porch into the living room, and her male companion waited on the porch and knocked on the screen door.

EG shouted, "Hi, Charles, come in."

He walked over and gave EG a warm hug. "I don't want to stay, but I wanted to see how you are doing and if you need anything. When Sherrie gave me the address, I didn't realize it was your house, EG." He turned to me and held out a hand. "I'm Chuck, Ms. EG is the only one who calls me Charles. You must be Claudia. I've heard a lot about you."

"I'm not sure if I'm flattered or if I should be nervous. You never know what kind of stories Sherrie and EG will spin."

"Don't be worried. It's not just these two. Aaron is my brother."

"Well, great, between those three maybe I—"

"All good stories," he said, smiling. He turned to EG. "I'm in town for two weeks so if you need anything, please let me know. In a couple of days, we will have some more pie for you." He gave EG another hug and us a quick wave and was out the door.

I turned and gave Sherrie a look that said I wanted an explanation.

"Give it a rest. I'm not out trying to pick up guys. Although . . ." Her eyes fell on Chuck through the window. "I was walking through the village, near the town square, when the thunderstorm hit. The door to BAR was open so I made a mad dash, trying to avoid the rain. Chuck was talking to Aaron, and he offered me a ride. How are you two? I can go upstairs to give you more time."

"No, stay here. EG and I are not done talking, but I'll tell you everything anyways. This way, I won't have to repeat it all."

"Are you sure?"

EG nodded. "Of course, if Claudia is good

with it, and I did invite you here for support. Let's sit down."

Sherrie sat at the head of the table, and I sat next to EG, our arms linked together. We brought her up to speed about me being adopted and EG being my birth mom.

Sherrie turned to me. "Are you ok?"

I nodded and smiled.

She hesitated before asking, "Are you sure? This is a lot of information coming from us."

I cocked my head. "Us?"

EG looked at Sherrie. "Did you tell her about Jackson?"

Sherrie flinched a bit. "I started to tell her, but we got interrupted."

"What? EG, you knew Jackson was trying to weasel us into your Chicago apartment?"

EG held up her hand. "Slow down. A couple of days ago, Sherrie called to ask how I was doing, and we got to talking and she wanted to know if I thought Jackson was being a dick. Those are her words not mine."

I stood up. "Next time, do you guys want to include *me* in the events of my life?"

EG took my hand. "Oh, sit down. You're not mad at us. Your friend here was looking out for you and didn't want to talk crap about your boyfriend unless she was sure. I figured you could use the moral support so I asked her to road trip it up here."

I slouched back down in my seat and mumbled, "All right."

"Are we good?" Sherrie asked.

I shrugged. "Of course."

"Can I ask another question? If it's too much, I'm sorry," Sherrie asked, looking at EG. Sherrie, while she was loyal and a great secret keeper, was also very nosy.

EG held up her hand, looking from Sherrie to me, and said, "Don't worry. I know the question, and the answer is more than just a man's name. I need to tell you the whole story."

EG'S STORY

October 1995
River Bend, WI
High School Homecoming Weekend

I had walked into Ellen's family home hundreds of times without knocking. She'd lived next door to me since her family moved to River Bend in first grade. We decided Ellen and Ellen Grace were too similar, so I declared myself EG.

Fast-forwarding many years, I knocked instead of going right in. We had graduated from River Bend High School a year and a half before. Ellen had gone to the University of Illinois Chicago, and I had gone to St. Thomas College in Minneapolis. We'd kept in regular contact, but now, stepping into Ellen's home, I felt it was time to start knocking and respecting other people's space.

"Hello, Mrs. Touras. Is Ellen home yet?" I said when Ellen's mom opened the door.

"Hi, dear. Come in. Come in. When did you start knocking? Give me a hug and then go upstairs and see Ellen. She got home ten minutes ago. I'm looking forward to the parade. Gosh, your mum must be so proud."

"Thanks, Mrs. Touras. Good to see you too. My mom is happy to have me back in River Bend, even if it's on a float."

I bounced up the stairs, walked into Ellen's childhood bedroom, and leaped on the bed. "I know we've been out of high school not even two years, but it's odd coming back here and sitting in your parents' house, waiting for homecoming weekend to begin."

"I know, it is weird. EG, can you believe it? You're grand marshal of the parade. Soak it up. Here's your fifteen minutes of fame! Forget winning the writing contest three years ago, a partial scholarship to St. Thomas College while having a full-time writing gig for *Matronly Mothers Monthly*. This is your shining moment—at the age of twenty. You are about to hit your peak!" Ellen giggled.

"Shut up. This is ridiculous. I don't know why I even agreed to come back here."

"Because you're a star and a local hero that put River Bend on the map. And Larry Lobal is stalking you on campus."

"Well, you should stop laughing because I got them to agree to put me on a float instead of a car. I told them to find more distinguished alumni. I said no to a convertible with me sitting on the trunk of a car with a damn scarecrow. They thought the float was a great idea and asked a large group of alumni to join me."

"Who did they get? I didn't get a call. Will your sister be there?"

"Your invite most likely came here instead of your dorm. That's probably why your mother has your tracksuit sitting on your desk." I laughed. "You can wear your track outfit or not, but you have to wear your medals from UI and the National Collegiate track finals. Anyway, no, Katie Lyn is not here. They're closing on a house in Minnesota, and she has some new work gig today in the Twin Cities. As for the others on the float, I forget a few of their names, but they got Teddy's brother, Christian, for his charitable work with Special Olympics. I'm just hoping Teddy will be here."

"Oh my god. You still have a thing for that guy? If he's here, he'll be on the float since he was prom king and valedictorian. You haven't seen him in years. I wonder if he hit his peak in high school. Maybe he's started losing his hair or got a gut."

"He is still soooo cute. I've seen him. I forgot to tell you, I ran into him six months ago at a party. We chatted for a bit before his snotty girlfriend pulled him away. He totally remembered me from that silly filmmaking class we had together in high school."

"Ohhh, nice. What's the agenda for the weekend, Miss Queen?"

"Stop with that Miss Queen shit. If you don't stop, every scarecrow I find will end up in your bedroom haunting you," I said.

"No offense but some of them are creepy."

"I agree, but I have to smile and talk about crows and scarecrows. My publisher has warned me several times to keep my comments short and polite. They don't want any bad PR for the magazine. On the flip side, if I mention the magazine and it gets printed in other publications or mentioned on TV, I get some type of bonus. Since I'm short on cash, I'm all about embracing the crows—flying or stuffed!"

"That's ridiculous. You are a one woman cash cow at the age of twenty, or should I say cash *crow*?"

"I was in the money until my scholarship from the Midwest Writers Guild went belly up. They're supposed to pay for tuition and books but are suddenly short on money—I don't know the details. They've paid up this semester, but after

January, who knows what will happen. One of the lawyers who works for the magazine is doing some checking into the guild to find the truth. He said I should think worst-case scenario. If they come up with the money, great, but I should consider myself on notice."

"That's awful. Can't you do anything? What about your parents?"

"As the lawyer says, 'It's hard getting money when the bank isn't open.' Whatever that means. My parents just bought the house in Florida, and they're waiting for the State to come through with the money when they take the land for the freeway. I think they also helped my sister with the down payment on her house. What about your family? Are they getting ready for the move before the bulldozers come in?"

"My mom is in denial about having to move, but my father has been looking at following your parents to Florida. He figures once Mom visits your parents, it will be easier for her to let go of this place. That sucks about money. Let's get back to a happy time or happy hour—what's the deal for tonight and this weekend?"

"Didn't you read any of the stuff? Anyway, it starts with the varsity football game tonight and some informal events at bars. Tomorrow morning is the parade, followed by the Lions Club cookout and baseball game. Which we have to go to."

"What? I don't do baseball," Ellen said.

"Yes, you do. At least you did senior year with a Mr. CJ Watson. Star pitcher for our beloved River Bend Fighting Crows!"

"Shut up. Don't remind me. Not my finest moment in my lineup of boyfriends."

"Don't worry, we're not playing. It's a mix of current baseball players, faculty, and alumni. We, as in anyone on the float, have to be there for the pregame ceremony stuff, and I agreed to throw out the first pitch. Don't laugh, but I get more bonus money if I wear a jersey with the magazine logo, a crow, and scarecrow on it."

"You have to be kidding me?" Ellen said.

I shook my head. "After that, we are free to party. The Lions Club cookout lasts until seven, and then there's music in the square. I think, at nine thirty, they want to shuffle everybody back to the football field for fireworks. The town is making a big deal of this because homecoming starts the one-year celebration leading up to River Bend turning a hundred years old. Sunday morning in the town square, some ladies group is putting on a pancake breakfast. Get dressed, and we can go to the football game. We can check out the alumni section to see who's back for the weekend."

I woke up that Saturday morning with my head a little fuzzy. I didn't know why no one had figured out that high school students should not help the Booster Club in the concession stands. Just because people were high school alumni did not mean they were old enough to drink. We had taken full advantage of a high school student's ignorance. I was lying in my bed when I looked over and saw Ellen asleep on the futon at the foot of my bed. I tossed a pillow at her to wake her up.

"What's going on?" she mumbled.

"I'm trying to figure out what happened last night. Should I be embarrassed to show up for the parade today?"

Sitting up, stretching, and yawning, Ellen said, "I think you're good to go. I remember you talking *a lot*. Especially to your boy toy Teddy."

"Did I say anything silly? Did I act like I was twelve and had a crush on the hunky-bo-hunk of a man?"

"No—well, you were slightly silly. Don't you remember any of this? You wanted to talk to Teddy but you did not want to seem needy, so you kept having these short conversations and then leaving and accidentally trying to bump into him. You sent me to talk to his friend Tommy to see where they were going after the game."

"Oh, that's right. Tommy. By the way, nice birthmark." I smirked. "Oh, that's not a birthmark—that's right, you can thank Tommy for that nice mark on your neck. At least I didn't make out on the slide in the Robertson's backyard."

"Give me a break," Ellen said. "At least I don't have to help judge the scarecrow competition today at the cookout."

"I did agree to that at some point last night. Well, at least it's another photo op with the baseball jersey on and more money. Maybe I'll be able to afford my books next semester."

"Let's shower and get dressed. I bet one of our mothers has cooked us a nice welcome home breakfast."

Late afternoon, I was wandering through the crowd, looking for Ellen, when I heard, "Hi, EG? How are the scarecrows?" I turned and saw Teddy standing there, smiling at me. "Did you see the one that looked like Principal Higgins. I swear it was going to walk off on its own. It is so lifelike."

"I saw his wife grab and toss it in the garage can when she thought nobody was looking. I think I can officially say I'm done scarecrows. Let me be honest with you. I know I should be grateful for the success of my book and that the town has embraced it, but seriously, one more scarecrow, I think I'm going to go nuts."

"I understand. If I get near them, my hay

allergies go nuts. I thought I was going to die up on that float today with all the hay. The whole time, I was trying not to sneeze on the candy we were throwing."

"Oh, is that why you were hiding on the back of the float? I thought I talked too much last night, and you were avoiding me. Sorry, if I babbled too much."

"Well, I was avoiding everyone because I was a wreck with all the hay. I was certainly not avoiding you," he said, blushing slightly.

"Really?"

"I was hoping to talk to you more last night, but I think I drank more than I thought. I kept losing you in the crowd. A group of us have decided to blow off this festival and go down by the river and have a bonfire. The city cleared an area for a new parking lot and a boat ramp. They haven't cleared all the trees they cut down, so there's plenty of firewood."

Just keep cool, I thought. *Don't say too much or too little and certainly don't lose him now in this crowd. Is Ellen watching this? Where is she? Does someone have a camera? Oh, crap, what is he saying?*

"We're telling some people to join us, then we're going to the store to pick up some beverages and meet there around seven thirty."

"That sounds great. Ellen and I would love to join the group. Where is the area you're talking about? Is it at the end of Mill Road?"

"No, that's slated for the picnic area the city hasn't started working on yet. Just a few more blocks over. If you want, I could meet you at your house and we could walk over together."

"That would be great. I can bring some blankets. Ellen may come with me if that's ok? I am on Maldine Avenue. The only blue house."

"Great."

He took a step towards me, and we were inches apart. Even with the crowd around us, everyone else faded away, and it was just the two of us.

Oh my god, is he going to kiss me?

His breath was warm on my neck as he whispered, "I was never trying to avoid you. I was—"

"EG, there you are! Oh, hi, Teddy." Ellen came bouncing out of the crowd.

Teddy didn't move. He stayed close, and it was comfortable.

"There's a bonfire at the river tonight," Ellen said.

"Yeah, Teddy was telling me about it."

"I was thinking of heading home to freshen up before heading down to the river. What do you think?"

"Good idea," I said.

I turned to Teddy, and before I could say

anything more, he squeezed my hand.

The corner of his mouth turned up in a smile. "Yes, I will see you at seven thirty." And with that, he turned and was lost in the crowd before I could blink.

"Did you see that? Did you see that!" I whispered.

"What's the big deal? Everybody is going to the bonfire."

"No, he was totally flirting with me before you pounded in on the scene."

We stood there for a minute, squealing like two schoolgirls.

"Let's go home and wipe off the day and get ready for a good night," I said.

"Hey, if he's coming to pick you up, do you want me there?"

"Yes, you have to be there. I already mentioned it, and I don't want to, I don't know, I, well, you will be a nice icebreaker. It's only a short distance. I'm so nervous. Let's go home and get ready."

"Ellen, it is nearly eight o'clock. Do you think he's coming soon? Forget it, don't answer, let's go. I'm tired of sitting on the porch waiting for him. I'll leave a note on the door that says we're gone."

"Ok, it's up to you. Let's grab the blankets and go. It'll take only ten minutes if we cut through the recycling center."

As we were walking, Ellen's friend from the previous night, Tommy, drove by and gave us a ride in his pickup truck. She was quite happy since I couldn't complain and have a sad mouth for the whole walk to the river.

It was actually nice once we got to the riverbank. About a dozen alumni including Teddy's friends Marcus and James but no Teddy. There were also a few high school kids, tagging along with their older siblings. Some of the guys had made a firepit and were pulling over logs to sit on.

"Hey, Marcus, I see you got a few scarecrows in the back of your truck. Is one your new girlfriend?" I said, laughing.

Marcus rolled his eyes. "Very funny, EG. Just stick to writing your fictional stories and leave the comedy to someone else. After the scarecrow competition this afternoon, the mayor suggested all the farmers and gardeners take them and make good use of them. My mother had me grab whatever I get my hands on for our fields. Some of them so lifelike. They are kinda creepy. Two of them didn't even have a pole inside them but could stand up on their own. One was dressed like that Eugene kid, the mayor's son. It looked like he made a life-size ventriloquist doll. Maybe if we put a dress on one of them, my brother could have a date for the dance next week."

"Be nice to your brother. I've got a better idea. If you don't mind, bring me one."

Marcus ran back to the truck and brought two over and handed one to EG.

"All right, everyone, can I get your attention?"

EG waited until she had everyone's attention. "I don't know about everyone else, but I'm pretty much done with these things. How about we sacrifice these two stiffs in the name of releasing the souls of all scarecrows. Marcus, light the arm of your scarecrow and touch it to mine, and together, we'll get this party started."

"Are you sure?" Marcus asked, striking a match.

"Sure. I don't think they have any voodoo power. Let's go."

The sun had set, and the flaming scarecrows set the wood in the makeshift pit ablaze. Everyone clapped, and one of the guys passed out beers and pulled out a radio. I was having a good time despite being stood up. I stood there enjoying the scene, and Ellen was lurking next to Tommy.

Someone tapped my shoulder and said, "I am really sorry."

I turned and saw Teddy standing there.

"Good for you" was the only reply I could think of in the moment. I wasn't mad, but I wasn't in the mood for any bullshit either—but, holy crap, he looked good standing there in Levi's and a blue flannel shirt. Did I mention his beautiful eyes and brown curly hair that anyone would want to run their fingers through?

"I get it. You're mad," he said.

"Not mad. I thought you were going to be somewhere, and you opted for other plans."

"Sorry. Can I talk to you over there where it's not so noisy?"

I let him lead the way to a pile of logs. We climbed on top and sat down next to each other. I was determined to not look at him for fear of melting. Our knees were touching, and that was all I could handle at the moment.

"Something came up. I can't explain it, but trust me, I'd rather have been with you." He paused for a moment. "Oh, I stopped and got you something." He reached into his coat pocket and pulled out a grape soda.

"What is this?"

"Well, I knew I blew it, and I wanted to do something for you. Do you still like grape soda?"

"Yes, but how did you know?"

"When we took that film class, you brought a grape soda every day. That's why I called you Radar. Why'd you think I called you that?"

"I figured you didn't know my name or that I always knew the weather or because I called you Loo."

"Trust me, I knew your name. Radar, from M*A*S*H, always drank grape Nehi soda."

"Oh, I totally get it now. Thanks for bringing me one, I appreciate the thought. I feel bad now. Do you know why I called you Loo?"

"I thought I did. You were Corporal Radar O'Reilly, and I was your lieutenant because I was the director of our little film."

"I should probably go with that story, but it was because I knew your last name translates to *pee* in Polish. L-O-O. Not L-O-U. As in, I have to go to the loo to pee. I have to go to the loo to *siusiac*."

"I can't believe someone finally figured out *Siusiac* translates to pee. I was always relieved no one had discovered it. There was one kid in our church who called me Teddy the Pee. His family moved away in first grade. Luckily, before I knew how to throw a punch. But how did you figure it out?"

"Maybe I was just trying to learn more about you then."

"Here, are you going to take it?" He held out the soda.

I took the can. "Did you run here? You seem a bit winded."

"Um, yeah, Kind of."

"How about I just hold it for a bit? So it doesn't explode when I open it." I laughed but stopped when I noticed his hand was swollen and had blood on it. "What happened to your hand?"

He pulled his hand back and looked straight ahead. "It's nothing. I was helping my mom with a project at the house and got a little banged up. It's fine. Do you want to sit here for a bit or join the crowd? It looks like that latest scarecrow is creating a lot of black smoke."

"Who knows what those kids stuffed in that thing. You know, there were over thirty of them at the competition."

"You created this monster, and River Bend has truly embraced it," Teddy said.

"Why don't we sit here for a while, at least until that beast burns itself out."

He was looking at me now, and he slipped his arm behind my back—either for balance or because he liked me, I wasn't sure, but it was nice. If I turned my head to look at him, I was done for.

He hesitated before he spoke. "So you're sitting here to avoid tar in your lungs or because . . . ?"

I looked at him. "Because I like sitting next to you," I said, my voice squeaking.

He leaned in and gave me the kiss of a lifetime—sweet and gentle but with passion. We stayed on the logs talking and kissing before we joined the others.

I opened the grape soda as we walked back to the bonfire.

Teddy went to talk to Marcus and James, and Ellen came bounding over. "Hey, you disappeared for a bit. Is everything all good? I see you're smiling, so something good must have happened."

"Oh, you know it, sista!" I said, smiling.

Teddy and I hung out for a while, talking with everyone, and someone announced the fireworks were beginning in ten minutes. We debated whether we would be able to see them since they were being set off in the high school parking lot. A few people left, and others decided the fire should be bigger.

Tommy and Ellen walked past, headed towards his truck, and over her shoulder, she said, "Don't forget my mom's blankets!" Teddy came over and took my hand. We stayed there for a moment with fingers intertwined, standing a few inches apart.

He squeezed my hand. "Do you want to see the fireworks or stay at the bonfire?"

I leaned into him and whispered, "I have a better idea." I stepped back, swooped up the two blankets, and walked past the logs we had been sitting on earlier. Near the edge of the parking lot, I stopped and said, "You don't mind if it's just the two of us, do you?"

He pulled me close, kissing me again. It was better than our first kiss. We stood there for a minute holding each other.

"Wow, it gets really dark away from the fire," I said as we started walking again.

He looked up. "I think the incoming rain clouds covered up the moon. I wonder if the fireworks will go off before the rain."

"I think we have time before the rain starts, but it's hard to see out here. I hope I don't trip."

"Keep holding my hand, and you'll be fine."

"So if I fall, you fall with me."

"You got it," he said with another kiss.

"Do you mind an adventure in the woods?" I asked.

"Come on, I think we can do better than the woods. The old park ranger station is up here. No one has much use for it since they decided to add the new boat ramp and parking lot. The rangers relocated to the north of Millard Street. There will be fewer mosquitos."

"Mr. Pre-Law Man, are you serious? Are we breaking in?"

"Don't worry. The lock was broken years ago. It's just an empty building, so the town hasn't spent money repairing it. It will probably be flattened in a few weeks' time when the tree crews get that far."

"Hey, I'm game for anything with you."

"Is that so? Anything?"

"Yup," I said, smiling.

We held hands and giggled as we made our way through the parking lot.

"Are you up for target practice?" I said.

"What do you mean?"

"Over there. There's another scarecrow by the wood pile. It must have bounced out of Marcus's truck when he pulled in. I bet you can't pick up that stick and hit it from here."

"You're really done with the scarecrow thing, aren't you? I don't even see it."

"I appreciate everything the story and the book has given me, but I don't need to hang on to them like a mythical god. It's over on the other side of the pile of rocks. You can barely see it, but there's some fabric or maybe it's just a tarp covering construction debris that moved with the wind."

"I don't see it," he said again.

"See Marcus's truck? Five feet to the right is the stack of logs. At the end of it is something round next to the rocks. It may not be a scarecrow, but it is a target." I looked at Teddy. "So game or no game?"

"You're on. You pick up that rock, and let's see who's got game. Loser buys the other one their pancake breakfast tomorrow," Teddy said, smiling.

We took a few throws before each landing a

solid hit. The scarecrow or whatever it was had not moved, and EG could only see something flapping in the wind. We looked for some bigger rocks.

"What are those things made with?" Teddy asked.

"Who knows? There were no real parameters set. The competition was everything from fun, ludicrous, and slightly sad. My vote went to the second-grade class because they had painted my name on the scarecrow's pocket. Here, take this brick. We each get one more throw."

We both struck the scarecrow, hitting its body—well, we thought we did, but we couldn't see far. We high-fived each other and kissed.

He picked up the blankets and grabbed my hand, leading me to the old ranger station.

The station was small, maybe 10x10, and completely empty except for some leaves that had blown in through the broken windows.

As we stepped inside, he asked, "Are you ok with this place?"

I pulled him to me, unbuttoning his shirt and kissing his neck. His hands were on my hips, slowly moving up.

"Yes, I'm sure," I whispered. "Are you, um, ah, prepared for this?"

"Yes," he said, stepping back and spreading the blankets on the floor.

We had a sweet, wonderful time—well, the

best we could have on a cement slab. As we lay there naked, we heard the echoes of the fireworks. Soon after the fireworks ended, we heard some noise. We froze, embarrassed by the possibility of getting caught, and laughed when we realized it was rain hitting the one unbroken window.

"We should probably get going, or we could be stuck here if a thunderstorm comes in," I said, moving to stand.

He pulled me back. "Would that be so bad?"

I smiled, feeling it reach my eyes. "We should go."

We got dressed and stood in the doorway, kissing, before we headed out through the sprinkling rain. Holding hands, we made our way back to the bonfire.

We were approaching the bonfire when I realized I only had one of Mrs. Touras's blankets. Teddy offered to run back and get it. He was back fifteen minutes later, looking pale and shaken, holding the blanket.

"Is everything ok?" I said.

"Yes." He didn't look at me and, instead, stepped toward a group huddling around the fire. "Hey, everyone, I heard the police are patrolling the area and will be here shortly."

"We're cool. We're not doing anything wrong," someone responded.

"I don't know if the bonfire is the real

problem or the drinking," Teddy said.

Half the crowd moaned and quickly started towards their cars and the footpath leading out of there.

Teddy raised his voice. "Hey, guys, I would avoid the path at the end of the parking lot. Why don't you head through the tall grass towards the high school so the cops think you were leaving the fireworks?"

"Thanks, man," a kid yelled.

"EG, are you ok?" Teddy asked.

I shook my head. "I gotta go!"

"But you weren't drinking. I need to tell—"

"That doesn't matter. I can't be caught here or be associated with any illegal matters. I can't lose the magazine job. I already lost the scholarship."

He held out his hand. "Oh-oh, I-I have t-to—"

"Can we talk about this tomorrow at the pancake breakfast?" I asked, taking his hand.

Sweat poured down his forehead, and he was breathing heavily. "I don't know if I can make it." He paused, finally looking at me, and took my face in his hands, then kissed me. "Goodbye," he said, stepping back. "I better get going." He turned and walked away with his head down.

I followed the group through the tall grass, went up the hill, and walked the few blocks to my street.

When I approached my house, Tommy was dropping Ellen off, and she met me in front of my house and we sat on the front steps.

"How was your night?" I asked.

"Tommy and I went to watch the fireworks and got stuck sitting with Abigail and Joe. That girl, Abigail, bugs me. She has always walked around this town as if she owns it. Why doesn't she stay away? I hope that's one person that doesn't return to this town after college. What does Joe see in her anyway? They've been together since sophomore year. Aren't they sick of each other yet?"

"Why do you let her bother you? I heard there is trouble at home for her. Parents are having trouble or her dad's in trouble. I don't know the whole story. My mom started to tell me one day, but we got interrupted and never went back to it."

"Whatever. They asked Tommy for a ride so we dropped them off at the bonfire. I went looking for you and Teddy. What happened to you guys?"

All I told her was "It was a great night, but then something switched and it ended abruptly. I don't get it."

"Don't sweat it. At least you finally got to make out with your high school crush, and it's over before you did something dumb like sleep with him." Ellen laughed.

Keep it to yourself, I thought. *It was sweet and beautiful—until it wasn't. Ellen doesn't need to know all the details, like the fact that I did sleep with Teddy.*

"Well, at least I don't have it tattooed on my neck, like you," I said.

"Shut up." She touched her neck, chuckling. "The hickey will be gone by sunrise. Plus, I don't think there's a future with Tommy. He was nice and all, but I think he has eyes for someone else."

"Oh, shit." I quickly stood. "I forgot a blanket again. I'll go back."

"I'll come with you," Ellen said.

This time, we took the shortcut down to the footpath. I was not worried about being caught with underage drinkers anymore. I was too preoccupied thinking about the way Teddy had said goodbye. It was so final.

We hadn't talked about seeing each other when we were back at school, but I had assumed and hoped this would continue. I guessed we'd call it what it was. A one-night stand with a hot guy.

By the time we reached the bonfire area, I felt content.

We approached the smoldering ruins and saw three guys and a girl getting ready to leave. They waved and offered us a ride, but we declined. Someone had placed the blanket on the logs where I had been kissing Teddy earlier.

"Hey, are you listening," Ellen said. "I have been talking, but you seem to be zoned out. Are you ok?"

"Ah, yeah. Just concentrating on where I am stepping. I don't want to roll my ankle." I lied.

"People clear out when you mention cops and it starts raining," Ellen said.

"Gee, I can't imagine why. At least the rain was short-lived."

"Let's cut through the woods. Pretty sure it's shorter than the path, and I think I hear other people cutting across the woods."

"Ok, walk this way and you can take the last scarecrow home as a souvenir. I went to the other side of the wood pile. "Teddy and I saw it earlier. It should be over here, but I don't see it. That's odd. I wonder where it went."

"They probably threw it on the fire like the rest of them."

I shook my head. "I don't know how anyone would have seen it."

A noise came from the river, and Ellen and I looked at each other.

"What was that?" I asked.

"It sounded like a splash. Who would be out there at this hour? I don't see any lights."

"Maybe just a rowboat. But don't they usually have lights?"

"But at this hour? Where would they get in? The boat dock isn't ready yet. If you drop in at Campbell Crossing, that's a long way to row at this hour. Most of the other boats are out of the water for the season," Ellen said.

"Maybe, I did see a boat near the old ranger station earlier. Maybe someone left the bonfire and decided to keep the party going, and they're out there having fun. I don't hear any other noise or music. Wait, I think I heard something in the woods. Let's get going and head through the tall grass."

It wasn't until the next morning that I saw the blood on my shoes.

CHAPTER TWENTY-ONE

CLAUDIA

"EG, that's quite a story." Taking a deep breath, I asked, "So a man named Teddy is my birth father?"

"Yes, but Teddy is . . . Well, there's a lot of the story that needs to come out."

A tapping noise sounded from the porch, and we jumped. Old Mayor Carl was banging his cane on the screen porch door.

Sherrie turned back to EG. "That must be what you heard last night. It wasn't rocks but the old guy's cane."

"Better let the man in. I don't think he'll go away," EG said, getting up.

"Stay put, EG. I'll get him," I said, walking over and opening the door. "Good to see you,

Mayor. How is the knee these days?" He extended his hand to shake to mine. Always a gentleman.

"Hello, Ms. Claudia. My knee is fine. Especially with all the pain medicine they give you these days. Mix it with a Scotch, and you definitely feel no pain. I need to speak with EG."

EG stepped onto the porch. "Afternoon, Mayor. Please come in and have a seat. Claudia, can you bring us some ice tea?"

I didn't know what to do for a second. There was no ice tea in the house. I didn't know if that was code for *don't leave me alone with this old dude or get out*.

EG must have noticed my hesitation. "Could the mayor and I have a moment alone please?"

I nodded, and Sherrie and I stepped into the kitchen.

"How are you doing? That was a lot of information to absorb," she whispered but didn't need to since EG and the mayor were in their own world.

"I'm ok. I need some time to process. I'm going for a walk. Would you mind staying here with those two?" It felt good to make a decision in the moment for me and not to worry about taking care of EG for a minute or thinking about Chicago or volunteering. Like I said, I had known I was adopted, but to have the final piece was something I needed to process.

"Sure."

EG raised her voice to the mayor, and we were able to hear her say, "I'm not sure what you think I know, and I really don't care what Abigail thinks."

The mayor raised his gruff old voice too. "Fine, if that's what you think. But I tell you, we all need to get together once and work it out. I am calling a meeting." He groaned as he was trying to get out of the chair.

"Claudia, can you give the mayor a ride home? We're done here." That was very uncharacteristic of EG to be so abrupt. The only other time I have seen EG be so short with someone was when someone had asked for her autograph, and she declined because we were in the middle of our dinner in a restaurant in Chicago. The lady had come over and started gushing and saying she'd just purchased her latest book and would love for EG to sign it. EG politely declined and offered to sign it later if she was still around when we were done eating, but lady kept insisting. EG unleashed on her about boundaries and common sense. The lady started to say something but was guided away by the manager, who had her leave before finishing her meal. I was impressed by her star power, but EG shrugged it off and said it had to do with the fact that she ate there thirty times a year when she was writing in her loft. The restaurant had nothing to lose by tossing out a tourist that would never come back. EG always downplayed her role as a celebrity and said she merely understood the economic value of choosing her over the irrational one-time guest.

"Is it far? I can maybe do it?" Sherrie said.

EG laughed. "It's less than a mile. You won't be rolling over two hundred thousand on this trip."

"I'm going for a walk if that's ok with everyone," I said.

The mayor was out the door, and Sherrie went out after him.

EG came over and gave me a big hug. "Are you ok?"

"Yeah, just taking in all the information. I know you said there's more, but can we do that later or maybe tomorrow?"

"Of course." She looked through the window. "Here comes Dr. Marie. It's up to you, but I do need to tell you *everything* and *soon*. Let her in and go for your walk. Take your time. Dr. Marie will not be here long, and when Sherrie returns, we will fix us a snack and relax."

"Why is the mayor bothering you? I do think it was him banging on your windows and not kids throwing stones."

"Don't let that little scene bother you. He is a good man. We just disagree about some stuff. I will explain what I know to you tomorrow. Now, go for your walk. Take my raincoat. I'm not sure we're done with the bad weather. Dr. Marie's here to look me over, so I'll be fine." She pulled her raincoat off the hook in the porch and tossed it to me and then shooed me away. *Am I somehow connected to whatever the mayor wanted to discuss?*

CHAPTER TWENTY-TWO

I dialed Jackson's number as I meandered towards the walking path that led to the river. He has always been good at balancing out a situation for me.

"What's going on?" he asked.

"A lot. EG and I had a big talk, and she shared so much with me. I just need to process."

"What is it? Is she sicker than you originally thought?"

"She's fine. Well, best she can be. She seems a little weaker than I thought she would be."

"Isn't that natural with chemo?"

"I was expecting tired, but she seems rattled. That's not what our talk was about though."

A car's horn startled me, and a second later, Sherrie pulled up next to me.

"Are you ok?" she asked.

"Yup, just going for a walk. Dr. Marie is with EG, but you can head back. Hey, how long are you here?"

"Tomorrow evening. I got to work on Saturday night. Call me if you want me to pick you up—as long as it's not too far."

"How about tonight we do something epic for the big rollover? Although . . . it might be a challenge in this town."

"Hello? Claudia? Are you still there?" Jackson said loudly on the phone.

I waved bye to Sherrie. "Oh, yeah. Sorry about that. Sherrie drove by," I said.

"She's still there?"

"Yes, until tomorrow. I wanted to tell you what I found out today."

"Isn't she staying a bit long? I think it's rude to put that much on you and EG."

"Why are you so concerned about Sherrie? I'm trying to tell you something."

"Well, to be honest, I always thought she was a bit pushy."

"Why are you trash-talking one of my friends? You have not said anything about her for the past year."

"I know she was your roommate. I didn't think you guys were that close. I just thought she was a bit of a storyteller. Couldn't always trust what she had to say."

"I don't get it. Why are you saying this?" As I said that, something clicked and I remembered the conversation Sherrie and I had started earlier today about the Chicago apartment and that she had more to tell me.

"Hey, are you still there?" Jackson said.

I snapped back to reality. "I'm here. Sorry, must have a bad phone signal. Can I ask you a question? Have you really been looking for an apartment or just hoping we could use EG's loft?"

"Both," he said in a flat tone.

"Oh." After another second, I put everything together. "I have to go now. Goodbye, Jackson."

I hung up and called my other roommate, Mia.

"How are you doing?" she said, the excitement from hearing from me was dull in her voice.

I paused before I said anything because I already had my answer. In the background, a song from the latest James Bond movie was playing—the same music I'd heard when I was speaking to Jackson.

"Hey, Mia, I'm good. The phone signal is not great, but I figured out what I needed to know. Maybe I'll talk to you later."

"Ok then, bye. Talk to you later," she said.

Holy shit. This was a lot to process. I got a

Teddy and lost a Jackson all in one day. They just didn't know it.

I stood there, dazed, and the rain started. I didn't have the mental ability to let my motions propel me forward.

If this had been a movie, this would have been the part when the camera would have panned out, the color becoming slightly dull, music starting softly, then getting more eerie, and I would look like a wet, lost puppy. The screen would cut to me lying on the ground as the car that had hit me drove off.

Well, this wasn't the movies, so no music was playing. But that car hitting me was absolutely true.

All I remembered from that moment was standing on the curb, hearing something loud, then some voices, and my head hurting.

Then, I was in a strange car and now, I was sitting in the hospital waiting room next to a man that looked familiar and a teenage girl I had not seen before. My head was not my only problem— my right arm was definitely not ok.

"Who are you?" I asked the man.

The girl answered instead. "I'm Mara. I saw you get hit and that car drive away. I waved down Duane here, and we drove you to the hospital. Don't worry, I used your phone to call your friend. She will be here shortly."

Duane nodded. "Miss, we met the other day at the Blue Daisy Diner. I helped you find Aaron. I'm Duane Schalski. I figured we would get here faster in my car than if we called an ambulance. You seemed to be able to walk if we helped you."

"You'll be fine. My aunt is a nurse here, and they are the best," Mara said, smiling.

"You talked to my friend Sherrie? Is she coming here?"

"Oh, no, I talked to Mia. I dialed the last number shown on the phone. I told her what I saw and that we were taking you to Memorial Hospital. I don't think she believed me at first, but then I explained the story several times and I think she overheard Duane yelling at me to help you. Don't worry, everything will be fine. I don't think there was any blood. You did land on your arm, which is looking funny, and we think you bumped your head. My aunt said the doctor will be here any second."

"Mara?" I said.

"Yes, what can I do for you? What do you need?"

"Mara?" I said again.

"Yes?"

"Pleeease. Stop."

She was rattling more than my head. I think Duane chuckled.

Thankfully, a nurse called my name.

I had a CAT scan for my head and an X-ray for my arm. I ended up with a mild concussion, and my right arm was fractured. My arm was being put in a soft cast when someone wearing blue came in.

"Hi, Officer," I said.

"Good evening, Miss. Actually, I am a deputy. To be precise, I am Deputy Holton Patrick. What can you tell me about the accident?"

"I can try to explain while they work on my arm, but I don't remember much of anything. Sorry. You should talk to Mara. Do you know if my aunt is here? Has anyone called her?"

"I did. I got everything, actually, a lot from Mara, but I need a statement from you. EG and another young lady are here. With the doctor's permission, they can come in when I'm done. Can you tell me what you know?"

"I remember standing there on the curb, and the rain starting. I had pulled up the hood on my jacket, so I didn't see much. I had been on the phone, and next thing I know, I hear voices, which must have been Mara and Duane. I kinda remember the car ride. I remember sitting out there waiting and Mara talking."

"Anything about the vehicle? What direction it was going, if it was turning, or if it swerved because of distracted driving?"

"I didn't see it at all because of my hood. Mara said she saw everything."

Deputy Patrick handed me a clipboard. "Can you write down your contact information, and then I will take your statement? A report is being filed, and we will update you on any progress we make."

I looked at him, waiting for him to understand I wasn't writing anything down.

"Sorry, Miss. You must be right-handed." He laughed. "How about you tell me the information, and I'll write it down."

After Deputy Patrick left, EG and Sherrie came in as the doctor was finishing my cast and hugged me. The doctor told them my prognosis and gave them instructions for how to care for me, then left the room.

I looked at EG. "I'm sorry. I should be taking care of you."

"Don't you worry. We got you," she said, touching my uninjured arm. "I called your parents and will keep them updated. They're going to come tonight, after they get Connor to a friend's house, instead of coming tomorrow."

"I'm so glad to hear that," I said, a grin spreading across my face.

Sherrie stepped forward. "While we were in the waiting room, I called and traded my shifts at the restaurant. So I don't have to be back until Sunday night."

"Well, how was it?" I asked.

"How was what?" they asked in unison.

"Your car rolling over two hundred thousand miles? Speeding to the hospital should be epic enough for you. You can say thank you to me for a nice story."

"Um, oh, that would have rocked it. We didn't think of that. After Mia called, EG tossed me her car keys, and we came right over. Didn't even stop to consider taking mine. Damn it!"

By the time we walked through the waiting room to leave, Mara and Duane were gone. I made a mental note to thank them for their help. I spent the ride to EG's explaining what had happened.

EG guessed some teenager had been driving and texting. Sherrie theorized a bank robbery getaway car had made a narrow turn, swiped me, kept going, and the robbers were now on their way to some mystery airfield, getting ready to take off for Mexico. I had no comment about that.

"You really didn't hear or see anything?" EG asked.

"No, I had just hung up the phone." I didn't feel like explaining what I had figured out about Mia and Jackson. I wanted to lie down on the couch and sleep through the night.

I got half of that. They had gotten me settled on the couch when a parade of people started coming over.

Jorge, EG's neighbor, came over to check on

her only to learn I was hurt, but he didn't stay long.

Sheriff Dalton was second. "I promise we'll catch whoever did this. I won't let him get away with it," he said.

"How do you know it was a man?" Sherrie asked.

"What do you mean?" he said.

"You said, 'I won't let *him* get away with this.' How do you know it was a man?"

"Very perceptive. It's a figure of speech. I don't know if it was a man or woman." In what appeared to be an effort to lighten the mood, the sheriff asked, "Did you ever consider a career in law enforcement?"

Sherrie's eyes grew wide. "All the time. I find it fascinating."

When he was leaving, my mom and dad walked in.

I could have sworn my face actually brightened. "It's so good to see you guys," I squealed.

They sat down, sandwiching me on the sofa. The hugs finally stopped, and my dad turned to EG and said, "You tell our darling our precious family story, and she ends up in the hospital with a broken head and a cast on her arm. Thank god, nobody ever told you where Jimmy Hoffa is buried. Who knows what would have happened to the family."

"Actually, we don't know *how* Claudia

ended up going to you," Sherrie said softly, looking at my dad.

"Yes, there is more *how* and *why* to the story. Why don't we finish up tomorrow? Claudia, you take my bed for the night. You'll be most comfortable in there. Katie Lyn and Matthew, take the upstairs bedroom. Sherrie, you get the couch in here, and I'll have the couch on the porch," EG said.

"I'll take the patio, but is it really bedtime?" Sherrie asked.

"Not at all," my mom said. "Except for Claudia. I'm assuming we'll have to check on you hourly throughout the night. How about I help you get fresh clothes on, clean you up, and get you comfortable for a shitty night's sleep."

"Amen," I said. "Although I am hoping the pain pills will help me sleep."

"Ok, while Katie Lyn helps Claudia, Matthew, get your bags from the car. Sherrie, can you find us something to eat while I talk to Jorge for a minute?"

Everyone jumped to their assignments as directed. A few minutes later, I was lying in bed. My mom and dad came in to ask if I was ok for the hundredth time.

"Yes, I'm fine. I just need some sleep," I said.

EG returned and came to check on me. "All settled in?"

"Yep, I'm good. What's Jorge up to tonight?"

"He's working on some project in his garage. I asked if he sees anyone trying to check on us that he would shoo them away."

"Who would come over here now?" I asked.

"You don't know this town very well yet, do you? The minute the word spreads that you got taken down by a hit-and-run driver and me with my chemo and your mother back in town, we will have more visitors, do-gooders, nosey biddies, and god forbid, more hideous food arriving on the doorstep."

My mom and EG walked out arm in arm and went to join Sherrie in the kitchen. My dad took the first watch and sat in the big green comfy chair next to the bed, quietly singing "Hit Me With Your Best Shot" by Pat Benatar.

That was the last thing I remembered about that night. I woke up many hours later feeling groggy. I could tell from the pillow and blanket on the green chair that my dad had spent the night. New concussion protocol did not require me to be woken up every hour, but I learned later that morning, my dad had woken up every hour to check my breathing and reported the update to my mom. The smell of breakfast and someone outside the bedroom talking on the phone got me out of bed, but it did not prepare me for what I was about to learn.

CHAPTER TWENTY-THREE

I got up and joined everyone at the table, feeling a little achy but able to move. "Where's the food? Why isn't anyone eating? Where's this breakfast I smell? I'm starving."

"Good morning, sweetheart," my mom said. "It's still in the oven. We're waiting on some fresh warm bread to be delivered. Why don't you shower? Everything will be ready in about ten minutes. I'll help you with your shirt. I don't know how much you can move."

"I'm ok. Stay where you are. Oh, actually, I need some clothes from upstairs. Can you bring something down?" I added, "There's now coffee in the house."

"Already got it. Thanks," my dad said. "Come here, we'll wrap a plastic bag over your arm so that thing stays dry."

My mom returned with a shirtdress and some underwear. "I figured this would be the easiest for you when you have to use the bathroom."

"The doctor said the swelling should come down quickly, and you'll have some use of your fingers while you have the soft cast on. Your mom is right, I don't think anyone wants to zip up your jeans every time you have to pee," EG said.

"Amen," Sherrie said and gave my dad a high five.

The shower felt great. Managing shampoo and conditioner with one hand was not so bad. I was wrestling the shirtdress over my head when something cold and furry rubbed against the back of my leg, and I screamed. *Shit, I don't need this.*

I looked down, and an adorable golden retriever sat, panting and staring at me. I heard a thunk and then a chuck and an "Oh, fuck," and I saw Sherrie and Aaron jammed in the doorway together, rubbing their heads. My dad was in the background laughing.

Aaron held out a hand. "Oh my god, I'm so sorry. I saw her push open the door and came in to get her. I didn't realize you were in EG's bathroom . . ." He gestured at me. "Half-dressed. When you screamed, I turned to leave, but Sherrie came running in . . ." He rubbed his head. "Sorry to you too, Sherrie."

She laughed and rubbed her head too. "I'm only forgiving you because this bread is so good," A chunk of bread was in her mouth, and crumbs sprinkled out as she spoke.

I finished getting dressed, walked into the living area, and saw Aaron standing by the dining table. "What are you doing here?" I asked.

"Your mom and EG asked my aunt for some fresh bread when I was at the café this morning, so she made me her delivery boy. I see you met Rita. Sorry again about that morning surprise."

"So this is Rita. The other night in the truck, when you said that blanket belonged to Rita, I thought you meant your girlfriend."

"You assume a lot of things about me."

Behind Aaron, Sherrie gave me two thumbs-up and mouthed *no girlfriend*.

"What was I to assume? You say a girl's name, and I'm supposed to know it's a dog? I was giving you more credit as a dude."

"That's fair, I guess. I thought you'd met her before because she's usually with me. This week, she had to spend a fair amount of time at home because she had a cone on her head."

"Did you get her spayed?"

"No, she had a few stitches after a lump was removed. It wasn't a big deal."

My mother patted the chair beside her.

"Aaron, you and Rita should stay for breakfast, I insist."

"Why sure, thank you, ma'am," he said.

After a nice breakfast, my mom and EG went to say hello to their childhood neighbor Ms. Lillyanne. Ever since they were young my mom said they had gone to Ms. Lillyanne's house and gotten apples from her backyard to make apple fritters. Today, they were taking her some fresh bread. My dad went to the hospital to straighten out the insurance information. He said the discharge papers had spelled my name wrong, and he wasn't having faith the insurance forms were completed properly by a lovely girl who had a big knot on her head. And then he wanted to stop by the police station to see if they had any updates.

That left the three of us, well, four if we counted Rita.

"Sherrie, would you like to go for a bike ride along the river? Jorge has several bikes and would be more than happy to loan you one," I said.

"I could walk you over and introduce you, if you want," Aaron said.

"I met him last night. Thank you for the offer." She looked at me "Are you sure? How can we leave you all by yourself?"

"I'm fine. I don't figure anyone is going to be gone very long. I just want to sit and relax on the sofa. I got my phone if I need anything. Plus, my mom and EG will be back soon."

Every time I said *mom* now, I just wanted to give her a hug. I didn't know what it took emotionally to adopt your sister's child, but I knew it was a special kind of love and I felt special to be a part of it.

I looked at the picture on the bookcase of my mom and EG holding Christmas wreaths they'd made three years ago after collecting pine cones and branches while drunk on spiked hot apple cider. Their arms wrapped around each other holding their wreaths like trophies. Giddy smiles show loved for each other and just pure joy.

"If you want to ride, you better go now before the rain starts again."

The three of them left, Sherrie promising to be back soon. I settled on the couch, grabbed a blanket and the remote.

Someone knocked lightly, and the screen door opened.

"Don't get up. It's just me. I must have left my keys in here," Aaron said.

"Come in," I sighed.

He came out of the kitchen, carrying the keys, with Rita following right behind. She jumped on the couch next to me and nestled her way to the pile of blankets.

"Sorry about that. She's been quite forward with you this morning."

"That's ok," I said, petting her head with my good hand.

"You'll have to stop petting her, or she will never leave."

"I'm good with that." I leaned in and got a couple of good licks from her. "Golden retrievers make for good therapy dogs, don't they?"

"I guess, but I don't think you're that broken."

"The hand and head are fine. I'm just processing some information, and this fuzz ball is a comfort."

"Are you ok? I know everyone keeps asking you, but your mojo is a bit off."

"Mojo? Now I have to worry about my bad mojo. I have a bump on the head, a battered arm, a crap load of information and a—"

"A boyfriend. I know, you told me." Aaron laughed. "What's with the eye roll? Just trying a little humor on the injured."

"Joke's on you, buddy. I don't think I have a boyfriend, or at least not for much longer."

Aaron motioned, asking to sit down on the other side of Rita, and I nodded.

"Great. Since I have known you, all I've heard from you was that you have a boyfriend; now, you have to adjust your opening line."

Brushing the hair out of my eyes for the hundredth time that morning, I turned and looked at him. "Sorry, this breakup is difficult for you."

"Take a little humor. You could use it."

"I know. It's a lot to process in the last twenty-four hours."

"You want to talk about it, or do you want some quiet? Don't worry. I'm good with either answer. I'm just a neutral person you can talk to."

"Thanks, but I think some quiet time would be good before the cavalry returns. Can I ask you to get me some water before you go though?"

Like a gentleman, he went to the kitchen and came back with some water.

"I don't get it. If you want to be with someone else, then go, but do you need two women?" I didn't know if I was just talking out loud, venting, or expecting an answer from the sky.

Aaron definitely didn't know if he should answer. He just stood there.

"I guess I could use a sounding board. Do you have someplace to be?" I said.

"I have a few minutes before I have to be anywhere," he said, sitting down again.

"Thanks," I said, frustrated, trying to juggle the water, the dog, the blanket, and the hair flying into my face.

He leaned forward, and his hand glided across my cheek as he brushed my hair back. "Can I get you a barrette or something?"

I laughed. "Barrette? Where did you learn

that fancy word? Do you have a sister?"

"No, a cousin. She runs the hair salon over on Broadway and Main. Over the years, I picked up some vocabulary. You got a problem with that?" He laughed, and his eyes sparkled.

"It's just interesting. I feel like a mess. I'm a little disheveled from getting ready with one hand."

"You look good," he said.

Heat rose to my cheeks, and I couldn't say anything.

He smiled. "Don't get all hot and bothered. I said *good* not *pretty*."

"Sure, go ahead and kick a gal while she's down," I said, giving him the side-eye.

"You are not out or down. I said remember your sense of humor. You do look—"

"I look fine. I get it. Now, tell me why guys are such idiots," I said, then told him what I had discovered about Jackson and Mia.

He listened without interrupting, and when I was done, he asked me a question I wasn't ready for. "Who are you mad at? Jackson, Mia, or yourself?"

"Myself? What did I do to me?"

"Hear me out. Be sad the relationship is over, but don't waste anger or energy on an a-hole of a guy."

"Interesting. Go on?"

"Are you mad at yourself for sticking with this douchebag after he left you with all those parking tickets and volunteer hours that *you* have to work? Are you mad at yourself because there were signs before now and you did not clearly see them? Are you mad because you're embarrassed?"

"Nice spin there, fella. My boyfriend cheats, and you ask if I'm mad at myself."

"Well?"

"You have a little bit of a point. Now what?" I said.

"You probably know what you should do and want to do, but you have to figure out how to do it and stick to what you want. It's not about whether you're ready to make a decision. That is facing you now whether you're ready or not. So you have to figure out what you'll accept about yourself."

"What? Explain that one."

"Sorry, I can't. Don't have time." He gestured over my shoulder. "Looks like the man of the hour is here."

I turned to look through the window, and Jackson was walking up to the house, with Mia of all people.

"I don't believe this crap," I mumbled.

"Well, I best be off." Aaron stood and mouthed *good luck*. "Come on, Rita." He headed out the door with a quick hello to Jackson and Mia.

They walked in and looked me over. Jackson sat where Rita had been and gave me a kiss on the cheek. Mia stood there, holding a box.

"How are you?" she asked. "I want to give you a hug, but I don't know if it'll hurt you. We stopped outside of Madison and picked up some donuts. I figured you'd prefer those to flowers."

"Thanks. I'm fine. Have a seat. I can't believe you guys drove up here *together*," I said.

"Of course. I had to see you," Jackson said.

Mia set the donuts down. "I was a little freaked out after we got the call from that girl who saw you get hit. It took me a minute to realize what she was saying. I called Sherrie right away, and she kept us updated. Where is she?"

I ran my fingers through my hair. "Everyone should be back shortly."

"So Aaron was here. Spending more time with him than me this summer. Should I be worried?" he said, laughing.

I ignored the question. "Actually, here comes Sherrie now."

She came in, and they had a mini reunion.

"Mia, Sherrie, do you mind if I talk to Jackson before everyone else gets back?" *Or before I lose my nerve*, I thought.

Sherrie nodded. "Oh, yeah, sure. Mia, let's go upstairs."

After they were out of earshot, I turned to

Jackson. "Why are you here?"

"What do you mean? We got a call you were run over by a car."

"We? You and Mia?"

"Yes. We were at the Tap Room when that girl called. Why are you so angry?"

"Do you think I'm that dumb?"

"What do you mean?"

I couldn't say the words I wanted to. I didn't want to ask the question, and I didn't expect him to confess. So I yelled, "Mia, Sherrie. Get down here!"

They ran down the stairs.

Sherrie looked at me intently. "Is everything ok?"

I couldn't look at anyone and studied my hands in silence. After a few beats, I looked up and said, "Someone tell me what's going on."

Sherrie stepped away from Mia.

I raised my voice. "Jack, right now. Tell me. Have the guts to tell me."

Mia looked at Sherrie for help, but Sherrie seemed to be trying to stay out of it.

"Sherrie started to tell me something, but I think I figured it out. I want to hear it from you both."

Mia shoulders slumped, and she let out a heavy sigh. "Oh my god, it's not what you think."

"Don't say anything, Mia," Jackson said, pleading.

"You want her thinking we're sleeping together?" Mia grabbed her phone and started looking for something.

"I can't believe you!" Sherrie said. "It's true."

Mia looked up from her phone. "*No!* Yes, Jackson and I have been getting together, but it's not what you think."

"How could you think something like that? Sherrie is spreading rumors," Jackson said.

"No, she started to tell me something, but we got interrupted," I said.

"Really? And you never thought to go back and finish the conversation? I'm guilty because of half a story?"

"What's going on?" I demanded again.

"Look, both of you, take a look." Mia looked between Sherrie and me now. "You guys have your golden birthdays this year. You'll both be turning twenty-three on August twenty-third. I, well, we were planning a surprise party for you both at 23rd Street Bar and Grill in Chicago. Jackson has been trying to call EG to get your family's contact information, but you were in the room each time he called. Here's my phone. Look at the emails marked SCBP—Sherrie Claudia Birthday Party. There is the bar menu. List of potential guests and other stuff."

"Really?" I said.

"Yes," Mia and Jackson said in unison.

"Oh," Sherrie and I said in unison.

For the next twenty minutes, Mia, Sherrie, and I said we were sorry one hundred times. I also retold my hit-and-run story. I felt much better. Better than I expected.

My dad returned as I was finishing up. "Well, hey there, everybody. I talked to the police. They don't have any leads. Mara's description of the car was that it's black with four doors. They are not sure if you were a target or if you were in the wrong spot at the wrong time. Mara can't confirm if you were stepping off the curb or if the car took the corner too short. She was full of lots of talking but few conclusions."

CHAPTER TWENTY-FOUR

I wanted some fresh air. Dad was going to wait for my mom and EG to return and insisted I promise not to go very far. The four of us headed out the door. Jackson and I were up front, with Mia and Sherrie behind us. Sherrie was giving a mini narration of everything she'd learned about the town since she has been here. Including the mileage between everything.

We got to the town square, and I said I wanted to walk to the river. Sherrie said she would show Mia around Jameson College.

Jackson and I walked in silence for a bit before he said, "I can't believe you thought I was with Mia."

"I'm sorry. It was a snowball of thoughts. I should have talked to you."

"If anything, I should be the one who's worried. Every time I turn around in this town, I see that dude. See, there he is." Jackson pointed.

I looked over. Aaron was in his truck, turning into the alley leading to the back door of his bar. He waved and turned out of sight.

I shrugged, and we walked to the river without saying anything else.

As we approached the parking lot and boat ramp, two old men were coming in from the river with fishing gear. They were about to leave in their truck when a teenage boy came running after them. The kid handed one of the men a tackle box. They were very appreciative, but the kid waved it off. Jackson couldn't believe the kid made that much of an effort in reaching the car before the old men took off.

I had stopped walking and watched the whole scene, having a moment of clarity. Everything that had been swirling in my head began to balance out. I saw the soup and flowers outside the courthouse not being for me but so Jackson could relieve his guilt. I saw the flowers he bought for EG not being for her but for her apartment. I saw my future and realized what I needed to do now. I felt the calm again. I felt lighter like something was checked off my to-do list that I did not know was on it.

I waited for Jackson to retrace the six steps

he had taken without me. When he came back, I said, "I'm done. Take me home."

"I want to touch the river. Can you believe I have never touched the Mississippi River?"

"Jackson, we're done here." I turned and walked back to EG's.

Jackson followed, but I could tell he was mad, which helped me make my point.

CHAPTER TWENTY-FIVE

An hour later, I said goodbye to Jackson. The girls came back from their tour of River Bend. My mom and EG were fixing soup and sandwiches for lunch, and Dad was going over the police report from my hit-and-run for the fiftieth time. I told Sherrie that, while I appreciated her being here, it was ok if she wanted to go back. I also suggested she give Mia a ride back since Jackson had left and would not be coming back. They seemed relieved to hear about Jackson and the breakup.

Little did I know, they'd made alternative plans. While they were walking around, they had run into Aaron, and he'd offered the apartment above BAR for the night. They were going to stay for the night and head back tomorrow. A band was playing at Draw Bar, and they wanted to go.

I called Mrs. Baron at Chambray and explained my absence today. She said she had known what happened before she'd had her second cup of coffee and told me to come in Monday and we would find some alternative jobs for me. Working one-handed was one thing, but working with my left hand was going to be a comical experience.

During lunch, everyone was trying to come up with left-handed jobs for me. Since I didn't, actually, couldn't eat the soup, I was done with my sandwich before everyone else. They all concluded I could replace one of the directional bronze scarecrow statues that point the way to the hospital. My family and friends were full of love, just not humor!

After lunch, Sherrie and Mia packed up, and my mom and dad offered them a ride to the apartment since the rain had started again. My parents wanted me and EG to have more time together.

The two of us grabbed some tea and settled on the couch on the porch. It was 2:00 p.m., but with the dark sky, it looked more like 9:00 p.m.

"How are you feeling?" EG asked.

"I'm ok. I don't know, I guess the weight of all this information keeps me off-balance just enough, but I got a handle on it all so far. Does that make sense? I'm a little sore from the fall, and my head is spinning with stuff. Everything you told me yesterday and what happened with Jackson. It's a lot to process, and I seem to be walking on a balance beam and have not completed fallen off yet. I may have gotten knocked down, but I am still walking the beam."

"Beautifully stated. I understand. I've felt the same way all week, and I think that's why I was so light-headed yesterday." EG paused. "But I need to tell you more, and it can't be put off."

She took a deep breath and stared out the screen window on the porch. After a few moments, she turned and looked at me. "I don't think it was an accident yesterday. I think someone intended to hit you. Well, at least, someone meant to hit me."

"I don't get it. Why?"

"You were wearing *my* green-and-blue-striped rain jacket, and you said you had the hood up. Someone thought it was me and saw an opportunity to either scare me or did a poor job of finishing me off."

"What? What are you talking about? Piece this together for me. Maybe it was you who hit their head."

"Let me finish the story from yesterday."

"Ok, I think I'm ready for more." I paused and took a deep breath. "Actually, I want more information."

"As I told you, Ellen and I went back for the

blanket. A few people were at the fire, and some noise came from the river and woods. It wasn't until I got back home that I realized that I had stepped in something. I thought it was mud until the next morning when I saw some blood. I didn't think anything of it until much, much later.

"The next morning at the pancake breakfast, some things were different. I couldn't explain it. Teddy was a no-show. Mayor Carl said the opening prayer and left immediately afterwards, not even waiting for everyone else to speak. Abigail walked around with her parents, smiling at everyone. Her dad got to the podium and announced the sale of some of their land to Seed Corp USA and all the jobs it would bring to River Bend. Everyone there was overjoyed.

"After he stepped down from the podium, he came over to my table and talked about me being the town's ambassador for this new phase in our town. I thought Abigail was about to faint. She went pale and cold. Despite the opportunity for making money, I knew I should pass up this opportunity. I suggested it should be Abigail for the position since she would be done with college before me and I still had two and a half more years.

"I left River Bend that afternoon not knowing that what had happened in the past twenty-four hours would have such a rippling reaction that it would lead to you and me sitting here.

"It wasn't until January that I realized I was pregnant with you. I was in a daze for a week before I called your mother. She came to visit for the weekend, and we talked about many options. I knew there was no way I was going to terminate the pregnancy. I also thought that my job working for a conservative magazine might be over since I was unwed and still in college.

"The next week, your mom and dad both came to visit with a precious offer and a wonderful gift for everyone. They offered to raise you. They were having trouble conceiving, but it was a little early for them to be talking about adoption, but then this presented itself. We had a long talk and decided it was a beautiful solution. You have to know it was not easy for me, but I knew Katie Lyn and Matthew would be the best thing for you, and selfishly, I would still be part of your life."

I squeezed her hand. I knew this must be hard for her to say out loud after all these years. She never seemed to be apologizing but gave me the facts, and I was ok with that. There was no need for forgiveness. Decisions were made, and they were good decisions.

"I said I couldn't decide until I talked to Teddy. I thought he should know. For the next several weeks, I tried finding him. I got his college phone number from his mother. That was the age before cell phones. When I called, his roommates said he didn't return for the semester, and they didn't know where he went. Your dad even checked out the story in case Teddy was avoiding some stalker chick from a one-night stand.

"We decided your parents would raise you as their own. They had just bought that house in St. Paul and were remodeling it. They were still living here and doing most of the work on the weekends. They didn't know anyone in the neighborhood, so when they showed up with a new baby, everything seemed natural. I opted for a home birth. The midwife had no idea that your parents' names were on the birth certificate.

"I finished the semester in a daze. Still writing monthly articles for the magazine and just wearing really big shirts. I spent that summer living with your mother and Mathew in their house here in River Bend and visiting Ellen, who stayed in Chicago for the summer.

"I think Mayor Carl figured out our little secret. Back then, he had a tradition of sending out a letter from the city to welcome new families moving to River Bend and to any family who had a child. When he was notified of your birth, he hand-delivered the letter because he had known your mother and me ever since we were small.

"When he showed up at the door, no one knew what to do. It was the five of us—me, your mother and dad, little you, and the mayor. It was a ball of awkward conversation. It was obvious that your mother had not given birth five days ago. He left, and we let out a collective breath. This was not a seedy backroom dealing, but we'd lied on the birth certificate. Your mother thought someone from the magazine could somehow find out if my name was on it.

"It wasn't until years later I heard about Teddy and realized more went on that night than I'd known about. He returned to college the following year. Doubled up on courses to make up for the year he'd lost. He changed his major and eventually went on to seminary."

"So he never knew about me?" I asked quietly.

"No. Not really."

"What do you mean not really?"

"He's not the man I thought he was and what most people think he is today. I have kept this secret of giving you to your parents for many years, but there are bigger secrets and stories out there. To be honest with you *and* myself what I thought to be the whole story is just what I know to be my truth. Sometimes I failed to realized other people have their side of the story and it probably involves me in ways I can not understand. And if it involves me it probably involves you too. "

EG's phone rang. She looked at the caller ID

and declined to answer it. She received a text seconds later and said, "We can expect company. Abigail and a guest are coming here now. I'm assuming it's Mayor Carl, but I could be wrong."

I now felt a weight sitting on me. I was trying to absorb everything I just heard. I snapped out of the self-reflection when I head a car pulled up to the house, and we looked through the window.

"That was fast," I said. "It's Sheriff Dalton and Mayor Carl, so I wonder who's with Abigail?"

Before the men could knock, EG was at the screen door, letting them onto the porch. Each one came over and asked how I was doing. Sheriff Dalton said they were still trying to figure out who'd hit me. EG opened the door to the house, and we all followed. Sheriff Dalton told her that they must talk this thing out as a group and implied with a nod that I wasn't part of the group.

EG started to protest, but I said it was ok. I would give them time, and we could continue our talk later. EG and I went to the porch, and I asked if she was ok with the men. I had an eerie feeling about this. I wasn't sure I felt comfortable leaving, but she assured me everything was fine. This was just something amongst old friends. I started out the door but turned back and grabbed an umbrella. I made sure EG had her phone and my number was one push away.

As I walked out the door, another car pulled up, and Abigail and Pastor Thec got out. I waved and kept walking. I looked back, and Abigail was watching me, as if she was wondering if I was coming back in.

I walked towards the river walking path, but if the heavy rain hit, I did not want to be caught far from town. I decided to look for Sherrie and Mia at the BAR apartment. As I approached the street, I changed my mind, wanting some time to myself.

I'll wander over to the library, I thought, looking around to get my bearings. Damn, Jackson was right. Every time I turn around, I see Aaron.

He was parked in front of his bar, unloading some items from the back of his truck. I waved and only got a nod. A few seconds later, Rita ran towards me, but Aaron called her back and she retreated quickly. Aaron held open the door for her, and she followed him inside. No wave, no smile, just a nod.

I didn't know why that bothered me. Maybe I was trying to divert my attention away from everything EG had told me.

I decided to ask if he was ok. Through the window, lights were on and music was playing. I tried the door, but it was locked. I banged and nothing. I tapped on the window and finally the music level dropped, and Aaron looked at me. I motioned to the door.

The locks clicked, and the door opened. Aaron stood there, looking at me.

"Hello," I said and waited for a response.

Nothing.

Using a funny low voice, mocking what he would sound like, I said, "Hi, Claudia, nice to see you again today. I hope you are feeling all right. Good to see you walking around. Well, where are my manners, please come in." That didn't earn me a smile, so I said in a sweet girly voice, "Why, thank you for the offer. Mighty nice of you."

He really wasn't moving.

"Are you being held up? Give me a sign if there's someone in there with a gun."

Nothing.

"Ok, I'll keep walking. Sorry to bother you."

"Are you by yourself?"

Whew, ok. Finally, I thought. "Yes."

"Ok, come in. Where's your man?"

"If you mean Jackson, he's gone."

"What do you mean gone? Gone for more rocks or gone *gone*?"

"He left. Why?"

"I don't like being called an asshole by some punk."

"What?"

"A few hours ago, I got back from the hardware store, and I was unloading stuff. I heard a car brake fast and some guy yell 'asshole,' and he sped off. I'm pretty sure it was the car I saw him in when I was with you earlier."

"Sorry, that was probably my fault. So you don't mind if I come all the way in, maybe past the doorway? The rain's picking up, and the umbrella is only doing so much to keep me dry."

He stepped aside, and Rita walked over and waited for me to pet her as I dropped the umbrella in the corner. Inside, tables lay on their sides and barstools were flipped over.

"Was there a bar fight in here?" I asked.

"I'm actually fixing the tables and some of the upholstery on the chairs and benches. I bought cheap when I opened this place, and now, I'm paying for it."

"So I take it you're not a fan of the sugar packet fix for wobbly tables."

He was still standing by the door as if he might leave at any minute or was hoping I'd leave soon. "I don't even have sugar packets on the premises. So do you want to explain why your boyfriend is a douchebag and it's your fault?"

"For starters, we have to give him a new name, like ex-boyfriend."

"Really?" He visibly relaxed, stepping fully back inside and sitting on a chair. "Here, have a seat," he said, handing me a flathead screwdriver.

"What's that for?" I asked.

"How about you scrape gum off those tables

while you tell me the story?"

I held up my right hand to remind him of my cast.

He smiled. "You got a left hand."

"That's true." I grabbed the screwdriver and sat down.

"So?"

"Oh, right. Well, I was wrong. Jackson was not cheating. Mia was planning a surprise party for me and Sherrie and needed Jackson's help."

Aaron turned to me. "So he didn't cheat and you broke up with him? What would have happened if he did cheat? Marriage?"

I laughed. "Nice sense of humor. No, I realized he wasn't the guy for me or the guy I want. I guess it was something you said earlier about how I saw myself in this relationship." I scraped gum off a table and continued. "Before I knew the truth about the party planning, I went over our relationship. I realized he was an ok guy and we had fun together, but he's not the type of person I want as a partner."

"How's that?"

"Like when we went for a walk by the river this morning. We watched a teenage kid run after some old fishermen who forgot some tackle down by the lake. I don't know fishing gear so I don't know if was worth ten bucks or one hundred, but I thought if Jackson had found the lures or whatever it was, he would have kept it. I want the type of guy that runs after people to return their things."

"So your type of a guy is a juvenile kid, jailbait."

"Shut up! You know what I mean."

"Stop. You're killing my table. I think you're doing more harm than good."

"This piece of gum is quite fresh. It's gooey."

"I swear Chuck did it this morning to annoy me. Just relax. You don't have to work. Can I get you a drink? Beer?"

"I'll take some water. Gotta stay away from beer until I'm off the pain meds."

He grabbed us two waters and came back and sat next to me, opening one of the bottles for me. "So you're done with him."

"Yup."

"So are you out trolling for new men this afternoon?"

"Whatever. That was nice of you to offer your place to Sherrie and Mia. Are they upstairs?"

"It's no big deal. That loft is part of the bar lease. I use it when I'm here late. I have another place out past the old Douglas Farm. I think I heard them say something about a movie. Should you be walking by yourself? Are you feeling that well?"

"I'm fine. The walk feels good, but I really had to give EG some privacy. There seems to be some mini crisis going on."

"Everything ok? Is it her cancer?"

"It's not her cancer, but I'm not sure everything is ok." I paused. "Can I share some stuff with you? It may help me sort through it."

"Sure." He sat back and just listened to me.

I didn't go over every detail, but I explained about being EG's daughter, the schmuck named Teddy being my birth father, and EG's urgency to tell me this now with all the weird stuff happening.

"What stuff? Do you mind me asking?"

"That's ok. You can ask. I'm here asking for you to listen so I guess questions are fine."

I told him about Mayor Carl coming over several times, Sheriff Dalton being in EG's house, all the phone calls from Abigail, and EG suggesting that she may have been the target in my hit-and-run accident.

"Interesting. What do you know about your birth father? Why the schmuck title?" Aaron asked.

I gave him the abbreviated version of the story about homecoming weekend and how Teddy left EG that night.

"I get it, but you made it sound like EG was ok with the one-night stand. If he never knew about you, it would be hard to blame him. He didn't walk out on you. I don't mean to defend the guy."

"Yeah," I said, "but why disappear for a few years and end up at seminary? You want to know the weirdest part? I think this all has to do with what they found in the river."

"The bag of bones? What makes you say that?"

"I don't know. Maybe it's just a feeling or the sense of urgency to tell me everything now. We have the whole summer together, and she's been a little weird whenever it's mentioned. She's used to all the gore and guts stuff. She writes about it in most of her novels. Anyway, they're all at EG's house now."

"What do you think the four of them are discussing?"

"Five," I said.

"Five? You said EG, Mayor, Sheriff, and Abigail? Are your parents there?"

"No, they went out. Abigail brought Pastor Theo with her."

"Pastor Theo?" Aaron raised his voice a bit and looked at me.

"Yeah, from St. Mark's Church in St. Paul? Do you know him?"

Aaron stood up, shaking his head, and kept looking at me. "Yes, I know him. Not very well. I just know who he is. He's from River Bend. His mother is an emergency room nurse over at the hospital in Kirkasaw County. Don't know about the dad. I think he has a brother somewhere in the state too."

He stared down at me, raising his hands in

the air, then combing them through his hair. He kind of yanked it like he wanted to pull it out.

"What," I said, shrinking in my chair.

He leaned over, put his hands on my shoulders, and gently said, "Oh my god, woman. Connect the damn dots!"

I stared at him.

I didn't get it until he started to say the words "Pastor Theo is Teddy."

"Oh my . . ." A heat wave washed over me. I put my head in my hands. Spinning. My head was not still. Spinning, it was spinning.

Aaron sat down next to me and rubbed my back.

"I got this same feeling back in the summer of seventh grade when I figured out I was adopted."

"You were pretty young when you found out. And you never told anyone you knew?"

"I accidentally stumbled on that tidbit one summer. I didn't know EG was my mom, just that I was adopted." I explained how I'd found out. "After the initial shock, I was oddly comforted that I had a secret piece of information. I knew what made me special. I thought it was cool, and it was like I had my own secret and a superpower. 'You can't fail me, I have super knowledge' or 'Don't pick me last, I know the family secret,' 'Don't strike me out, I know adult-level secrets.' I know that's crazy thinking, but I was only eleven at the time. I had the superpower of knowledge. My friend and I also thought swimming in chlorine would be good for our acne, so I'm not sure about the superpower knowledge of a preteen girl."

After a few minutes of silence, I said, "I want to go back to EG's."

"Are you sure? You can stay here as long as you want. I can give you some quiet time," Aaron said.

"No, thanks though. I'm going now." I stood, and he was next to me. "Thank you, for everything."

After a few seconds, he stepped back and offered me a ride, which I gladly accepted.

As we approached the house, we could see all the cars were still there.

"Do you want me to come in with you?" he asked.

"No, I'm good. I'm not sure they even want me there. I just want to see EG and get a look at Pastor Theo. I don't know if *look* is the right word but I want to see them, EG and Pastor Theo."

"Do you want me to wait in case they ask you to leave?"

"Nah, if EG says everything is good and they still want some time, I'll go upstairs or visit Jorge next door if he's home. I wonder where my parents are."

"I think it'll be a while before they're back. I talked with them this morning at breakfast, and it will be a bit before they return."

I slid out of the truck as the storm picked up. I had been gone fewer than thirty minutes, but it felt like a lifetime. As I stepped into the screened-in porch and took off my jacket, I could see, through the windows, the five of them standing in the living room around and the police report sprawled across the dining table. I saw Pastor Theo and realized my feelings or lack thereof had not changed. Now, I just wanted to get to EG.

I opened the door, and all five of them turned and stopped talking.

EG immediately walked over and hugged me.

I whispered, "I figured it out."

"Finally," she whispered.

In the background I saw Mayor Carl motion for everyone to sit at the table. EG put her arm around me and lead me to the table.

The sheriff and the mayor were sitting opposite me. Pastor Theo was on my right at the head of the table. EG was on my left and Abigail next to her.

Abigail spoke up first. "EG, this is for us. Not for everyone."

"I must agree," Pastor Theo added.

"I agree too," EG said. "But this concerns her

too. Let's put the police reports away. We have gone in circles for twenty minutes without saying much but implying what people may or may not know. We need to start from the beginning. I don't think everyone here has all the information." Then she looked at me and softly said, "*This is the why.*"

She squeezed my hand and looked at everyone. She waited and finally said, "Where should we begin?"

Sheriff Dalton cleared his throat. "EG, this is tough for me and my position. I have had a hard time reconciling my part in this with the oath of office I took several years later."

Mayor Carl put up his hand. "Thomas, it's ok. EG is right. Once we walk through that night, once and for all, we will *all* understand that Claudia belongs here."

"Thank you, Mayor. OK, now let's start. You and especially Sheriff Dalton know the law better than any of us, but we must agree to do what is right both lawfully and morally," EG said.

I watched each of them sitting there, quiet and still. They seemed to be reflecting internally for no spoke for a minute. I realized they had come here wanting something, but when the truth was ready to be told, the weight of it seemed to hold them back.

No one did or said anything until Mayor Carl spoke up again. "Are we ready?"

Everyone nodded, and an unspoken bond of unity was sealed.

CHAPTER TWENTY-SIX

Pastor Theo looked at EG. "Twenty years ago. I was, um, well then." He cleared his throat and started again. "Remember I was late getting to your house before the bonfire? I never told you why."

"You said you were helping your mom with something and you hurt your hand."

"Yes." He pushed back his chair and leaned forward, placing his elbows on his knees and clasping his hands together like one might do in a prayer of anguish. He took a deep breath and rested his head on his folded hands for a moment before he looked up. "I don't know if you remember my father. He was not around very much or very long. My mother kicked him out of the house when I was around five years old. He stayed in town for a few years, and after that, he popped back in whenever he felt like it. He always had a hand on the bottle, other women, and the gas pedal. A few times, he cleaned up his act and my mother let him back, but each time, he failed."

Mayor Carl put a hand on Theo's shoulder. "Son, he failed you as a man and as a father."

"I appreciate the understanding, Mayor." Pastor Theo had everyone's eyes pinned on him and continued. "He was rumored to be living in a shack several towns east of here. My brother and I only believed he was close when we saw a bruise on our mother's neck. That night, he came back to the house. Looking worse than I had ever seen him. He probably dropped 40-50 pounds. He was a shell of a man. I would have not recognized him if I'd passed him on the street. The drinking and living life as a bum took its toll on him physically and mentally.

"I walked in on him attempting to have another go at my mother. I pulled him off her before he could strike her again. I hit him several times and made it clear that if he ever returned to that house or even this town, he would live to regret it. He left, but I'm not sure where he went. I didn't even know if he had a car. I took my mother and drove her to her sister's house a few miles away in case he was stupid enough to come back."

"That's how you hurt your hand," EG said.

Pastor Theo nodded and continued. "We

met up at the fire. We were talking and decided to leave the group for a bit."

EG was squeezing my knee and holding her breath.

Pastor Theo paused. He was blushing, trying to catch his breath. "As we were walking, we decided to throw rocks, bricks, and sticks at one of the scarecrows that was behind a wood pile. I didn't think anything of it. After our walk to the ranger station, we rejoined the group at the bonfire. And then I had to return to the ranger cabin to get one of the blankets. On the way back, I decided to grab that scarecrow to throw on the fire, but it was then that I discovered what"—he took a slow deep breath—"what brings us here. I'm sorry I got everyone involved. I am so sorry."

He looked to the mayor, Sheriff Dalton, EG, and then Abigail. With his voice wavering, Pastor Theo said, "EG, that was no scarecrow. That was my father."

Frozen, Everyone was frozen but this news seems to only hit EG and me. The others had known. No one spoke and I made the connection and in a whisper I mumbled. "That... that discovery. In the river was your..."

It was Abigail's outburst that got the most reaction from the everyone. "Yes, Claudia. We are talking about a dead man here. That bag of bones is why *WE* are here. I am not...

"Stop, Abigail." Mayor Carl cut down Abigail while speaking for the group. "It's ok. Let Teddy continue."

After a moment of silence, Theo raised his head, his eyes were red and his voice was a bit unsteady. "He must have wandered down to the river and passed out. It was so dark that night, we never realized what we were doing. I'm more ashamed to admit that I'm not sure I would have stopped if I'd known it was him." His head turned down to the floor and then rested on his fingers that were still laced together in a fist, elbows on his knees. He rocked back and forth trying to steel himself to say something else, but nothing else was able to be voiced.

"We understand. He was a bastard of a man," Sheriff Dalton said.

"It doesn't make it right," Theo said. "I knew immediately that the man was dead, but it took me a minute to realize it was my father. I also knew I had to get everybody out of there."

EG squeezed my arm. She was pale, shaken, and looked like the wind had gotten knocked out of her. Trembling, she said, "That's why you made up the story about the police trolling the area. I wondered how you found out about the police being there."

"I had no clue. I just had to get rid of as many people as possible. I figured whoever didn't leave would be too drunk or distracted by the fire. We had no bad intent in our hearts, EG, but I also didn't know who would believe us. I'm sure the neighbors had heard the fight between me and my dad. My aunt's neighbors had seen me when I'd taken my mother over there after I got my father out of the house. I tried telling you once that night, but you insisted on getting out of there because you couldn't jeopardize your job. I was making decisions so fast and without thinking. I didn't know if I could ever look at you and think about that night as you would think of it. I knew I would think of the blood on my hands and my conscience."

A tear rolled down EG's cheek. "I didn't know that happened. I thought of a thousand different scenarios because, the next morning, I saw blood on my shoe and, later, discovered you'd disappeared from school and town."

Abigail shook her head. "You really had no idea? The way you looked and talked to me at breakfast the next morning? Don't tell me you have been living with a clear conscience all these years. I saw you in the woods! This is our story."

EG's sorrow, guilt, and grief turned to anger, and she looked pointedly at Abigail. "Of course, I didn't know. How could I imagine this? Is this the meaning of your little bookend story? Did it make you happy knowing I'd killed someone? You sit up on the hill and try to twist me into this horrible person. All for what? So you don't have to go at this alone! Will you be quiet for a minute, and let me realize what I am a part of here?"

That outburst kept everyone frozen. The look on Abigail face was shock but I don't know if it was what was said or how she was spoken to. I don't think I have moved an inch since I sat down. I was tensing up. Abigail leaned back away from EG when she spoke but she had her feet practically glued to the floor.

I noticed no one seemed comfortable. Ever since the mayor had sat down, he kept his cane between his knees and the table, and his hands were firmly placed on top as if he was trying to stake the cane into the floor. The sheriff, while not in uniform, still had his gun in his ankle holster. He had on a short-sleeve buttoned-down shirt, but it was wrinkled and his hair looked like it hadn't been comb. Both of which were very uncharacteristic. He looked shaken before we sat down. Teddy was still hunched over, but the rocking stopped during EG's confrontation with Abigail. EG turned away from her and seemed to be the only one looking at everyone and then finally put her head into her hands and rested them on the table. I slid out of the chair, stepped into the kitchen for some tissues for EG, and returned and heard Pastor Theo say, "That's not why we are here. Both of you, please calm down. EG and I did it and unwittingly pulled you all in."

Mayor Carl spoke up again. "Son, hold on one minute. You don't know it was the two of you. I was with old Sheriff James when the neighbors called in a report about a commotion at your house. It was no secret what happened when your old man came back to town. He figured by the time we got to the house, he may be gone. I was done with all my responsibilities for the day. I was tired of the crowds, and I told Sheriff James I would drive around and see if I could spot him. Sheriff James gave me one of the police radios, and I started driving around.

"I spotted him several blocks from your mother's house. You were right. He was a mess. The drinking did him in, but I think there was more. On his wrist was an ID bracelet from a hospital."

His hands still clasped tight and his knee bouncing nervously, Pastor Theo said, "Even if he was sick, that does not make up for the fact that while he was passed out, we stoned the man to death. There was all that blood."

The mayor held up a hand. "I approached him, and he had nothing to say. I asked if I could give him a ride somewhere. He said something incoherent and kept walking. I got back in the truck intent on following him, but he walked towards the woods. At that point, it was too dark to follow him on foot. The radio Sheriff James had given me was not working, so I headed back to the fireworks to report what I had seen. He thanked me, but he and his team were working the fireworks area, directing traffic, and watching for drunk drivers. I decided to check on your mom and drive around a bit, and that's how I ended up seeing you guys at the bonfire."

Sheriff Dalton spoke next. "I had dropped Joe and Abigail off at the bonfire and took Ellen home. I thought the bonfire would go on for a bit, so I went back, only to find a handful of people. I was having a beer and talking to Joe when Abigail said something about Ellen probably coming back for her blanket. I didn't want to get into it with Ellen about why I had dropped her off and went back to the bonfire, so I took off for the woods and that's when I stumbled upon Teddy."

Sheriff Dalton is Tommy, I thought. *Wow, so many revelations this week.*

"I tried to get you to leave, Tommy. I begged you to leave," Pastor Theo said.

"I know. You did everything you could think of. You even said you were meeting a girl there."

Theo glanced at EG.

"But you looked awful. I could tell something was wrong. Then I saw the blood. I made you tell me. I know I could have left. That night standing with you, I was content with my decision to help you. I made peace with my role even before I knew the whole story. You said the words *my father*, and I knew right then and there. I was your friend, and I was not going to leave you. I have held onto the feeling all these years. I struggled when I took my oath, but I remember helping you, my friend, and that helped me move through my career in law enforcement. I made the right decision."

Pastor Theo put his head back in his hands and waited in silence. He whispered, "Thank you."

"We were standing there, trying to come up with a solution, when Abigail came over," Sheriff Dalton said.

"I was trying to find you because Joe was getting drunk and would not walk me back home. I was hoping to catch up to you, Tommy. I saw you two and knew something was wrong," Abigail said.

"You did not help the situation. You flew off the handle when you saw the blood on Teddy. You would not walk away. You demanded we tell you what was going on, or you were going to start yelling. Then you really freaked out," Sheriff Dalton said.

"I know I didn't handle any of it right. You have to understand my situation. My family was in serious trouble."

"Your family?" EG asked.

"Yes, all the showboating I was doing—I was always going over the top with how great everything was for us. Some of that was because I was a spoiled brat back then, and then I learned things. Our family was in deep debt, and my parents' marriage was a joke. This had been going on for several years. We were on the brink of losing our house and the manufacturing plant. Then, out of nowhere, my dad got an offer for the majority of our land and the plant. The company wanted a town with dependable workers who had a good Midwest work ethic. It was not a high-profile company. You throw in a murder, and that would have been the end of everything for me and my family. And that factory did this town lots of good. I too am content with my decision to help that night. No regrets."

"I am assuming, Mayor, you went down to the riverbank later that night," EG said.

Pastor Theo spoke up. "Yes, he did. Abby, Tommy, and I were coming up with a plan for what to do with my father. I remembered seeing that old boat down by the ranger station earlier that night. We needed some type of sack to put him in. That's when the mayor pulled up.

"Abby said she had an idea and to wait for her signal. She came out of the woods, pretending she had gone to the bathroom. She greeted the mayor and said she was happy to see him. Earlier in the day, she had seen the enormous duffel bag holding all the baseball equipment in the back of the truck. The two of them chatted for a bit, and then she walked him over to the fire. As they walked away from the truck, she waved us over, and Tommy and I grabbed the duffel bag. No one noticed. Mayor Carl talked to the guys at the fire a bit and left."

"That's when Ellen and I came back," EG said.

"We know," Theo and Sheriff Dalton said together.

"We had dragged my father to the water and heard you guys coming down. We lay in the tall grass and waited for you guys to leave," Theo said, sitting upright with his right knee bouncing.

"We heard some strange noise in the water and woods," EG said.

"Yeah, I almost shit myself when you walked over to where Teddy's dad had been minutes before. If there was a full moon or clear skies, you would have seen the trail we made. That noise was probably the duffel bag rolling into the water and us trying to stop it," Sheriff Dalton said. "Abby convinced everyone to leave. The handful of guys left were all drinking age, but she made up some story about the illegal fire and said the mayor would probably have Sheriff James swing by."

Abigail leaned forward. "I told Joe I was going to walk with some girls as the boys headed home. I walked in the direction of the woods but stopped when I knew I was out of sight. Tommy went to get the boat and pull it up to us. Teddy and I looked for anything heavy to weigh the duffel bag down. I took all those baseball bats and sports equipment and threw them in the river." She looked at the mayor. "Sorry." She sounded like a little girl apologizing for something she didn't fully understand.

Pastor Theo continued. "Tommy walked up fifteen minutes later, pulling the rowboat. We put my father in that duffel bag with some heavy cinder blocks left behind by the construction crew, and whatever else we could find. We paddled out to the middle of the river and let him sink to the bottom."

Abigail looked from Sheriff Dalton to EG and then to me as she spoke for the three of them. "It was a bad night. We all made decisions that night that we had to make peace with."

"I think it helped direct me to law enforcement. I wanted to do right for those who can't help themselves. Whenever I wrestle with my conscience, I think of your mother, Teddy. Back then, I never thought law enforcement did enough for her," Sheriff Dalton said softly.

Pastor Theo nodded in agreement.

Mayor Carl tapped a finger on the table. "I guess I made peace with it too. I knew something went on that night. The next morning, I went back to the riverbank where the fire had been. I saw a few baseball bats washed onshore and didn't realized they were mine until later. I went to put them in the bed of my truck and realized my equipment and duffel was missing.

"After I left the riverbank, I drove around a bit more before the pancake breakfast. I spotted an unfamiliar old beat-up truck parked near the woods. It was unlocked, and the keys were still inside. I went through the personal belongings and confirmed the truck belonged to your dad. I didn't know what condition he would be in and if he should be driving. I took the truck and hid it in my garage. I figured if he was sober, he'd come looking for it and I would return it to him.

"Obviously, he never went to the police. After a week, I went through all the stuff. I found some medical records and insurance information. I don't know if it makes a difference, but your father was sick. Real sick. From what I read and recall I don't think he had much time since he wasn't getting the treatment he needed.

"After a year, I finally gave the truck to a friend of mine who runs a youth camp up north. He took the truck with no questions asked and understood no answers would be given."

Pastor Theo sat back in his chair. "I never told my mother or brother. Although Christian asked a lot of questions. I came back to the house close to dawn. I stayed by the river until the sun started coming up. I don't know what I expected to see or do. I was recalling everything I'd done that night."

"That next morning was almost worse than the night," Abigail said. "I was running on adrenaline. Thankfully, no one had noticed I'd gotten home in the middle of the night. That morning, my father was so excited about announcing the new factory coming to town. I figured I just had to get that damn breakfast done with, and I could be on my way. Once again, I had to put up a front that we were a happy, perfect family. What a joke we were living, and god forbid, the people in town knew anything different. Thankfully, Joe was too hungover to realize I was so shaken. I went back to my dorm that night and stayed away for several years.

"I stayed with Joe all those years until he passed away and never told him what I was a part of that evening. He never had a clue or, at least, never let on if he knew something.

"I tried to balance my personal karma when I sold our family land so cheap to those developers who built Chambray and to Jameson College for its new dormitories. I was hoping to put something positive into this community.

"We know that he was not much of a man and I didn't kill him, but we erased him from the earth. This is not something I take lightly. No matter how big or small a person's contribution to the world might be, that person still should not leave it without a word of recognition that he was once a part of it." He voice faltered but continued. "We made him a ghost."

It was at this moment I realized how much this must have weighed upon her all these years. She realized at some point making a death invisible was taking away a man's dignity, even if he did not earn it as a father or husband.

After a minute, Abigail regained her composure. She straightened up and sat like she had a book balanced on her head. She placed her hands flat on the table and looked out the open window behind the mayor. "Believe it or not, several years later, I went back to the riverbank. I said a prayer and tossed a small cross into the river. It didn't make sense, and maybe I'm fooling myself or trying to justify my role, but it helped me make peace."

Mayor Carl spoke up again. "I never said anything to Addie or Eugene. I told them I picked up the truck real cheap and thought about fixing it up as a fun project. Eugene was away at college and never had an interest in cars, so he didn't pay any attention to it when he was home. Addie thought it was a silly hobby that never took off."

EG gestured around the table to everyone. "That brings us to today. We've looked at the police report and the preliminary autopsy report."

"There is nothing that connects us to any of it," Abigail said. She had been bouncing between remorse and guilt, but was now leaning in for self-protection.

That doesn't mean we shouldn't do anything," EG said.

"She's right, Abigail. Teddy's mother and brother deserve to know. I don't know about any criminal charges after all these years. That man was dying, almost dead before he came to town, but that does not erase the facts of the accidental stoning and hiding a corpse. I don't know the law here," Mayor Carl said.

Pastor Theo nodded. "They do deserve to know. I think, after several years, they came to realize that my father was never coming back. They moved on, but still, I need to tell them my role in what happened. I did not return to school that fall. I traveled a bit. I guess you could say I was hiding and dealing with what happened. I came back from time to time. Each time, I wanted to tell them what happened, but I couldn't. Once, I made up a lame story about hearing about my father living in some town a hundred miles away. I thought that would put my mother at ease about him not coming back here. I won't go into details about my life for the next year, but I came out of it with a new path of becoming a pastor."

"So you could grant yourself forgiveness." Abigail sneered.

"No, like Tommy, I wanted to do something helpful. The law and law school were too depressing. Through my travels, I did volunteer work. Building houses, cleaning beaches, planting trees, but I knew something was missing. I volunteered to help a town clean up after a terrible hurricane and stayed in a church that was housing volunteers. I became close to the pastor there, and I liked how he was able to comfort those who had lost not only their possessions but their hope in the future and god," Pastor Theo said, looking at Abigail.

We sat there absorbing everybody's role in what had happened.

After a minute of silence, Sheriff Dalton said, "I never had a case that dealt with the stealing and disposing of a corpse, but I did some research. A person can be fined up to twenty-five thousand dollars and be sentenced to twelve years in prison. I asked a lawyer some questions."

"What? You got someone else involved?" Abigail barked. "You should have told us you involved someone else. Protecting yourself. How could you?"

The sheriff held up his hand. "Take it easy. I talked to one of the State district attorneys that I have worked with in the past. I presented him the case from a lawman's perspective. I wanted some information on what the State's take on this would be. We do that all the time on different cases. As I said before Claudia got here, it is still a matter of jurisdiction. Wisconsin currently has the case, but it could swing to Minnesota." He paused and looked at them one by one. "Although, as far as what *we should* do, that really doesn't matter."

Abigail pointed to the reports. "Those reports show no DNA on the canvas bag. There was no identification found."

"I don't know about bone DNA testing yet," Sheriff Dalton said. "EG, do you know anything? Have you done any research for your books?"

"No, I haven't. I've dealt with blood, bullets, and bomb explosions. I don't know the technology about bones that's out there today or what's to come in a few years," EG said. "It doesn't matter what the State can determine or prove at this point. We said we have to figure out what we should do, not what we have to do to protect us."

"You sound like you've made up your mind to confess everything." Abigail pointed at EG. "You don't get to do that. This involves everyone here.

Well, almost. I'm still not sure why Claudia is here."

CHAPTER TWENTY-SEVEN

EG locked her arm around mine and took a deep breath. She looked at Mayor Carl, and he nodded. "You knew, didn't you?" she said.

"Yes and no," Mayor Carl said. "I didn't know the whole story. I had put the pieces together over the years. I knew you and your family to be good honest people. I didn't believe it was my right to interfere. I was still dealing with the truck, technically stolen, sitting in my garage, with my limited knowledge of what happened that night, and my lack of forthcomingness with Sheriff James. I guess I chose to step out of it. So I'm assuming no one else here knows."

EG shook her head. "I just started telling Claudia everything the last few days."

"You're talking to Claudia. Tommy is

talking to a State lawyer. Theo, did you confess anything to a fellow pastor? Tommy, you tell Jean anything? Why can't you folks keep it to yourself?" Abigail said, rising from her seat.

Sheriff Dalton stayed quiet and unmoving. Theo was watching this play out.

Mayor Carl waved Abigail down and pushed himself up with his cane. He took a step from the table and looked out the window to the clouds and rain. With his back to everyone, he finally said, "EG, it's time."

All eyes landed on EG. She took a deep breath and looked at me. The only noise was the breeze coming through the windows from the incoming storm.

I put my arm around her for a hug. "It's ok."

EG looked at Theo. "In the beginning, I thought a million times to tell you. I rehearsed what I would say. Decisions had to be made and made fast. Once everything fell into place, I was ok without you knowing. Maybe that was because I couldn't find you, but I also felt like that was part of some greater plan."

"Oh, holy hell," Abigail mumbled, raising her hands to her mouth, clearly figuring it out faster than Theo.

Maybe that proved he was my biological father. It had taken Aaron practically calling me a dumbass to figure out that Pastor Theo is Teddy.

EG looked down at her hands and back at Theo. "We have been discussing the horrible events of that night, but something beautiful came out of that evening."

Theo leaned forward with his elbows on his knees again and looked from EG to me and back. He seemed to be slowly connecting the dots. "Are you telling me that . . ."

"Claudia is your daughter."

No one spoke for a moment. Then Theo and EG stood up and hugged for a long time.

Still holding each other in a light embrace, he said, "I-I, um, oh. W-wow."

"It's ok. I know this is a lot for you. I know you know Claudia, but let me introduce her to you as your daughter."

I stood up, and he came forward and put his hands on my shoulders. We looked at each other, and together, we said, "Hi," which seemed to get a chuckle out of the group at the table. We hugged for a moment and sat down again.

He shook his head with a shocked smile. "With all the things I expected to come out of today, I did not expect a . . ."

"A daughter," the sheriff said, sitting back down. "EG, you kept that from him?"

"It took me several months to realize I was pregnant. I tried finding him, and as he said, he took off traveling. My sister and Matthew offered to raise the baby, and I knew that was a beautiful plan. They were struggling to have a family, and I would still get to be part of her life." She turned and looked at the mayor. "We never meant for you to get involved. We were scared when you came to the house, thinking you'd figured everything out. You were so kind, and we appreciated your silence."

"That's ok. I figured it was none of my business whose name was on that birth certificate."

Theo was still shaking his head. EG and I sat once again with arms locked, looking at each other and then at the mayor. He looked as if he had a confession of a lifetime.

Sheriff Dalton stood up and broke the ice. "Well, I guess we now know why Claudia is here. I could use a drink."

"I think that is a good idea," EG said. "Claudia and Abigail, why don't you go in the kitchen and see what I have to drink. Maybe see if there's some food for us to nibble on."

Abigail seemed a little put off about being sent to fetch beverages but went with me anyway, probably figuring I needed help with my one good arm.

Mayor Carl and Sheriff Dalton were hanging around the table talking about something.

EG turned on several lamps since the rain clouds made it appear much later than what it was, and she and Theo moved to the corner of the living room, where they talked quietly. I watched them together, and they looked comforted by one another. I felt no connection as part of a trio with them. I have my love for EG but did not see the three of us as a unit. They talked quietly and hugged until I returned with beer for the sheriff and Theo. I returned to the kitchen to give them more time.

Abigail had poured herself wine and remained in the kitchen getting food together. EG and I stuck to mineral water.

The mayor declined beer as well, saying it didn't mix well with the pain medicine for his knee. "Speaking of mixing pills and beer, EG. I owe you an apology. The other night, I had a few drinks at home after getting the first police report. It set me off. After all these years, for the bones to be discovered, I was a mess. I came over here, and I think I knocked on the windows looking for you. I hope I didn't scare you."

"I was a bit unnerved for a moment. I was soundly sleeping and thought some kids were throwing rocks at the window. It's ok. We've all been shaken by the news. Hell, I almost fainted when Eugene brought the first report over here, and I didn't even know my role in it. He mentioned an envelope with Teddy's name on it, and it struck a nerve."

Abigail came back with a nice tray of cheese,

veggies, and crackers. She had even sliced some of the bread Aaron had dropped off this morning.

Sheriff Dalton had his chair pushed back, tearing apart a slice of bread and looking at it like a puzzle he had to put back together. "Now what? We are no closer to figuring out what we should do than when we started this conversation."

"We do what we've been doing all these years. We keep quiet. What difference does it make? We all made peace with it one way or another," Abigail said.

"I don't know about that," EG said and her voice cracked. "I haven't had time to even think about my role in the death of Teddy's father."

"I agree with EG. Just because silence worked doesn't mean it's right. We don't know if anyone else knows anything. Someone else may come forward. There were several people at that bonfire late that night," the sheriff said.

"No one can pinpoint the death to that particular night. Any report is going to be vague on the year much less that night," Abigail said.

"You are right about the date, but what about DNA in the bones? I don't know yet if they're able to link the body to Teddy or his brother," Sheriff Dalton said.

"But that still doesn't make them suspects, only grieving family members," Abigail said. "Tommy, who else was by the bonfire later that night?"

"I'm not sure. When I came back from dropping you off, it was Marcus and two or three other guys. EG, do you remember?"

"When Ellen and I came back, I saw Marcus and his brother, Tim, with his date. They were getting ready to leave in Marcus's truck. I don't know who else was there."

"I do," said the mayor. "It was the Peterson twins. I talked to them for a minute and asked them to make sure the fire was out. I left and must have missed you and Ellen by a minute or so."

"Mayor, when you left there, the twins followed you. We saw EG and Ellen coming back, and I told Joe I wasn't getting in the truck. It was an easy way for me to slip away from them and go back to help Teddy and Tommy," Abigail said.

Sheriff Dalton said, "That's right. I don't think they saw anything. The twins came late, and once they figured out the bonfire was pretty much over, they wanted to get out of there and see if they could get into a bar with their fake IDs."

"So that's it?" Abigail said. "It's just us. And Claudia."

"But we heard something in the woods that night," EG said.

"Are you sure it wasn't us, the three of us hiding in the grass? You said you heard a splash," Theo said.

"We definitely heard something in the water, but I heard something in the woods. And, no, I don't think it was an animal. It was too sharp of a noise and no other movement. I didn't think too much of it because I had no idea what was going on. I was still surprised that the scarecrow, which I now know was your father, was not there."

"So are you suggesting that someone witnessed all this and never said anything?" Theo asked.

"I don't know, but I wonder if it has anything to do with Claudia getting run over. That's the other reason I think she should be here. I think she got pulled into our mess when someone mixed up the two of us."

"How are you connecting these two situations?" Abigail asked.

"It was raining when she went for a walk. I gave her my green-and-blue-striped rain jacket. No one else has a jacket like that. I've had it for years. She had the hood up, and with the profile glance, she does look like me."

"Could that be true, Sheriff?" Mayor Carl asked.

"I saw the report Deputy Patrick put together. Anything is possible. It could have been intentional or an accident. We don't know if there was an intended target or not." The sheriff continued with EG's theory. "Why target just EG?

There were four of us. Really, three. Mayor, you only had an incidental involvement that night. Has anything happened to any of you recently?"

Everybody shook their head.

I sat upright. "May I say something? Abigail, you said you have been out of town, and you are somewhat protected up on the hill with staff and residents walking around."

"Why should that matter?" she asked.

"You and EG have the least to protect. Breaking the law in any regard is bad, but look, they could lose their careers. Even if no charges are filed, being associated with this could be damaging for them. Sheriff Dalton has an election coming up in a few years. Think how this could impact what people think of him regardless of the job he has done."

"Are you suggesting that one of them came after you?" Abigail said, pointing towards the men at the table.

"No, not at all." I paused and looked at them. "Right?"

They all laughed and shook their heads.

"I'm saying that is why they're not as big of a target. I do want to ask what you were doing in the house when we returned from Rochester, Sheriff."

"Claudia! Stop!" EG said, aghast.

Sheriff Dalton looked stunned, dropping his

shoulders, and waved off EG. "It's ok. I deserve that. I have to admit that I was looking through your old files. Remember a year and a half ago when you asked me here to answer questions about police work for a book you were writing? I noticed how detailed your research notes for your books are. There were notes and material on everything from blood analysis, DNA, decomposition, bullet testing, and so much more.

"I have read every one of your books, and you used the information superficially. I thought you were testing me about that night twenty years ago. I had started my campaign for county sheriff and was getting attacked from my two opponents that were former colleagues and friends of mine. All that rubbed me the wrong way, and so you suddenly fell into that category of people I didn't know if I could trust. The other day when I stopped by, you were vague and distant. My job has taught me to be suspicious of everyone, so I came back to see if you had . . . well, I don't know what I was hoping to find or not find."

EG stared at her hands for a moment before she spoke. "I get it. We all start acting funny, regardless of our careers, when we're involved in something like this. I was prepared this summer to tell Claudia about giving her up, which made me beyond nervous about losing her. I wanted to do it on my time and my terms. Then, the four of you start coming over and insisting I knew something about what Bill Wallace had dug out of the river. None of you came right out and said it, but you all were trying to pull me in. I was ready to face my truth about giving up Claudia and who her father is, then I had to face the fact the blood I found on my shoes from that night had me involved in something I couldn't comprehend."

"I didn't mean to spook you. Sorry for invading your home. We're all on edge."

"I appreciate that, and I now understand what we're dealing with here. And, for your information, I do use all that research. I write the slasher-horror book series under the pen name Mo Robert Earl. It's not my best work, but it has paid me well."

Abigail clapped. "Great, now that we're all caught up on what you two have been doing, can we get back to that night?"

I leaned forward. "I didn't mean to accuse any of you of running me over, but could there be anyone else involved?"

"We made sure everyone was gone. We saw Marcus's truck leave, and Abigail said she saw EG leave through the woods before we started collecting anything heavy to weight down the duffel bag."

EG sat upright. "We didn't go through the woods. Ellen and I left through the tall grass.

Remember I said I heard something in the woods? It couldn't have been us you saw. Abigail, are you sure you saw something?"

"Definitely. We couldn't hear anything with the roar of the river. The rain clouds started to break up, and pockets of moonlight started to give us some visibility. We were hiding behind the logs, and I peeked and saw something moving. I assumed it was you."

"Who could have been in the woods that night?" Sheriff Dalton said.

"Anyone," Mayor Carl said. "More than half the town was at the fireworks. There was so much movement, no one would have seemed out of place if they'd been seen wandering around. With the afternoon festival in front of city hall, half the streets were closed. Everything around the high school was also blocked off for the fireworks, and with the tree clearing at the riverbank, most people were walking. Everything was a mess, so seeing someone outside their regular neighborhood would have been no big deal."

"No one would have been hanging out in the woods at that hour. Everyone scattered pretty quickly, and with the rain, I don't believe anyone would've come to the river at that hour," Pastor Theo said.

Abigail stood and paced the room. "We don't know if another person saw what happened that night, which means we don't know if Claudia getting hit has anything to do with it."

Sheriff Dalton watched her pacing for a few minutes before looking back at everyone else. "It is awfully strange to have a hit-and-run in this town. Only things we usually deal with are stupid college kid pranks, trivial shoplifting, and the occasional drunk driver."

EG held up a finger. "If there was someone else in the woods, why sit on that information all these years? Wouldn't it be better to put us in jail? Who has something to gain from our silence?"

That statement slammed everyone into silence for a minute. The only noise was rain hitting the house at a steady pace. The wind was getting stronger and the thunder louder as the heart of the storm came closer to River Bend.

EG broke the silence. "Abigail, where have you been?"

Abigail stopped pacing and glared at her. "Are you asking me for my alibi for yesterday afternoon?"

"Sit down. I was concerned. Claudia said you have been gone. I was curious if anyone tried to get in your cottage or tried contacting you while you were gone."

"This is all getting to me," Abigail said, slowly sitting down.

"We are not going to play the blame game. I

don't think any of us tried taking out either one of you ladies," Pastor Theo said.

"Fine," Abigail said.

"That leads us back to the original question Thomas asked. Now what?" EG said.

"My vote is we do nothing," said Abigail.

"Impossible." Theo shook his head. "I have to tell my mother and brother. I have waited too long."

"You know that will put the burden on them. Keeping the secret," Abigail said.

"They have nothing to gain. Despite being the ugly human being that he was, he was still a husband and father. Why would they say anything? There is no insurance money. It would be a relief to them. They would have no reason to say anything. I can tell them the discovery in the river last week was my father and leave all of you out of it."

"You never know how people will react." Abigail resumed her pacing.

Theo started to speak again, but Sheriff Dalton said, "Listen to him. We aren't talking about random people. This is his mother and brother."

"What if they want to claim the remains for some type of burial? There will be questions," Abigail said.

"I'm willing to handle anything that comes my way," Theo said.

"Sitting here, *we* can't decide what to do, and you want to involve more people. Just because he was your father doesn't mean you get to speak for the group," Abigail said.

"We can't stop anyone from talking. Listen to me. We can't start turning on one another. Especially now with Claudia nearly getting run over, we need each other more than ever. We can't keep this buried. Someone out there may know what happened," EG said.

Abigail went to the window and stared outside. "Why now? Why do we have to go through this again?"

Sheriff Dalton walked over to Abigail and put his arms around her, comforting everyone at the table with his simple gesture.

Until the smack of gunfire pierced the air.

CHAPTER TWENTY-EIGHT

Sheriff Dalton pushed Abigail to the floor but tripped, and they ended up half on the sofa and half on the floor. The rest of us reacted a second later after we realized it wasn't thunder but a gunshot. Mayor Carl slid off his chair and held his knee. Theo dove towards me. I pulled EG down towards the head of the table and away from the front door, and the three of us huddled together.

Sheriff Dalton was the first to his feet after he'd untangled himself from Abigail and the sofa. He went to the front door, motioning for us to stay down. He cleared the porch and what he could see of the yard and went outside. The heart of the storm was now overhead, and lightning flashed through the window. The room lit up for a moment, showing shock and disbelief on everyone's face.

Sheriff Dalton poked his head in the door. "I don't see anyone. Stay down." He grabbed his phone. "Holton, I need you to come to 803 Thirteenth Ave. No lights or sirens, but it's urgent. A shot was fired into Mrs. Graham's home. No one injured. I saw taillights headed south but unsure if the car passed the house or not. It's too dark for make and model. I'll wait for you to walk the perimeter. Call Wyatt and have him come in for backup patrol. I will notify dispatch of your movements and my position."

The mayor moved over to Abigail and put his arm around her.

Sheriff Dalton came in, crouching and staying away from the windows. "You have an umbrella?"

EG nodded and pointed outside. "Take what you need, it's on the porch."

He was about to step out, but he eyed the window and walked to it slowly. We all could see the glass like a spiderweb. He looked at the opposite wall, and our eyes followed his line of sight—a bullet hole.

A minute later, we heard a car door slam, and the sheriff waved in Deputy Patrick, who was dressed for rain. He surveyed everyone in the room, and the two men stepped onto the porch.

We relaxed slightly as the men walked around the house, but we didn't move far from our positions. They came back a few minutes later, stopping on the porch to shake off the rain like a dog getting out of a lake.

Deputy Patrick let Sheriff Dalton take the lead. "I think the shot came from the road. We didn't see any footprints. With the rain and mud, there would be some trace if someone was out there. Holton here"—he gestured to Deputy Patrick—"will call the tech guys, and they'll assess the situation a little better than I can by eyeballing the scene. There is a bullet hole in the window on the porch that lines up with the living room window and the wall. I'll let the tech guys pull the slug from the wall, and that will give us some type of starting distance. Either from the street or sidewalk."

"Now what?" Abigail asked.

"You can all get up. I don't believe you're in immediate danger. Holton will take statements from each of us. Deputy Wyatt will be here shortly and will sit out front and watch the house."

The deputy stepped forward and motioned for Theo to follow him to the kitchen.

"Well, Mayor, I'm having a drink now. What about you?" EG said, breaking the tension.

The side of his mouth turned up in a grin. "I think that would be ok now."

She looked at Abigail. "I guess you've got an alibi for this one."

"Screw you" was all Abigail said, but she finally smiled.

EG and I sat on the love seat, and the mayor and Abigail sat on the couch. Sheriff Dalton remained standing.

Mayor Carl rubbed his hands on his pants. "Sheriff said it, EG said it, and Abigail, so I guess it's my turn to say it. Now what? What do we do now? We are no better off than we were several hours ago."

"I disagree," EG said. "I think this little episode proves we must do something."

"Do you think whoever is out there wants us to go to the police? Don't you think they're trying to silence us?"

"What should we do? Give them the power? Are they willing to kill each of us for our silence?" EG said.

"We are missing an important fact here," Sheriff Dalton said. "I don't mean to put more fear into you, EG, but this is your house, and we don't know that shot was not intended for you. From the street, in the rain, the shooter could have thought Abigail was you. I'm sorry to ask this, but since this is the second incident, is there anything I should know about, outside of our situation?"

"Like what? That I got a hitman on me? Don't be ridiculous!"

"Come on, Thomas. This is EG. What would

someone have against her?"

Theo came into the living room, motioning to the mayor that Deputy Patrick was ready for him. He gave Mayor Carl a hand getting up from the sofa and handed him his cane. "What's going on here?"

"We're trying to figure out if EG has a double life and who wants to kill her," I said.

"I'm trying to figure out the angles of the cases. We don't know if all this is related. Yes, some very strange things happened simultaneously, but we have to figure out if they're related or not."

EG held a hand up. "I get what you're saying. I don't have a double life. I have never been threatened or involved in anything illegal or crazy. The most eccentric thing I do is write novels."

"She didn't know about her involvement with my dad until this afternoon," Theo said softly.

Everyone paused what they were doing and looked around the room. A collective sigh of relief seemed to go through the room when they realized Deputy Patrick was still in the kitchen. The five of them wanted to conclude this on their own, but the stakes had gotten higher with the gunshot.

A car door shut, and each of us tightened up for a second. Sheriff Dalton looked out the window and waved Deputy Wyatt Baumann in.

Deputy Baumann said, "The tech guys won't be able to get here until morning. They're working a big accident over in Jacksonville. I'll patrol the area and stake out the house overnight."

"Is that necessary?" EG asked.

"Yes. He has an unmarked vehicle. Most of your neighbors will be in for the night due to rain," Sheriff Dalton said.

"All right, but please tell Jorge next door what's going on. He'll figure out something is wrong if he sees someone patrolling the area. He'll either make a call to you guys or take matters into his own hands. He is protective of the neighborhood—I mean that in a good way—don't get all weird about it."

Sheriff Dalton shook his head. "Not a problem. We'll talk to him. He wasn't home when we did the perimeter walk."

The sheriff spoke with the two deputies on the porch for a few minutes. Wyatt left to patrol the area, and Holton continued taking statements. EG moved everyone into the kitchen, and Deputy Patrick into the living room.

"All this activity and talking has made me hungry. It's the first real appetite I've had for a few days. I should take advantage of it. Mayor and Claudia, have a seat at the island. Theo, go in the fridge and grab anything we can use to make sandwiches. Abigail, can you get the plates and silverware? I will grab some glasses and maybe some Scotch."

"Amen," Abigail and Theo said together.

That seemed to put everybody at ease for the first time since we'd heard the gunshot.

I was the last one to give a statement, and EG had a sandwich cut up in tiny bites waiting for me when I returned.

She shrugged. "I figured you couldn't handle a large sandwich with one hand."

"Good point." I paused. "I feel like part of this group because I want to ask *now what?*"

Sheriff Dalton returned to the kitchen. "Holton's gone." He made a sandwich but didn't eat.

We watched him, waiting for him to speak.

"Ok, folks. We may be on the clock now to figure out what we should do. We have to assume that little gunfire has to do with our particular situation."

Theo struck the counter with his palm. "I'm done with this. I'm leaving you all out of it and going to first tell my mother and brother, and then I'll go down and see the district attorney in Kirkasaw County. I've been thinking about this. There's no need to involve any of you. I'll tell them I ran into him again as I was leaving the riverbank, one thing led to the next thing, and I struck him until he collapsed. I grabbed the duffel bag and took him out to the river."

"I don't think you need to go that far. Fine,

if you need to tell your family, that's one thing, but why go to the police?" Abigail said.

Theo raised his hands. "Because it's the right thing to do."

His words hung in the air.

"I'm ok with that," Abigail said.

Mayor Carl tapped his cane on the floor to get everyone's attention. "We appreciate what you want to do, Teddy, but you're forgetting our little pistol-packing shooter out there."

"He's right," EG said. "We may not get to decide how this ends. Someone out there is making our decision for us. We have to face whatever comes our way. Teddy and I can leave you all out of this. I now understand what I did. Maybe my conscience is fooling me, but I'm content with coming forward. I am not going to let someone else control my destiny, *and* it is the truth. I'm not going to live with someone controlling my life. I want to shut down whoever has come after me. I'd rather face the courts than live in hidden fear."

"You're trying to be noble, but don't forget if you come forward, Thomas and I also have to come forward. Do you really think there's a witness out there and that Claudia's hit-and-run and now this little incident are all related? We came here to figure this out together. You don't get to make that decision. I say we wait and see if what's happening now is connected to that night. No one can force our decision," Abigail said in a demanding hushed tone, seemingly too shaken to speak her truth loudly.

"I am not waiting for the clock to run out," Theo said. "We take the power away from whoever is out there. Once I come forward, they will not be a threat. Witness or no witness. I don't care. Maybe I made up my mind before I even returned to River Bend today. Are we just sitting here looking for absolution from each other? I am not going to live teetering on the truth and what someone may or may not know."

"I'm going with you, Teddy," Sheriff Dalton said.

"No, you're not."

Sheriff Dalton put one hand on his hip and held the other up. "Yes, I don't care what happens to my job. I want to make it right with the law and myself."

"Before, you said you made peace with what happened. You were a great friend that night. You did more for me in those few hours than anyone has ever done for me in all my life. I cannot let you and will not let you put your career in jeopardy. We have the truth of that night and the truth of today. They don't have to be inclusive of each other. I don't want someone out there controlling what and how we conduct our lives."

"He's right," Mayor Carl said. "You are a

decent man, Thomas. We've all made tough decisions, but we have led honorable lives."

Sheriff Dalton threw his arms up and walked around the island. "So what? What is the perfect formula? Three good deeds for every one sin? Maybe if we break one of the commandments, we donate to charity. We break a civic code, we do twenty hours of community service? Hide a body, destroy evidence, and we get to live peacefully? Teddy takes the fall for all of us?"

Mayor Carl rubbed at his forehead. "I don't want him to do this by himself, but it might be the only answer."

"I don't know," the sheriff said with a heavy sigh.

EG took Theo's hand. "We can't have you go this alone. We—"

CHAPTER TWENTY-NINE

We heard a commotion outside, and Sheriff Dalton put up his hand to silence us, but we were already stone quiet and frozen.

"Get down!" he said.

I exhaled. "Sheriff, that's my friend Sherrie. She's ok."

He looked at EG and she nodded, and we all relaxed. Deputy Baumann walked Sherrie to the door.

Sheriff Dalton waved them in. "It's ok, Wyatt."

Sherrie shook off her wet coat, gasping for breath. Her eyes met mine as she looked at the six of us in the kitchen staring at her. "I got some news. I think we know the car that struck you. Why are you not answering your phone? What is going on here? Should I be here? What's with officer hothead out there? What's with the broken window?"

EG pulled Sherrie into the center of the kitchen, wrapping an arm around her. "Sherrie, this is Pastor Theo, Sheriff Dalton, Abigail, and Mayor Carl."

She brought her hand up in a wave. "Hi, sorry to barge in. I thought you would want the information, but I feel like I'm interrupting something, and seriously, what's with the cop out front?"

"It's ok. We had a little incident," EG said.

"Another person?" Abigail said.

"Take it easy. Everybody in this town is going to hear about the gunfire. Just because nobody came running out of their houses does not mean my neighbors didn't hear anything. Plus, when the tech guys get here, it will be obvious something happened."

"Gunfire?" Sherrie said, clutching her chest.

EG rubbed her back. "Yes, but we're all ok. Nobody got hurt."

Sherrie turned to her. "Should I be here?"

"Yes. You said you had information about Claudia's hit-and-run." EG took her by the arm and sat her down at one of the island kitchen chairs.

Everybody waited for her to start.

"Yeah, I do, but seriously, can someone tell me about the gunfire and deputy hound dog out there?"

"We aren't sure if it was a random drive-by or if someone here was an intended target. That's why we have Deputy Baumann posted outside and patrolling the neighborhood. Now, Miss, you said you have some information for us."

"Um, ah, well, I think so. Mia and I were eating at the Blue Daisy Din—"

"Really, on a Friday? Stay away from that place on Fridays. The substitute cook is there," Mayor Carl said.

"Mayor!" Abigail said.

"Agh, leave him alone. Everyone in town knows that. Besides, it's Tuesday and Wednesday during the summer, so Chef Jerry can coach Little League," EG said. "Go on, Sherrie, tell us your story."

"Ok, we were there eating, and I saw Mara and some friends. She's the girl that saw the hit-and-run—I saw her at the hospital after the accident. No one else was in the diner, so we heard everything she said. She was looking at different types of cars online, trying to figure out what kind of car hit you.

"She was out past her curfew last night, sneaking home, and saw someone washing their car at the car wash. She thought it was funny they were washing their car at that hour and with all this rain we've had. The closer she looked, the more she realized the car looked like the one from the hit-and-run. She knew it couldn't have been the actual car because she knew that driver, but she thinks she can identify the make of the car." Sherrie paused, took a breath, and looked at each of us, seemingly waiting for applause or approval.

We all stared at her. She hadn't given us the actual information about the car.

"Well? Are you going to leave us hanging? What was the make of the car?" I asked.

"Sorry. Didn't I say that? She believes it's a four-door Mazda. It's not much, but I thought it might help. Mia stayed there to see if Mara would say anything else. We're meeting at the loft later."

Abigail turned to Sheriff Dalton. "Does that help?"

"Any information is useful, but I'm not sure how much we can rely on her identification. I'll have someone question her later. Can you all give me a minute? I want to talk to my deputies." The sheriff pulled out his phone and went to the porch, closing the entryway door behind him.

EG started to hand Sherrie a plate, and Abigail said, "EG, we're not done here."

I understood, and thought Sherrie did too, that Abigail did not want her there.

Sherrie nodded. "If you don't mind, I think I'll change into some dry clothes. I got wetter than I thought I would when I ran over here. Claudia, do you have anything I could wear?"

I nodded. "Pick out anything in my room."

Before Abigail could shove Sherrie out the door, EG said, "Go ahead. If Mia doesn't mind waiting, you can change and dry your hair."

"Thanks," Sherrie said. She looked at me and mouthed *gunfire?*

I nodded and mouthed back *all good.*

We regrouped for a minute after Sherrie left. Sheriff Dalton came back in, looking stoic.

"Everything ok, Thomas?" Mayor Carl asked.

"Yes, just trying to get the information out to the field. How is your friend?"

"Fine, she was surprised to be stopped before coming into the house, and you hear the word *gunfire* it takes a moment to process. She's upstairs changing clothes."

"We have to figure this out now. I'm sorry, but I think Theo has the best approach to this," Abigail said.

"Because you free yourself," EG said.

"We're all in this. If he wants to tell his mother and brother, we can't stop him. He seems set on also turning himself in. What can we do to stop him?" she said.

Mayor Carl looked at Abigail. "You're cheerleading his cause because it benefits you. Come on, we're all adults. I'm old enough to be a parent to each of you, so I want you all to listen closely—we need to do what's right. I will go with you, Theo."

Abigail pointed at Mayor Carl. "All you did was hide a truck. Maybe you knew something, but you didn't know everything. You are retired. You don't have much to lose! Maybe a pension?"

"Neither do you," EG said. "What do you have to lose? Your good family name? You're the last of your family left in this town. Your own son only visits once a year."

Theo paced the kitchen. "I am not going to allow any of you to be involved in this further. I should have done this years ago. I don't know why I thought I could keep it buried. I'm ashamed that I didn't tell my mother and that it took a stupid fisherman for me to do what I should have done years ago. I made peace with God many, many years ago, and now, I need to do it with my family." He walked into the living room.

Abigail walked after him. "So that's it? We— or *you*–just decided what's going to happen!"

"You'll be fine. Let him go, Abigail," Sheriff Dalton said calmly, putting his arm around her.

The rest of us stayed behind in the kitchen, watching them. We jumped when the screen door slammed shut and the front door opened. Jean, Sheriff Dalton's wife, stood there, dripping wet.

CHAPTER THIRTY

"Jean, what are you doing here?" Sheriff Dalton said with a twitch.

Theo took a few steps towards them, gesturing towards her. "What kind of job is your deputy doing out there? This is the second person to get in here. Are we all going to have to spend the night here?"

Sheriff Dalton dropped his arm from Abigail but didn't move. "Teddy, this is my wife, Jean. You remember her from River Bend High, I'm sure."

Pastor Theo hung his head. "I'm so sorry. We're a bit on edge here. It's been many years. How are you, Jean? Sorry for the abrupt hello." He stepped forward but stopped.

She hadn't moved or loosened up to return his greeting. She looked shaken and pale.

Deputy Baumann came in. "Sheriff, I saw it was your wife, so I figured it was ok."

"That's fine, but please no more unannounced visitors. I don't have my radio, so you will have to call my cell phone," Sheriff Dalton said. He turned to his wife, nearly as pale as she was. "What is it, Jean?"

She looked like she had aged twenty years in the last two days, unsteady on her feet, hair dripping wet, face white as a ghost, but her voice was strong and unwavering. "What do you mean? What? Don't treat me like this. I'm tired of it! I've spent more time thinking about this than any of you. You all have moved on. Why can't you let this go? Teddy, damn it! Just because old man Wallace found those bones does not mean we have to do anything!"

"We?" Abigail said, her voice squeaking.

In a mocking tone, Jean said, "Yes, *we!*"

Pastor Theo looked at the sheriff intently. "You said you didn't tell Jean. Is there anyone else you didn't tell?"

"He didn't tell me anything! He didn't have to. I've been listening to you idiots discussing this for days. I'm tired of all this. I'm tired of the chasing, the hiding, the secrets," Jean said, shaking a little more than before.

Sheriff Dalton stepped toward Jean and, with a comforting voice, said, "What do you mean?

Tired of secrets?"

Jean held up a hand. "Stay there. Don't come close to me. I'm done. I heard everything." She shook her head. "Don't look at me like that. I've been the wife of Mr. Thomas Dalton, sheriff of River Bend, for many years. Yeah, I pick up on stuff. I read all the case files that come through. I can access the state crime databases. I know all your passwords. You are not the only one who can plant listening devices, Tommy."

As Jean continued, her voice had a slight tremor. "That's right. I know them. I'm his wife! Not you, EG, and especially not you, Abigail. I was the one who stood by him. I was the one who cleaned up after you idiots, protected your secret as much as any of you, but I wasn't invited here, was I? Nope, poor little Jean was sent to visit her sister when the shit hit the fan—or should I say—when the bag of bones hit the riverbank? Tommy, I know you sent me to Milwaukee to get rid of me. I'm done being pushed around. Let's solve this now."

"It was you," EG said, everybody turning to look at her but not daring to move. Our bodies were frozen and I heard my heart pounding with the rain. "You. It was *you* that night in the woods. You witnessed everything."

"That's right. Give the lady a medal. I'm finally included in something. That was supposed to be the weekend I finally got my Tommy.

"You guys nearly ruined it all. Joe had talked about getting so serious with Abigail. He and Thomas were the only ones that were ever nice to me. I think I even talked Joe into proposing to you, Abigail. I knew that'd be what stopped Thomas from running after you like a puppy, and he could be mine. Then EG and Ellen showed up that weekend, and Ellen was all over him Friday. That was it for me. I was done."

Theo stepped forward. "Jean, what happened?"

She raised a shaking finger to her chest, and her voice trembled as she said, "I was stuck in this town. My family couldn't afford to send me to college. My grades didn't get me noticed, and I was never good enough for any team. I was invisible, but my sweet Tommy was always nice to me. I was determined to make him mine, but Miss Abigail strung you along before you finally dug your claws into Joe and then you jumped to Ellen. I was done."

"What happened that night?" Theo asked again.

"I took my father's gun."

No one moved.

Jean's eyes grew wide. "I st-stayed here. I m-made this town what it is today." She paused and took a deep breath, clearly trying to collect herself. "You know that phrase 'Keep your friends close and your enemies closer'?" In a mocking tone, she continued. " 'Oh, Abigail, why don't you work on the historical society with me? EG, do you have any books I can read?' I got those scarecrow statues put all over this town. I thought that might push you out of here. You know what they say about crows. They remember who feeds them. I fed you ladies so much, but did you give me anything back? I came back from Milwaukee and found EG's food in my house. I saw my Tommy going into this house. I heard him calling Abigail, saying they needed to meet. You are trying to take my Tommy again."

Her words were coming one on top of the other, her shaking growing worse with each moment. She looked at her trembling hands and shoved them into her coat pockets.

Sheriff Dalton stood frozen. Theo stepped forward again, but the sheriff held his hand up, motioning him back.

"Jean, what happened that night?" EG said softly.

"I saw Tommy driving Ellen around. I took my father's gun." Tears trickled down her face. "I don't know what I was thinking. I headed towards the river, wanting to get away from everyone. Of course, I didn't know about the bonfire. Why would anyone invite me? I was in the woods, and this man came out of nowhere, babbling, and came after me. I was scared."

Sheriff Dalton stepped towards her. "Jean,

what happened next?"

Jean held out her hand to stop him. "Stop there." She pulled a gun from her coat pocket.

We all gasped. My mind was spinning but blank at the same time.

"Get back everyone!" she shouted.

"Easy, Jean," said Sheriff Dalton. "I have my gun but I don't want to use it. Put your gun down and come to me."

"Stop, don't move," Jean cried. The gun wobbled in her hand. "That man came after me. I was mad, I was lonely, I was scared. I tried walking away, but he grabbed my hair. I don't know what happened, but the gun fired and he dropped."

"It was you!" Abigail shouted, bringing her hand to her mouth.

"Stop it!" Jean yelled, her finger trembling on the trigger.

From the stairs behind Abigail, Sherrie said, "What's all the noise . . ."

We all startled, having forgotten she was upstairs. The gun went off in Jean's shaking hand.

"Holy shit!" Sherrie grabbed her arm. Sheriff Dalton lunged and forced Jean's arms together in an embrace and restraint at the same time, drawing the weapon out of her hands slowly. She cried and shook fiercely.

Theo and Mayor Carl went to Sherrie. EG and I stood there frozen, in disbelief.

"It grazed you. You'll be fine. You're very lucky," the mayor said.

Sherrie's eyes looked glazed. "It kinda stings. No, more of a burning sensation."

As I walked over to Sherrie, Sheriff Dalton was rocking Jean in a big bear hug. He looked shaken and like a shell of a man.

Deputy Baumann came running in with his gun drawn, Jorge behind him.

Mayor Carl held up his hand. "Deputy, everything's ok. Please put your gun down."

"Wyatt, here's the weapon that was fired." Sheriff Dalton handed the weapon to the deputy.

EG waved Jorge in from the doorway.

He gave her a hug as he surveyed the room. "What can I do for you?"

"I think she needs to have her arm looked at," Theo said, gesturing to Sherrie.

Jorge looked at her, wide-eyed. "Do you need me to call an ambulance?"

"I don't think so. It's not so bad. It must have grazed her. It'll be faster if we drive," Theo said, looking at Sherrie for confirmation.

Sherrie nodded, a blank look still on her face.

Sheriff and Deputy Bauman agreed it was ok for them the leave the scene.

"Ok, come with me. I'll drive you," Jorge said.

Holding Sherrie's upper arm, Theo stepped

away from the stairway. Sherrie stepped off the last step towards Jorge, wobbling a bit.

Pastor Theo caught her. "Whoa, slow down. I think your adrenaline is dipping. Hold on to me, and Jorge will get his car."

Jorge nodded to her and started for the door.

"Wait," EG said, a bit too loudly.

I was sure everyone in the room was wondering what could happen next.

She looked at Jorge and Sherrie and, in a softer voice, suggested, "Sorry, why don't you take Sherrie's car. It's on the street, and no one is blocking it." She looked at Sherrie like a kid in a candy store and whispered, "It's a seven-mile drive."

"*Yes!*" Sherrie whispered. She leaned in and gave EG a kiss on the cheek, and they giggled quietly between themselves.

"Can I go with?" I said, but didn't wait for an answer.

We walked through the kitchen and out the back as not to disturb Jean and the scene in the living room. Jorge grabbed a kitchen towel and gave it to Theo to use on Sherrie's arm. I looked back, and Mayor Carl and Abigail had collapsed in relief on the couch. EG was watching Sheriff Dalton and Jean. He was still holding her, and Deputy Baumann was talking to him, pulling Jean away.

Theo guided Sherrie, applying pressure to

her arm. Jorge took her car keys. Sherrie and Theo sat in the back, and I rode shotgun as Jorge drove to the hospital.

We pulled away, and another patrol car pulled up. This time with its lights on.

After a few miles, Sherrie said, "Claudia, could you move the front seat up so I can watch the odometer?"

Jorge and Theo seemed confused until Jorge hit the steering wheel with his palm. "It's on 199,994, hot damn! EG always knows best."

We cheered as the car rolled over two hundred thousand miles.

"Hell of a story!" Sherrie yelled, clapping her hands, then wincing at the pain.

Pastor Theo and I looked at each other and smiled.

CHAPTER THIRTY-ONE

Jorge dropped us off at the emergency room and went to park the car.

As we walked in, the same doctor who had looked at my head walked past. "You again?"

"Nope, I got a new one for you," I said.

He motioned for assistance, and someone came with a wheelchair for Sherrie.

She handed me her purse. "My insurance card's inside. Can you fill out the forms for me? Don't worry about calling my parents. They're on an airplane, and I don't want them to get a voicemail that I was shot when they land. No matter how you word that message, they will panic."

I nodded, and Pastor Theo went to wash his hands. I paced around the waiting room and called

Mia to give her the update.

By the time I hung up with Mia, Theo and Jorge had returned.

Jorge looked around the waiting room, at the one lone guy waiting to be seen, and back to us. "You all want something to drink?"

I nodded and sat down. "Yes, thank you."

Pastor Theo sat next to me. "I'll take something cold, Jorge. Thanks."

Jorge left, and neither of us spoke, the ticking clock counting off the minutes. We mindlessly stared at the baseball game on the single TV.

"Hell of a story," he said.

"Yup, hell of a story."

I laughed. He laughed. We laughed. There were no other words for a while. Then, out of my peripheral vision, I saw him shake his head.

"With everything that's happened, I don't think I processed all the new information yet. I have been consumed with my father," he said.

I looked down at the floor, staring at nothing, and considered my feelings. "It's ok." And I meant it.

"I had no idea. I'm sorry."

"I know. I'm ok. I don't hold you . . ." I didn't know how to finish that sentence.

"So, I guess it's my turn to say 'Now what?' "

We both laughed again. He leaned towards

me to bump shoulders. It wasn't a hug. It wasn't a high five. It was an endearing way to reach out to someone. We giggled, balancing the weight of the heavy information we'd all learned.

"I need to call my parents and give them an update," I said.

Theo gave me a quizzical look.

"To tell them where I am and about Sherrie. They'll want to see her. I'm not going to tell them what you all were discussing."

He nodded. "I appreciate that, but it does affect you in ways we probably don't understand at this point. We can discuss everything later."

CHAPTER THIRTY-TWO

As I made the call to my parents, a deputy walked in to take our statements.

After we'd all given our statements, the doctor came into the waiting room and approached us. "Sherrie was indeed lucky. It was a graze. Her arm will hurt for a while, but she'll fully recover. She will be discharged soon."

I held a hand to my chest, breathing a sigh of relief. "Could I go be with her?"

"Of course," he said, gesturing for me to follow him back.

As soon as I got in the room, Sherrie asked, "What was that all about anyway? Why did she have a gun?"

I hesitated for a minute. "They're all old friends and decided to get together. Oh—Pastor

Theo is Teddy, can you believe that?"

"You've got to be kidding me." She shook her head, fixating on that for a bit, and then asked, "What about Jean though?"

"She's mentally unstable," I said, shrugging.

Sherrie gave me a deadpan stare with the straight follow up. "No shit."

"She was jealous over her husband, Sheriff Dalton, thinking he was having an affair or something, and it probably set her down a dark path. None of us saw that coming. Not even the sheriff."

That got another "No shit" from her. "That was pretty scary."

"Yeah, I'm glad everyone's ok. I had no idea what to expect."

Forty-five minutes later, Sherrie and I stepped through the big double doors that separated the waiting room from the triage and recovery areas. My mom and dad were talking to Theo. Mia sat in a chair to the side, waiting for us.

I stopped walking and held Sherrie back, watching them. As they said goodbye, Theo gave my dad a handshake and a one-arm man hug, and then he hugged my mom in one of those embraces that could make someone melt. My mom wiped away a tear and embraced my dad as they watched Theo leave.

"Are you ok?" Sherrie whispered.

"Better than ever." I smiled.

CHAPTER THIRTY-THREE

My dad informed us that were going to Jorge's house. EG's house is now technically a crime scene and Jorge had generously offered his house to everyone. Jorge and Theo had driven Sherrie's car when they left the hospital.

By the time we got there, the rain had finally let up, and it was 7:00 p.m., but it felt like midnight. With the dark, rainy day and everything that had happened, I felt like three days had passed.

I hadn't been in Jorge's house in several years and was quite shocked to find it all torn up.

Jorge must have seen the look on my face. "I'm in the middle of a renovation. Come in. Sit. It might be a bit dusty."

Sherrie and I plopped down on the sofa and took the drinks offered to us. Abigail and EG came in, and EG sat down next to me. Abigail went to the kitchen and came back a minute later with a glass of wine.

EG looked across me to Sherrie. "How are you?"

"I'm feeling fine. Don't worry about me."

"What about the others?" I asked.

"Mayor Carl went home, and Theo went to his mother's house in Franksville," Abigail said.

I understood the hidden message that the earlier conversation from EG's house was done for the night.

"What about my friend, the pistol packer?" Sherrie asked.

I didn't know whether I should laugh or scold her.

Before I could react, EG said, "They took Jean into custody, but I'm not sure if they went to the hospital or the sheriff's office. I don't know how much access Thomas will have to her or if his position will help or inhibit him from seeing her." She shook her head. "Anyway, my house is off-limits probably until morning."

Jorge offered his house to my parents for the night and said he would go to his sister's house.

"Since pistol-packer Jean is under surveillance, I guess I'm ok without a bodyguard," Sherrie said.

"Someone can stay at my cottage," Abigail said, which I thought probably surprised everyone and EG accepted.

Jorge handed my dad the keys to the house. "Call me if you need anything. Stay as long as you want. Help yourselves to anything in the kitchen. Abigail, EG, you want a ride?"

They gladly accepted, and Abigail stepped out of the house with a quick goodnight to everyone and to no one in particular. I got a big hug from EG after Sherrie got hers.

In the end, I went to the loft with Sherrie. Abigail and EG went to the cottage, and my parents drove Mia to her parents' house an hour away. My dad was determined to have at least one of us girls leave River Bend unharmed.

As my parents dropped us off at the loft, my dad said, "Aaron is waiting for you upstairs. Yes, you will have a bodyguard for the night."

Mia ran in to get her suitcase, and my parents got out of the car and gave us more hugs.

With all this hugging, one might think something big happened today.

"I don't like it that you haven't called your parents yet, Sherrie," my mom said.

"I know but they are flying home and I don't want to leave a message— 'Hey, I got shot but all is good.' I'll call them as soon as I know they will answer. I promise I will call."

We said our final goodbyes, and Sherrie showed me the way upstairs to the loft. I was pleasantly surprised to find the building clean and not smelling like a bar. We walked down a long hallway, passing two doors before we reached the loft.

Mia was walking out with her stuff when we reached the door. "I have something to confess. I should have said something before, but I didn't know how, and with everything going on, I didn't know when was the right moment. I'm guessing this isn't a fine time either, but you should know that Jackson did make a pass at me. I blew it off and he took it well, but that's why I think he was so willing to drive up so early yesterday and agreed to take me to my parents' house after we saw you. I didn't say anything when you accused us of cheating because we were planning the party and I didn't want to be a part of your anger for him. I know it's crappy not telling you because I didn't want guilt by association. I'm sorry. You seemed so relieved to know he wasn't cheating, I didn't want to ruin that for you. I'm telling you now in case you have doubts about your breakup."

"I appreciate you telling me. My hesitation about the breakup is coming from something else, but what you told me helps."

After a few more hugs and a goodbye to Mia, we walked in and found Aaron on the sofa with a book and a beer, with Rita at his side. She got up and sniffed us before sitting down on my feet, waiting for me to pet her.

Aaron called her back. "I hope it's ok that I'm here. Claudia, your dad asked that I stay to make sure you two are ok. He said you had a big night."

Sherrie and I looked at each other and rolled our eyes.

He waved us in. "Come in. Why are you standing in the doorway? Are you hungry?"

"I could nibble on something. I think my stomach is funky from the medicine and not eating much," I said as we walked to the kitchen table.

The loft was a big rectangle-shaped room, a real loft-style apartment. The "bedroom" was a bed on the left wall. There was a huge sofa and one leather club chair that looked as old as this town but very comfortable. The kitchen was simple but had everything one might need. The highlight was a whopper of a stove-oven combo that seemed slightly oversized for a place this small, almost as oversized as the TV on the wall. An old round table with four mismatched chairs sat in the kitchen area. The giant windows overlooking Main Street were the best feature.

"Mia and I noticed all the pie before. Can I have a piece?" Sherrie asked.

"Of course. Claudia, do you want some?"

"Do you have anything less sweet? Something like bread or crackers?"

We sat at the table, and I wiggled it.

"What are you doing?" she asked.

Aaron stopped cutting the pie and turned towards us. "Go ahead and wiggle it. It's not going anywhere. And it's gum-free. Chuck hasn't been up here for a week." He looked at me, the corner of his mouth turning up in a grin.

As Sherrie devoured the pie and I had some bread and cheese, we filled Aaron in on the highlights of the night.

"I don't know if I should believe you, but why would you make up something like that? When you guys are done, you can take the bed and I'll take the sofa."

"I know, crazy story that we know to be true. Sherrie, do you have any clothes for me?" I asked.

"I don't have many clean clothes left. I wasn't planning on staying so long. Whatever I have is yours."

"I got some sweats and a T-shirt if you want," Aaron said. "Take what you need from the closet. There's not much to choose from, but everything in there is clean. There might be a new toothbrush under the sink."

"Smooth move. Keeping the place stocked up for your lady guests," I said.

He shook his head. "They're the free ones

the dentist gives you."

Sherrie went in first to change, and I called my parents to update them so they'd stop worrying.

I was pleasantly surprised to find the closet neatly organized and the bathroom spotless. I grabbed a T-shirt and cutoff sweatpants that were slightly too big and had a hard time tightening them because of my banged-up arm.

I found Sherrie arranging the bed. She had gathered extra blankets to support my arm and pillows to support her bad arm. She looked exhausted.

I'd forgotten with everything going on that she'd also had a ridiculous forty-eight hours. If all that was going to happen to anyone though, I would have expected it to be her.

Thinking of the last few hours brought a realization. *Until Mia mentioned Jackson, I haven't thought about him since this afternoon. Shouldn't I be sadder than this? Guess that means I made the right decision, despite what happens this fall.*

Aaron had turned off the TV and was on the couch, holding a paperback book, and Rita was at his feet. He looked up. "The main light switch is next to the door. Tell me if this reading light bothers you."

Sherrie turned off the lights and climbed into bed, and I got in on the other side.

"Sherrie, is there anything I can do for you?"

She shook her head and promptly fell asleep.

I was tired and still a little sore from getting knocked down yesterday, but I was unable to sleep. Forty-five minutes later, I sat up. The light above Aaron's head was still on, but the book was on the floor and I saw the rise and fall of his chest. The soft glow of streetlights streamed through the large windows, casting shadows in the loft. The bedroom area was darker since the bathroom and closet blocked the last window.

I got up and wrapped a blanket around me the best I could and walked to the windows.

Rita came over and sat at my feet again, and a minute later, Aaron got up from the couch.

"I hope I didn't wake you," I whispered.

He walked over. "Nah, are you ok? Do you need anything?"

We sat down on the big window seat, our backs on opposite posts. I rested my head on the window, and he put his legs up and stretched his feet out to my side.

"I'm fine, just processing everything."

"I'm assuming there's more to the story than what you and Sherrie shared before."

"Yup," I said, nodding.

"I figured that much but didn't want to ask too many questions."

"I appreciate that. I haven't told Sherrie

much. She thinks Jean is a nutcase and doesn't know what we were discussing before the shootout at EG's. I just need time to process it all myself."

"Can I ask, and you don't have to say, were you right? Is the bag of bones found in the river connected to all this?"

I took a deep breath and looked out the window for a bit before I answered with a nod.

"That's probably all I'm going to get from you, and that's fine. I understand."

"Give me some time, and I'll tell you what I can."

He nodded, and we sat in silence for a bit.

"Even with EG being sick and all this ridiculous stuff happening that I could've done without, I'm happy I got to know you."

"Yeah, I get that," he said, and we laughed together.

I stood up and he followed suit. We stood side by side, looking down at the street where people were leaving Draw Bar. We were watching and looking at nothing at the same time.

"I think I'm ready for bed," I said.

We turned and were inches apart, facing each other. I couldn't bring myself to look up, but I couldn't get myself to step back either. He wasn't moving, and I didn't want to move.

He put his hand on my elbow and whispered, "Claudia, aren't you going to bed?"

"You're standing on my blanket."

"That I am," he said.

We stayed like that for what seemed like an eternity.

Sherrie rolled over and snored loudly. We laughed, and he finally stepped back.

I walked towards the bed, and he headed back to the couch. I paused and whispered, "Aaron?"

"Yeah," he whispered back.

I didn't know what I wanted to say.

He whispered again, "I know, crazy day."

And with that, we both whispered, "Goodnight."

CHAPTER THIRTY-FOUR

EG

"Did you have to slam the car door so hard?" Abigail said.

"Sorry. It's been a long day," EG said.

"I'm still on edge. Between our soul-searching and two gunshots, I think I'm done for the night."

"I get it. It's been a chaotic day. How long does it take to open your door?"

"Here we go. Come in before I change my mind and have Jorge come pick you up. The guest bedroom is the second door on the right. I'm going to have a glass of wine if you want to join me," Abigail said.

She took out an open bottle of Chardonnay

from the refrigerator and poured two glasses. She handed one to EG, who was seated in a wingback chair. She sat on the sofa and put her feet up on the coffee table. A stack of EG's book *The Scarecrow* toppled over.

"I'm going to need a lot more books once it gets out about those bones being tied to River Bend," Abigail said.

EG peered at Abigail over her wineglass. "Screw you."

CHAPTER THIRTY-FIVE

CLAUDIA

I woke up at six thirty the next morning to Rita licking my face. I managed to push her off with my one good arm, and she moved on to Sherrie.

Even though the bathroom and closet walls blocked the streetlights at night, they did nothing to block the morning sun flooding through the large windows.

Aaron was fiddling in the kitchen as we stumbled out of bed. "Sorry, Rita has a habit of waking up folks. Are you guys hungry?"

I ran a hand through my hair. "Yes, how long have you been up?"

"Just long enough to take Rita for a short walk and start on breakfast. Are you good with scrambled eggs and toast? Coffee is brewing."

"Thanks," we answered and sat down.

I called my mom, knowing she would have been up by six, and she reminded me to have Sherrie call her parents.

When I ended the call, Sherrie held her phone up and laughed. Mia, who had been home for less than ten hours, had texted her nonstop overnight. She was already hoping to come back, insisting she could play nurse and/or bodyguard for us.

Sherrie finished breakfast first and went to shower. Aaron and I sat there for a bit in an uncomfortable silence.

I was successful in getting butter on the knife, but I could not get my bread buttered one-handed. "Ugh," I moaned. "I can't wait until I get this cast off."

He took the knife from me, smiling. "Let me help."

As I ate, heat rushed to my face each time I looked at him. Nothing had happened last night, but I felt silly when I looked at him.

He cleared the table when he was finished and did busywork to avoid the stillness.

Sherrie finally popped out of the bathroom with a wet head, carrying some shorts that she tossed my way. "I found these for you."

"Thanks, but I'll put the dress back on and

shower at EG's. Those shorts will be hard to maneuver when I go to the bathroom."

"Sounds like a plan. Let me grab our stuff," Sherrie said.

"If you give me a minute, I can help carry your stuff. Let me get ready for a run real quick," Aaron said and disappeared into the bathroom.

Sherrie scrambled to my side. "What is going on with you two? Breakfast had a strange vibe. Did something happen? Was Jackson right?"

"Shh! No, nothing happened, but I don't know. Remember I had a boyfriend less than twenty-four hours ago. But we did have a moment or two."

"That's it. A moment or two. Damn, Mia and I had a bet that something happened."

"Shh, quiet. Here he comes."

"What are you two whispering about over there?" Aaron asked.

"Just guessing what you put in your scrambled eggs." Sherrie giggled. "Ready, everyone?"

Aaron drove us back to Jorge's, and he noted, "You girls are suddenly quiet. Cat got your tongue?"

"No, just trying not to interrupt the beautiful morning drive," Sherrie said.

"Just curious if you are going to share what you were giggling at back in the loft."

I looked at him with as serious a look as I could muster. "If we tell you, we will have to kill you, and with PPJ out there, who knows what will happen."

"A PB and J sandwich is going to attack me?"

"It's P-P-J—as Sherrie named her—Pistol-Packing Jean," I said.

"Maybe I don't want to be a part of your humor. I might suggest easing up on the pain meds," he said, shaking his head.

But I heard the laughter in his voice.

CHAPTER THIRTY-SIX

Thirty minutes after we arrived at Jorge's, we were allowed back into EG's. Once again, my dad wrapped my arm in a plastic bag so I could shower, this time singing Queen's, "Another One Bites the Dust."

EG was still at Abigail's, and after I showered, my dad gave me a ride over there. Mom and Sherrie stayed at EG's and waited for Sherrie's parents. My mom had found them a room, and they would arrive soon.

During the drive, I asked, "What's going on? What have you been doing since you got here? With so much going on, I didn't ask where you were yesterday."

"We're working on a special project. We'll tell you about it once it's confirmed."

I turned to him. "Special project?"

"Yup, no hints, no clues. If you don't pay attention when we tell you things, you'll have to wait," he said, smiling. "Don't bother calling your brother; he has no idea."

For the rest of the ride, I tried to figure out what the project was but couldn't come up with anything.

I arrived at Abigail's, still clueless, and said goodbye to my dad. He had a twinkle in his eye.

This special project will bug me for the rest of the day.

Mayor Carl was on Abigail's porch, waiting for her to open the door. "How is Sherrie doing?" he asked as I walked up.

I waited until we were inside to answer because I figured EG and Abigail would also ask. Abigail directed us to the kitchen table where I started filling them in on Sherrie and her parents' decision to come here. She poured the three of us coffee while EG fixed herself a cup of tea.

There was a knock at the door, and I stopped talking. Abigail went to the door and let Pastor Theo in. He looked like he'd slept only a few hours.

"Morning, everyone," Theo said.

"Pardon me for saying this, but you look like hell," Mayor Carl said.

"I don't doubt that. I feel ok. Just tired," Theo said.

"What happened?" Abigail asked.

Before Theo could speak, there was another knock at the door, and Abigail went to open it.

"Is it all right that I come in?" Sheriff Dalton asked. He seemed hesitant and slightly surprised to see us all there. He had the same clothes on as the night before and appeared to be minus his ankle holster and gun.

"Yes, come in," Mayor Carl said on everybody's behalf.

At Abigail's direction, Theo walked with her to the little library area and pushed two chairs closer to the small kitchen table so we could all sit. Sheriff Dalton asked to use the bathroom and then returned to the table, sitting a few inches outside the circle. Abigail poured him and Theo a cup of coffee.

"Well, Tommy, these folks here just told me I look like crap, but I think you got me beat. How are you? Jean?" Theo said.

"Last night, they booked Jean with a misdemeanor charge of firing a weapon. The charges can and will probably change once the district attorney looks at the case. Because of her behavior and physical condition, they moved her over to Bauxton Medical Center, where they can evaluate her and balance her medication. I was hoping to see her this morning but wasn't allowed because they said she's resting. I'm not sure if that's true or not. I've been up all night thinking about each of you and what to say to you. I don't have anything more than I am sorry."

"I'm the one who's sorry," Theo said. "It all started with my family."

"But it was Jean who shot your father and let us carry that burden all these years!" Abigail said.

"I'm sorry to ask, but did Jean say anything more about that night?" EG asked.

"I rode in the back seat with her when we went to the station. From what I could piece together, it sounds like her depression started much earlier than I thought, and that weekend was the final straw. So many of us on that damn float parading our successes.

"She thought things were never going to change for her. I think she intended to kill herself that night. After she shot your father, Theo, paralyzed in fear, she froze in the woods.

"Everybody started showing up for the fire, and she just watched everything. She saw you guys throwing rocks at your father. She heard you saying it was just a scarecrow. She was waiting for everyone to leave, hoping to push him in the river. And you guys know the rest. That's when we all came into the picture.

"We covered up the crime she committed. She took that knowledge and something happened to her. I can't explain it. I saw her a few years later, and she seemed like a new person. Confident, sweet, and caring. We started dating and were married before I even finished the police academy. She never wanted to leave this town and got herself elected to the town council, put up those damn scarecrows everywhere, and became a model citizen. All the while, she was hiding the vicious secret that she was sick."

"You really didn't know?" Abigail asked.

"Not the full extent. I saw the medication and the bills, but I never understood how much she depended on the pills. She had one episode a few years back when she stopped taking the medicine for a bit, but still, I had no idea how deep-rooted her instability was until yesterday." He grew quiet for a few beats, then turned to me. "Claudia, I am so sorry."

"Me?"

"Yes, Jean was the one who hit you."

Mayor Carl looked at him, puzzled. "But you don't own a Mazda."

"Jean's sister does. They switched cars so Jorge could work on it. Mara was correct in her identification. I think Jean thought you were EG and . . . I don't know how to finish her thinking or logic.

"Jean got it in her head she was some type of secret detective because I let her read the crime reports, and believe it or not, she was a pretty good sounding board sometimes. I didn't realize she'd access the state database with my password though." He sighed. "The crime scene guys found a microphone in your house, EG, in a book. I'm guessing that's what she was referring to yesterday when she mentioned listening to us."

"Oh my god, unbelievable," Abigail mumbled.

Sheriff Dalton shook his head. "I'm taking a leave of absence. Lieutenant Prahloc will be in charge. The State will watch me like a hawk and review all my cases to look for any interference from Jean."

Theo cleared his throat. "Before any of you ask *now what*, I need to tell you guys that I spoke to my mother and brother."

The room was silent, everyone waiting for him to say more.

"It was good, bad, ugly, and the right thing. My brother made the two-hour drive, and I told them together. My mother said she always suspected something because I suddenly dropped out of college and lived a vagabond lifestyle. My brother was angry because I didn't tell them sooner."

Abigail leaned forward. "What did—"

Theo held up his hand. "I didn't mention any of you. I did tell them about Jean shooting him. I figured that may come out. Sorry, Tommy. I said he attacked, and she defended herself. I told them I stumbled upon him at the fire and panicked because of the fight earlier and decided to dispose of him. Which is the truth as far as I'm concerned. I did those things. Who cares if I had help? I'm going to tell the authorities the same thing. I'm going out of your jurisdiction, Tommy. I want it done."

"Are you sure?" EG asked.

"I've thought long and hard. Mayor, you took a bum's truck. No one will care. Abigail and Tommy, all you did was help me move a body. EG, we now know we didn't kill him. There is no reason for anyone of you to be involved anymore. Let's just be done," Theo said.

"What about your family?" Mayor Carl asked.

"This morning, the three of us went to the river. Mom said a prayer of peace, and we left in silence. We're good. Our past is done, and we have peace forever in our hearts that that man will not haunt us anymore. Christian already drove back home, and I think my mother is truly finally at peace. We're good."

"That's not what I meant," the mayor said.

EG shot me a look, and I looked to Theo. I hadn't seen it before. His wedding ring.

He's married. Oh my god. Hell's bells, of course he's married. He talked about his wife and kids in his sermons. I have half siblings. I realized he was talking.

Focus.

"I'll tell my wife what I told my mother and brother. I'll also have to tell the church leaders. I'm not sure what kind of charges I'll face for taking a corpse and not reporting it. If the church decides to let me go, that's fine. A colleague has offered me a teaching job at a liberal arts college in New Hampshire. He is the type of guy that understands things beyond the rulings of the church and can balance a person's moral decision, ethics, and the law. I've turned him down several times, but it might be time to take the job."

The room again was silent. The relief and disbelief were nearly palpable. I didn't know if anyone had anything left in them.

Abigail shifted in her seat. "So that's it? We're done?"

"I guess so," the mayor said.

Everybody slowly stood up but didn't make any effort to leave the kitchen. Theo eventually moved the chairs back to the library.

It finally felt like a new day. Some things still needed to be settled, but we had answers and relief.

"Thomas, I don't know what we can do, but if there's anything, please let us know," EG said.

The mayor put his hand on the sheriff's shoulder and giggled. "While Jean is gone, if you need any meals, I can have Eugene and Rhonda deliver some casseroles the ladies made."

That made the sheriff laugh, which made everybody else laugh.

"What have you told Eugene?" Abigail asked.

"That we were helping you with some town history project," Mayor Carl said.

Sheriff Dalton and the mayor were out the door first, followed by Theo. EG and I were the last to leave.

Abigail walked us to the door. "EG, what are you going to do now?"

EG walked through the door, and without looking back, she said, "Write a book called *Now What*."

Before she closed the door, Abigail said, "Screw you."

CHAPTER THIRTY-SEVEN

Theo offered EG and me a ride back to her house. No one spoke, but it was a comfortable silence. All the rain clouds had disappeared, and the sun was out.

We pulled up to EG's house. Jorge and Phil were there replacing the window.

EG and I walked towards the porch, but Theo asked that we wait. He asked me if he and EG could have a moment together. They stood at the front of the car, and I stopped and leaned against the rear door.

I couldn't hear what they were saying, but they were smiling and crying. It ended in a warm embrace, and she turned to go in, nodding that it was my turn.

Theo walked over and leaned on the car next

to me. We watched EG as she walked towards her house.

"I don't know where to begin," he said.

"I get that. It's all new to me too," I said.

"I have to talk to Melanie, my wife, about what I need to do with the authorities. I also have to, I mean, I want to tell her about you."

I nodded. "I understand."

"I want to know you, but I don't want to interfere," he said.

"Thank you," I said.

We briefly hugged, and he stepped back, holding me by the shoulders and looking at me. "Who would have guessed that when I got that phone call from Abigail about the discovery in the river, I would come away with a daughter?"

"God has a plan," I said.

"You're stealing my words." He smiled. "We'll be in touch."

I nodded again, smiling, and said, "Good luck with everything."

Theo looked at the house and EG on the porch before he got in his car and drove off.

I was five feet from the porch when EG shouted. "What's going on?" I said.

EG stood on the porch, hands on hips. "Phil is refusing my money."

I held up a hand between them. "Listen. I've been in town long enough to know how this works.

Phil, you take EG's credit card and charge her for the supplies. For the labor, she'll make sure you get two pies."

Jorge laughed, and I turned and looked at him.

"Jorge, you also get a pie for all your hospitality and three books of my choosing," I said.

EG waggled her finger at me. "Don't make pie promises you can't keep."

"Don't worry. I'm good with my pie-negotiating skills."

CHAPTER THIRTY-EIGHT

After Jorge and Phil left, EG and I dropped ourselves onto the couch, my parents took seats at the dining room table and were watching us as if they were still processing everything and Sherrie was plopped on the other couch admiring her arm bandage while waiting for her parents to arrive.

I looked at my father. "What's in there?" I said, gesturing to the large envelope he held. "And where have you guys been?"

He looked at my mom, and she said, "You might as well tell her. It's not really a secret."

He dipped his head towards her. "Ok then. The envelope has lease agreements we need to evaluate. We've been looking at investment opportunities."

"Here? In River Bend? No offense, EG, but

River Bend?" I asked.

"Well, not River Bend in particular, but it's one option because of the freeway access and that new industrial park out on Hwy 29," my dad said.

"We've been thinking about going into business with Lesley and Jan—Aaron's mother and aunt."

"A book café?" I asked, confused.

"An industrial kitchen, producing a high volume of cakes and breads. We're in the early stages of looking at different sites," my dad said.

I studied them for a moment. They looked serious. I turned to EG. She shook her head, shrugging.

"You're not kidding?" I asked.

"Why would we kid you? Remember? We told you," my mom said.

"Yes, we did," Dad said.

"You said something about investment properties. I thought you meant a vacation rental home or maybe a duplex in the city. Wow, color me impressed."

My mom was nearly glowing, her excitement apparent. "We're looking for a central location so we have access to both Wisconsin and Minnesota markets. Aaron has been very helpful in scouting locations for us."

"Good for you guys. Speaking of pie and bread. Do you have any here? I'm hungry," I said.

We all moved to the kitchen, settling around the kitchen island, and my mother pulled out stuff for ham sandwiches.

EG, Sherrie, and I took the stools while my mom cut up some fruit. My dad stood between me and EG, holding the lease agreements.

"I know what happened the past few days has been enlightening and unnerving, but I can find the silver lining," EG said. She paused for dramatic effect. "No one has said cancer, chemo, or treated me like an invalid. While I don't wish the past few days on anyone, the cancer break has been nice this last forty-eight hours."

"That is an enlightening, truthful spin to take on everything," my mother said.

I took a deep breath. "That's speaking truthfully. On that note, I must add my truth. My job this fall is not really a job. It's a four-month internship with no guarantee of a job offer at the end. I assumed I was getting an offer from Albor Company, where I worked last summer, but that never came through. This is all I could find in my field. I'm the one who suggested Jackson and I live together so I could afford a place in Chicago. I figured I would work at Colton and look for a permanent job and, hopefully, have something secured before the internship ended and Jackson had to return to school."

Everyone stared at me. I thought they were

waiting for the second half of my story, but I was wrong.

"Interesting," my dad said.

My mom put her hand on mine. "Thank god. I was so worried you were going to take him back. I thought you would backslide when you started missing him. We never were crazy about him, but hanging on to him for rent support is a curious choice."

"I agree. Slowly, I am thinking in the right direction. Give me some time this summer, and I'll figure out what I will do."

Sherrie, as usual, had something to add to the conversation "Speaking of telling your truth, I am . . . I should probably tell you, um, that I . . . well, that I shot a man."

My mom and EG froze in their spots, and my dad suppressed a laugh when I muttered, "You mean 'You shot a man in Reno.' "

Apparently, my dad was the only one to get my Johnny Cash reference?

"Just kidding! I wanted to be part of this tell-your-truth conversation. Wow, you should see your faces!"

A piece of bread flew past Sherrie's head. I turned, and EG held another piece of bread, ready to throw again as she laughed. Sherrie smiled, ducked, then got up, and walked towards the front door.

"Where are you going?" I asked.

"My parents just got here and parked under that tree with all the crows. I'll have them move the car."

"I think it's fine." I laughed. "Our friend, the pistol packer, PPJ, with her two gunshots probably shook that tree loose of crows for a while."

CHAPTER THIRTY-NINE

Sherrie's parents stayed for lunch, then headed to the hotel. My parents left soon after that but would be back Monday to be in court when Jean appeared.

My dad would hum "Na na na na hey hey goodbye" anytime someone mentioned Jean and her court date. Those lyrics were written by the band Steam. Nobody knew the whole song, but it is always sung to send a message to a losing team—but thanks to my dad, I actually knew all the lyrics. He was always on-point with his song choices although they were sometimes inappropriate.

EG and I walked them to the car, saying our goodbyes with extra hugs. We stood in the sun, listening to the birds for the first time in a few days, and we walked back into the house. We plopped down on the sofa next to each other.

"Are you good?" she asked.

"I think I am. It's a lot to take in, but I was always good with the decision you and my parents made. I just have to figure out what it means to me that Pastor Theo is my birth father."

"You are something special," she said, squeezing my hand.

"Right back at you. I'm relieved to know no one else will be coming after you. You look a little glum. Are you ok?"

"I'm thinking about Jean. I feel sad for her. All these years living with all that. All the heartbreak in high school and trauma of Teddy's father coming after her. She built a better life for herself, but it was all based on that night. She tried controlling everything."

"Do you really think Sheriff Dalton had no idea?"

"What makes you say that?"

"He seemed more shaken than even Abigail, and that's saying something. He should be used to tough situations. That's his job. He admitted to looking through your files only after being questioned about it. But why come here when he has access to the whole state legal system?"

EG patted my knee. "You should stay here this fall and do some writing. You spin a good story from inferring other people's truth. That is one part of writing. Filling in the gap for your readers, but in real life, you have to listen and know when to trust your gut about people. I don't think he knew about Jean's involvement. He's like the rest of us who were a part of something for one night. In that moment, he sought to do what was right, and that was to help his friend. Right or wrong by legal standards—it didn't matter that night, he did what was right for his friend. I believe him when he said he has struggled between the law and helping his friend."

"Profound. That is all I can think to say right now, profound. Maybe enlightening. So you can see I am no writer? I'll leave that to you."

"Sounds good. I'll keep writing. I think I hear your phone buzzing. I'm assuming it's either Mia or Sherrie."

It was a text. "Actually, that was Kay, from Chambray Center. She wrote, 'hit-and-run, gunshots at EG's. Whole story = pitcher of margaritas.' I love small towns and the chain of gossip."

"You go call the girls. I think I'm gonna say thanks to Jorge and maybe go for a walk or sit on the patio and put my feet up."

"Sounds like a plan. I think I'll go for a walk," I said.

We stood up, hugged, and she went out to the patio.

She yelled, "Walk, my ass. You are going for

a *walk*! Say hi to Aaron for me."

How did she know before me? I did have to return his clothes. I grabbed them and headed out the door. EG waved as I walked past Jorge's house.

CHAPTER FORTY

A block away from BAR, I realized I was slightly nervous.

What if he's not there? I don't even have his number. Sherrie or Mia might have it. No. There's no way I'm asking either one of them. They'll ask too many questions.

As I approached, his truck was pulling into the alley behind the building. He waved, but I didn't know what that meant.

Should I come around back or will he open the back door and come through the bar and open the front door or was that just a wave? What should I do? Seriously, how did I make it through four years of college?

I stood there until finally he opened the front door.

"Hey," he said, leaning against the door.

"Are you out of breath?" I asked.

"I wanted to catch you, but I didn't know which way you were going."

"You were looking for me? I have your clothes."

"Oh, the clothes."

We stood there, waiting for the other to speak.

"Do you have a minute? I want to show you something cool." He stepped back and gestured inside.

I nodded and followed him in. "Something *cool* to show me? Is that the pickup line that works best for you?"

"Why, is it working?" he said, glancing back at me with a smile, and whistled to Rita. "Come on, girl."

Damn, he got me.

Aaron locked the door and started up the stairs. "Follow me. It's all about timing."

When he opened the door to the loft, Rita hopped up on the sofa and Aaron pointed towards the bed.

I stopped in the doorway. "That's your move? Point to a bed?"

"Trust me and come here." He went over to the windows and pointed to the brick wall across the loft.

An amazing shadow created by the spiral of city hall and the steeple on the Methodist and Lutheran churches was cast on the wall. The town was a living panorama shadow in his loft.

"That's pretty cool. You have my permission to use that pickup line again."

"Do you want me to?" he asked.

We were practically in the same spot as last night, but this time, we stood side by side, not facing each other. The shadow moved slowly with the setting of the sun.

"What do you mean?" I said.

"Do you want me to use that pickup line on other women?" he said and turned to face me.

I kept watching the shadow, not looking back at him. I didn't say anything. I couldn't.

After a few breathless moments, I squeaked out, "Not really."

"Claudia, I want to do something I've wanted to do since I handed you that pie in the cooler."

"Really?" I said, my face growing hot. "I think I might be ok with that."

"Might?"

"Maybe more than *might*. Maybe I thought about it too," I confessed.

"Really?"

"Probably sooner than I should have, but yes."

I turned, inches away from him. He put his hands on my face and pulled me in.

I put my one good arm around him, and he kissed me.

We kissed. We kissed. We kissed.

We stayed like that for some time.

I will have to tell Sherrie and Mia. But not now.

Oh, good hell, if I tell Kay, this may also get me free tacos with those margaritas!

CHAPTER FORTY-ONE

EG'S ENDING

I know this is not right—as her aunt and an overall decent human but especially for being a writer—it's not appropriate for me to write this. This is Claudia's book, a story she wanted to tell.

To be a good writer, one must have a great imagination or—how I look at it—be a great liar. I guess that's why I've been so successful. I can lie, and I do it quite well.

The story does not finish sweetly with Claudia and Aaron kissing. I need to tell you more.

Sorry to ruin the romantic ending, but truth trumps love. This is how the story really ends.

CHAPTER FORTY-TWO

I lied to Claudia because I was too scared of the truth. Sheriff Dalton had been lying to us all.

This morning, he had talked about listening *devices* and so had Jean yesterday.

Yes, more than one. They'd both let that slip. Yet the police had only found one at my house.

While we were at Abigail's cottage, he kept staring at the bookshelf. I believed he was trying to figure out how to retrieve the second device.

Claudia did not have a run-in with the ghostly Gray Lady—Sheriff Dalton was going through Abigail's cottage, just as he searched my house, but Claudia interrupted him when she delivered the food.

I needed to know if he had been covering for Jean or using Jean's disease as a cover for something he'd done. How far back did his betrayal go?

CHAPTER FORTY-THREE

I sat on Jorge's couch, telling him about what happened at my house with Jean.

When I finished, Jorge went into the kitchen and came back with two glasses of wine.

"It's a bit early for this. Don't you think so?"

"Not after that story."

"You're right. Thanks."

"Plus, I don't think your story is over," Jorge said and nodded towards the door.

Abigail was walking over from my yard. Jorge let her in.

"Good afternoon, Jorge. Hello, EG," Abigail said. "Your front door was open, but there was no answer when I knocked. I figured you wouldn't be far. Do you have a moment? We need to talk."

"Again. Now?"

She took a deep breath and hesitated, wringing her hands. "I don't think it's over."

I nodded. "Let's go back to my place."

"Can we talk here?" Abigail asked Jorge.

"Of course, you ladies take all the time you need. I'll be in the garage. Abigail, take this glass. I just poured it, and from the looks of it, you could use it." Jorge handed her the glass, grabbed his safety glasses, and left us on our own.

Abigail downed half the wine and settled herself in a tall wingback chair. When Jorge's electric saw started grinding in the garage, she said, "I thought you would decline to see me if I called, so I came to see you. I don't know how to say this, so I must be direct with you, EG." She stared out the window, not looking at me as she spoke.

"You never hold back. Why are you hesitating now?"

"I can't believe I have to say it."

I wasn't going to let up, needing her to say it first because we or maybe just I am thinking some pretty bad things about our friend, and I don't want to carelessly toss my suspicions out there.

"I don't think it's over," she said again. She sat there, still staring out the window, and took another sip of wine. Then she looked directly at me. "I think Tommy is more deeply connected with this story."

"I do too," I said flatly.

"Why are you sitting there and letting me confess this if you think the same thing?" Abigail said.

"Just because I had my doubts doesn't mean they are the same as your thoughts."

Abigail put the wineglass on the side table, stood up, and walked around the room. Stepping over construction debris, she paced for a bit, then stood behind the chair.

Breathing a sigh, I relented. "Fine, I'll say it. Jean mentioned listening devices. More than one. I don't think it was a slip of the tongue. Thomas said the crime tech guys found one. I think there is another one in your house somewhere. I'm assuming in a book, or is there something else Jean may have come into contact with?"

Abigail didn't respond.

"Jean also said 'especially not you, Abigail.' She did not like either one of us, but she had it bad for you. You should be thankful that Sherrie interrupted us when she did."

Abigail had her hands resting on the top of the chair and looked hopeful that I would keep talking. When I stopped, her shoulders slumped, and she heaved a big sigh.

"You're going to make me say the words," she said.

I nodded.

"Yes, Tommy and I were having an affair."

She walked around to the front of the chair, sat down, clearly relieved to have spoken those words. She picked up the glass of wine and finished it.

"Now that you finally said it, let's back up a bit, and we can lay it out for each other and figure out what to do."

CHAPTER FORTY-FOUR

Abigail and I sat there for a minute, not saying anything. She put down the empty wineglass and reached into her pocket and pulled out a locket necklace. She held it up for me to see it before she clutched it in her hand.

"This is my locket. It was missing. I am very careful with my jewelry. Everything has a place in the jewelry box. The locket's value is not high, but it is sentimental to me. Joe gave it to me several months before we got engaged. I think he did it to see if I was disappointed that it wasn't an engagement ring. He was testing the waters. I thought it was sweet that he was so nervous to ask me to marry him.

"It went missing six weeks ago. I know I put it in the jewelry box. Before you ask, the chain did

385

not break and slip off me. I never wear it to bed. Today, after the five of you left, I went to the guest bathroom. I dropped a tissue into the garbage but missed, so I bent down and saw this on the floor. Hidden but not hidden."

"Thomas used the bathroom," I said.

"So did you last night and this morning," she said. She must have seen the look on my face and waved it off. "No, I don't think it was you. I just want to tell you who's been in my place. Delores, my housekeeper, was there two days ago. That woman is a saint and honest. If she had found it, she would have cleaned it before I got home and told me immediately. There is dirt all over the locket and in the clasp."

"Are you suggesting Thomas put it there?"

Abigail nodded. "Earlier this week, I was talking with Mayor Carl by the river. We saw Tommy leave the woods. He didn't see us or anything for that matter. He had something shiny in his hand. I believe it was my locket."

"You think he took it because Joe gave it to you, and tried hiding it in the woods?"

"Jesus! EG! For a mystery writer, you can be unimaginative."

"Don't snip at me. Remember, you came here looking for me. Now, fill in the blanks for me and speed it up. Wait—I think we need more wine before you continue."

"You're right. We need more wine. You also said you had worries about Tommy."

I went to the kitchen, grabbed the bottle of Chardonnay from the refrigerator, and filled our glasses with generous pours. I carried the bottle to the living room and left it next to Abigail and went back to the couch. This time, I sat on the end closer to her, tucking my legs under me as if I were a child poised to hear a good story.

I raised my glass for a toast. "Here's to being civil to each other. No more gunshots. And to ending this saga."

Abigail raised her glass and clinked it against mine. "Amen."

"About a year and a half ago, Tommy and I started getting together. At first, it was just friendly conversation over coffee or the occasional drink. It was not meant to be romantic and, really, never became romantic. It was two friends who wanted company, some passion, and no commitment. I think he was looking for a friend. We knew our relationship would never progress beyond the occasional rendezvous, and that was fine for both of us. I know it sounds unbelievable, but Tommy does love Jean. He would never leave her or want to hurt her. I know the irony of everything I am saying, so spare me any lectures.

"I haven't ever stopped loving Joe and don't know if I want to ever put that past me. I occasionally date but more for the company than courtship. I shared all that with Tommy. I think he respected me more for hanging onto Joe's love. He wouldn't take that locket out of spite."

"So what are you suggesting?"

"Jean was in my place—at least, I think she was—and I think she took it. She probably found out about Tommy and me and wanted to hurt me. She knew the locket was from Joe. My jewelry box sits on my dresser unlocked. Tommy has a key to my place. She could have found it."

"That's a lot of assuming," I said.

"In April, I went to visit my son and his wife for a weekend. The following Monday, my neighbor Shelly made a comment about me being out late. When she saw the confused look on my face, she said she saw me coming in late Friday night, and she asked if I was sneaking in from a hot date. She was woken up by her sick dog and had to get up to take her outside at one a.m. She looked out her window and saw *me* enter my apartment. She's always asking about my personal life, so I thought she was fishing for information. She said she noticed my car was gone when she and Earl came back from dinner and thought I must be out on a date. I never put too much thought into it until later. I hate gossiping neighbors."

"Right now *we* are the gossiping neighbors. And by the way, did it ever occur to you that some people are just friendly and would like to get to know you? If you would give more people a chance, maybe you would not be looking at Thomas for some *company*."

"I thought we toasted to being civil to each other."

"You have a fair point, but so do I. Let's keep going. I found Thomas in my house this week. I don't think anything is missing, but I haven't really looked. He claimed he was looking through my old research files." I shook my head. "And I don't know what Jean would have against me."

"Oh, come now. Don't be so naive, EG. You've got it all. People are jealous. Don't make me spell it out. You've got a great career, are beloved by the community, a community that you helped make famous, and you had empathy from everyone when you became a widow. You do everything with such grace, people either want to be you, be near you, or shoot you out of envy."

"Well, that is a fresh spin on my life. I'm not sure what to say to that. I haven't ever given much thought about what people think of me."

"Don't be modest. It's annoying."

"Does anyone see that I am a single, aging woman, living in a small town by myself?"

"Don't get mad. This isn't the time for a pity party. And remember, I'm in the same spot, except I'm in that damn senior center."

"Touché," I said. Everything that was said stung a little.

"It took me a while to understand why I stayed in River Bend, but do you know why you stayed?" She paused, perhaps unsure if I would answer. When I didn't, she continued. "We must have been a threat to Jean. She has been trying to compete with her past."

Why had I stayed all these years? I wanted to flee now. I enjoyed my life, but this town had limits. Had I kept myself here because I couldn't move past giving up Claudia over twenty years ago? Had I been waiting for Teddy to find me? Why was I spinning all this now? A tidal wave of emotions steamrolled me in that moment.

"Hey, snap out of it." Abigail waved her hand in front of my face and brought me back to our conversation. "I'm saying someone like Jean may be jealous. You are also a big part of her story. If it wasn't for you and those scarecrows, the events of the past few days may never have happened."

"Are you blaming me for Jean losing her mind?"

Abigail poured the rest of the wine in our glasses. "Not really."

"Careful what you say."

She raised her newly filled glass and waited for me to do the same. "Here's to being civil."

"Amen. We are not doing the blame game.

A sick person will probably lose their mind no matter what happens. We just happen to be part of Jean's mental puzzle that was falling apart on her. Tell me how you think Jean took your necklace but Thomas is to blame.

"Tommy was acting funny these past few months. We only saw each other maybe three times, but he was needy and reminiscent. He joked about what would have happened in high school if he'd had the courage to ask me out before Joe did. He said he was thinking about asking me to prom, but before he could say something, Joe had made his move. He always felt guilty for wanting to ask me out and could never say anything to Joe since they were best buddies. I think Joe's death hit him as hard as it hit me."

"Do you think he saw the necklace in his house?"

"I'm not sure. During one conversation, he mentioned something about Jean. She was out of town for a few days, and Tommy had been drinking a lot one evening. He never drinks more than two or three beers, but that night, he went out with some guys from the Rotary Club and came to my place drunk at one a.m.—in his uniform, no less. He walked in, kicked off his shoes, and plopped down on the couch. I was mad and tried to get him to leave, then thought it would be better if he slept it off and snuck out quietly in the morning."

I held up a hand. "I mean this respectfully — get to the point. I don't need a play-by-play."

Abigail motioned for me to stop talking. "I am getting to the point. As he was lying on the couch, he started to say something about Jean and souvenirs. That's all I got out of him before he passed out. The next morning, he was very quiet and didn't know what I was referring to when I asked him about the night before. After that, we saw each other once or twice before old man Wallace found—"

"Before old man Wallace found the bag of bones and our new reality," I said.

A minute passed in silence.

"You think Jean was collecting items or evidence and Thomas found out?"

"I think she buried the stuff."

"What?"

"Think about it. You're the writer. All those horror books you write, where is your imagination?"

"You read those books?"

Abigail looked like a kid who'd gotten caught with her hand in the cookie jar.

She giggled. "Once I found out that Mo Robert Earl was you, I picked up the first one in the series and then I kept reading. It's not bad work, and to be honest, I like them more than your mystery stuff. I've always had a thing for scary movies, and the books are kinda fun and scary."

"Damn, that may be the biggest surprise of the weekend. You like slasher-horror books for teenagers. Mrs. Abigail Montgomery Worthington of River Bend has a secret vice!"

We clinked our glasses again, laughing.

"We're out of wine. Let me see if Jorge has any more," I said.

Abigail followed me into the kitchen. There was no more wine, but we found a bottle of halfway decent Scotch. I got out some glasses, and Abigail pulled two barstools from under a plastic sheet. We sat at the makeshift plywood kitchen island. Jorge's saw was still grinding away in the garage.

"So back to our story. You think Jean buried items."

"In the woods. I don't know what's out there, but if I had to guess, that's where Jean took her souvenirs. She couldn't keep them at home."

I was slowly starting to see Abigail's thought process. "You're saying she went to the woods to hide things. Thomas found out and took your necklace but didn't know how to give it back to you? So he put it in the bathroom, hoping you'd stumble upon it?"

Abigail nodded.

"Why the woods?" I asked.

"Really? Put it together, Ms. Mystery

Writer."

"I'm a fiction writer. I make stuff up. The truth is crazier than anything I can write. You say she went to the woods." I was slowly realizing that Abigail might be right. "That's where this all started for her."

"After she shot Teddy's father in the woods that night, she changed. She morphed into another person," Abigail said as she shifted on the uncomfortable barstool. "You said you also had doubts about Tommy."

"Did you see him the last few days? I mean, really look at him. He was unshaven and seemed not as pulled-together as usual," EG said. "Why are we sitting here?"

"Let's go back into the living room."

"No, why are we sitting in Jorge's house?"

"The whole listening device thing has me spooked. I feel better knowing Jorge is close," she said.

"I feel more comfortable here than your house. What if Tommy is looking for us?"

"What do you mean? Looking for us? Why would Tommy come after us? Do you mean come after you?"

"I don't know anymore. My nerves are shot. I got through the whole ordeal yesterday without wetting myself, but finding the locket today has put me over the edge. I think we should go to the woods."

"Go to the woods and what? Hold a séance? See if the trees will talk to us?"

She gave me a look. "Remember, *civil*."

"I'm being civil with a side of humor. You want to walk in there and see if we can find where Jean has buried stuff. What if it was just your necklace?"

"We won't know unless we look."

CHAPTER FORTY–FIVE

"If we're going to the woods, let's go now before it gets dark. I want to go home to get a jacket though. The mosquitos will be bad after all the rain," I said.

"I can't believe you believe me. I thought you would brush me off."

"Like I said, I had my concerns too."

We walked out the front door, and Abigail turned to go to my place.

"Wait, I want to say goodbye to Jorge and thank him," I said.

I was only gone ninety seconds, but when I came out of the garage, Abigail was gone. I started towards my house, and Abigail came out of Jorge's, carrying two red plastic cups.

"I figured we could use something for the woods." She handed me a red plastic cup of Scotch.

"Just because it was my idea does not mean I'm comfortable walking in there to find . . . well, whatever it is we're going to find."

We walked back to my house. In my bedroom, I put on a light sweatshirt, and when I bent down to put on some socks, I realized I was a little wobbly. "We should take it easy with the Scotch."

I waited for an answer and got nothing.

"Abigail?"

Nothing.

My insides knotted up. *Why does she keep disappearing?*

"Abigail?" I said louder.

"I'm using your restroom. Stop shouting."

"I was saying we should take it easy with the Scotch."

Her reply was a bit slurred. "I agree. I just took a two-minute pee." She came into the room, smiling, her cheeks flushed.

I shifted to steady myself. "I have to admit, I've enjoyed our time this afternoon. You gave me a lot to think about. This past week, we have spoken more and spent more time together than we have the past two decades. You're fun to hang out with when you're tipsy and have enlightening insights into my life."

"Let's get one thing straight. I am not tipsy. Mrs. Abigail Montgomery Worthington is not

398

tipsy; she is civil."

"Did you just make a joke? I love it. It only took twenty years and two gunshots, but Abigail found her fun side."

"Be quiet. Do you have a sweater for me?"

"I've got a raincoat."

"Nice try. Is that *your* sense of humor? Putting me in the coat that Claudia was wearing when she got run over."

I grabbed a sweatshirt for her, silently hoping she would change her mind about going to the woods. Then I realized I was just hoping we were wrong. I came to conclusion that we needed to accept that the fate of our old friend had probably been set through his actions and not what we were about to uncover. Plus, at this point, I probably would have gone without her.

CHAPTER FORTY-SIX

We left my neighborhood on foot and walked in silence. We approached the riverbank and woods stopping in the parking lot and looked at the boat ramp. We stood side by side not daring to face each other or maybe not willing to face what we might find.

"This area was just being developed back then," Abigail noted.

We watched a barge float down the river and the waves bounce on the shoreline. Each ripple hitting the shore was like another flashback of that night many, many years ago. We each took a sip of scotch.

"How much do you think about that night." I asked.

"Too much or maybe not enough. What

about you?"

"More than I can explain, but I am sure it is very different then your version of that night. I have not really had time to process my role in what happened that night. For me, that night was all about becoming pregnant and Teddy dropping out of my life as fast as he reappeared that weekend. I had no idea what you all went through and have been living with all these years. I knew something must have happened, but I could never conclude anything close to the truth."

"All these years I was bitter towards you for not having to live with my guilt, and I never thought you had a story greater than mine. As I am standing here now, I can't imagine how that night lingered for you." Abigail continued. "Claudia is a beautiful girl. What you must have gone through that year, I can't fully understand."

I squeezed her hand and gave her a warm smile.

"Let us move forward but I'm not sure what it will prove if we find things," I said.

"I think it will give me peace. If we find stuff, I'll know it was Jean and not Thomas."

"We may not find anything. We don't even know what we're looking for. If we find something, that could prove Thomas knew how sick Jean was and was covering for her."

"He is always protecting people."

"I haven't told you my concerns yet. Thanks for asking by the way. I sat and listened to you talk about your affair and the locket. You could have asked why I didn't think our saga was over."

Looking straight ahead, in a quiet tone, Abigail said, "This is not a competition."

"What if Thomas was setting up Jean."

Abigail was raising her cup to take a drink but stopped. She turned and stared at me. "Well now, that is the mystery writer in you coming out. Tell me your theory."

"I think Thomas was using her. I told you I found him in my house, and you may not know this, but he was in your house last week when you were gone. I'm pretty sure it was him now. Claudia was there delivering groceries. She forgot something, so she went back to the main kitchen, and when she came back to your cottage, some papers were moved. She chalked it up to the ghostly Gray Lady or being absentminded.

"I think his offers to go with Theo to the authorities were hollow sentiments. Thomas knew Theo would never allow him to jeopardize his career.

"I also don't think Jean could do all that stuff she said she did without Thomas knowing about it. The listening devices, accessing the state database and collecting souvenirs while living with Thomas. I think he knew how sick she was and used it to his advantage."

"But why? Why would he need Jean?" Abigail asked.

"I don't have that all figured out. I'd be curious to know what happened in that election he talked about. It was a tight race, and suddenly, it wasn't and he won by a large percentage.

"I believe he loves her, but I think he loves you more. After Joe died, you became available again. He was a ball of raw emotion. People compartmentalize feelings, and unless you deal with them, those feelings will always be there. Some people don't know how to let go.

"I think he set her up to save himself. She was the backup plan if he needed one."

Abigail was silent for what seemed an eternity.

"Anytime you want to say something would be fine with me," I said.

"Just a lot to absorb. We don't know anything for sure."

We stood there, listening to the river flowing and the birds singing after the rain.

"Why don't we see what we can find." I said, unsure if it was a question or statement of fact.

CHAPTER FORTY-SEVEN

We walked to the edge of the parking lot and slowly stepped onto the dirt.

"What do you think we should look for?" Abigail asked.

"Why do you think I have all the answers? I didn't even know we were going to do this until a few minutes ago."

"You know this stuff."

"If you think being a mystery writer has prepared me for this, you are wrong. Stop thinking I have the answer key."

"I think you have the answer key because you're smart and have common sense."

I stopped walking and looked at her.

"Don't get all modest again. I admire the work you do. Actually, I'm jealous of all the things you've accomplished."

"I don't know what to say. That's kind of you."

"Seriously, it's probably the Scotch talking, but I have confessed so much to you, why not everything? Your writing, your teaching writing to high school kids and doing writing workshops, and how you connect with everyone in town is something I admire. Sometimes I wish I could be in that circle of yours."

"You have been nothing but a bag full of surprises today."

"At least I'm not a bag full of bones." Abigail clasped her hand over her mouth. "Oops, too soon?"

"Mrs. Lincoln, the play was wonderful, and it's never too early for a joke. You waited twenty years and now two jokes in one day."

We stood there giggling like two schoolgirls. I grew quiet when my thoughts circled back to where we were standing, and Abigail seemed to feel the same, a look of unease on her face.

I burped up a little Scotch. "Well, let's rock and roll. I don't think too many people have been through the woods the last few days because of the rain. We should look where the ground is disturbed or something looks overly covered up."

"We should think about the layout of the woods twenty years ago. Yesterday, Jean talked about watching the bonfire. Do you think she went back to the same spot?"

"That's a good insight. See, you're smart too," I said.

"I never said I wasn't smart. I was just admitting that I thought you were smart."

"Wow, from funny girl to smart-ass in one afternoon. I think we could be friends after all."

"Great! I give you a compliment, and now you're hanging on me like some needy best friend," Abigail said, smiling.

"That night, the trees had been cut but not cleared, and the bonfire was at the end of the lot."

"About ten or twelve years ago, they expanded the lot. We may not have to go that deep. Let's start to the right near the riverbank."

We walked about ten feet from each other, not saying much. Light streamed through the tall branches, and the trees cast long shadows. We kicked up wet leaves and turned fallen branches.

Abigail stopped walking for a moment. "I think that night defined my life as much as it did Jean's."

I didn't respond, unsure if she was speaking to me or thinking out loud. I had my own experiences that night, but I could not imagine what she, Teddy, and Thomas had lived with all this time. That night, they drew strength from friendship, fear, and the will to do what they thought was right.

Regardless of their reasons, they still had to face the knowledge that they erased someone from the earth. The three of them didn't kill Teddy's father, but they let his life and death disappear.

Abigail started walking again. "So much of my life I was a puppet to do what my parents thought was proper and what a girl was supposed to be. After that night, I knew I had the strength to do whatever I wanted. After a few months passed, I had the guts to face my parents and confront my dad about their marriage."

I paused to let Abigail say what it seemed she had been thinking over the past day and, really, twenty years.

She continued in a peaceful tone. "Joe never knew what happened. He thought going away to college changed me into someone he wanted to marry. Little did he know, it was one night in this town that changed me."

"You always had that strength in you. That night was a catalyst. The same as Jean. Maybe she had always had issues. Something can make or break you. It's what you do with it that makes the person."

"I'm not sure I agree with that. That night changed me. I found something I don't think was there before. I think people can change, not just grow up."

"Maybe you have been living with guilt guiding you," I said.

Abigail stopped walking. "I haven't thought about it like that. I always hoped I lived right regardless of that night. When I moved up on the hill, I purposely took a cottage with a view of town instead of the river. After all this time, I still can't look at this place and not think about it. I was . . ."

She walked over to a small thorny bush. Next to the bush was a log that looked like it had been there years. "What about this? Come take a look. You can see the river and the edge of the boat ramp."

"You might be on to something here. Yup, you are smart," I said.

"What happened to being civil?" she said, trying to stifle a laugh.

"My buzz is wearing off." I smiled and showed her my empty cup. I put it on the ground and grabbed a big stick and snapped it in half. "Take this stick, and let's clear some leaves."

We spent a few minutes clearing the bush and came up empty.

Abigail put her hands on her hips. "This was a long shot. I'm not sure this was a good idea." She sat down on a fallen tree and put her foot up on a large rock.

"I disagree. I think we're on to something here. What if we move this branch and roll that rock aside? Do you see how it's lying there? Does it look like it has extra leaves around it to you?"

I squatted and used my hands while Abigail pushed with her leg, and the rock easily moved. She lifted the log that was stuck in the mud. The ground was different near the area where the rock had been resting. We picked up our sticks again, brushed a thin layer of dirt away, and found what we were looking for.

We got up and just stood there. A light breeze blew in off the river, and light was still coming through the trees. I wasn't sure I wanted to touch it, but we couldn't turn away. I'm sure Abigail felt the same. We moved closer together.

"Before more gunshots," she said.

I realized it wasn't a toast, but a little prayer. She took a gulp, then gave me her cup, and I finished the Scotch.

"And ending this saga," we said together.

CHAPTER FORTY-EIGHT

I knelt down, and Abigail sat on the log. We brushed away some dirt. A man's watch lay there, and a tin box wrapped in a plastic bag was underneath it. I pulled on the box, and it came away easily from the dirt. Roughly the size of a sheet of paper and probably four inches thick, the box had some age to it but was still sturdy, but the plastic bag was from the local grocery store.

I removed the box from the bag, and we stood.

Abigail mumbled something, perhaps saying a different prayer. I held the box as she lifted the cover off. We didn't move. We both were most likely in shock that our wild guess was right.

Abigail brought her hand to her mouth. "Oh my god, oh my god, oh my god."

A small porcelain statue, a ring, a dollar bill, and other trinkets lay in the box. I put the watch inside, and Abigail took it from my hands.

I removed a large manila envelope from the hiding place. Inside it, "Sheriff Williams" was scrawled across a white business envelope with photographs in it.

Photographs I probably did not want to see.

I reached into the manila envelope to pull out the other documents, but Abigail nudged me.

"Be quiet. Don't move. Look up," she whispered.

Someone was at the edge of the woods, trying to back out. The person didn't seem to be spying on us but trying to hide from us. Abigail handed the box back to me.

She took a step and directed her voice to the shadow. "It's too late, Tommy. We have it all here. You might as well tell us."

"I'm here walking. Clearing my head. Just like you ladies." Thomas stepped toward us.

"Save yourself the embarrassment and the dance. We have the box," Abigail said.

"What are you talking about?"

"Give us more credit than that. You came here for this." Abigail stepped closer to him, clearly having no intention of letting him go.

He slowly made his way closer, wearing the same clothes he'd worn this morning, which meant the same clothes as yesterday, but this time, there was a bulge around his right ankle.

"How did you know?" Thomas asked.

"It was a guess. Are you going to tell us what's going on?" I said, startling Abigail.

She seemed to have realized this was bigger than just her and Thomas.

"Give me the box," he said in a flat voice.

"You know we can't do that," Abigail said. "Now tell us what's going on."

Thomas stayed silent and unmoving. He didn't seem to be calculating his next move; it seemed, instead, that everything was crashing in on him. He'd lost everything—Jean, his job, and now Abigail. It was the moment of fight-or-flight.

I shifted my feet, and Abigail reached over and held me still, taking control of the situation. She had lost Tommy, a friend of years past, her lover of today, and a connection to Joe.

The look she gave him said she was not about to let him fool her. "Now tell us what's going on."

Thomas's shoulders sank. "I didn't know what was going on. You have to believe me."

Abigail glared at him. "Don't give us that crap. This is not the first time you've been here."

"You have to believe me. I didn't know what Jean was doing. I found out about the box a few weeks ago."

"Why should we believe you? What is all this stuff?"

"I'm not sure. I think Jean has been nicking stuff from people she felt threatened by. She was always jealous. You heard her. She wanted to be included. I tried to give her everything. Nothing ever seemed to satisfy her. She's not like you, Abigail. When she thinks she's exposed or in danger, she falls apart. She doesn't stand up like you." Thomas paused. He took a few steps towards us and stopped when he was about ten feet away. "I think she realized I was in love with you. That I need you. Especially now." He held his hand out to Abigail.

"Don't come near me," she said, her voice faltering a bit.

Thomas took another step closer.

"Stay where you are," she demanded.

Something switched in his eyes. I wasn't sure if Abigail saw it. Tears rolled down her cheeks.

"Abby, come here," he said, still reaching out to her.

She shook her head. "No."

"Then give me the box. Let Jean have some dignity. Let her recover peacefully. She is getting the help she needs. You don't need to make it harder for her."

Abigail didn't say anything, and that seemed to be answer enough for him. He took another step closer. "Do what's right for Jean, for me, for us. We have something special."

I took a step towards him. "This is not about Jean."

They appeared to have forgotten I was there.

Thomas's face turned bloodred. "Stay out of this, EG. It's got nothing to do with you. Abigail is going to give me the box, and everything's going to be fine." He looked at her intently and took another step forward.

I needed to snap Abigail back to reality in case she was wavering. I didn't have anything to lose with my wild guess. Well, I did have something to lose—my life—but I had to continue. "I saw the envelope with the former sheriff's name on it and the photographs."

Thomas turned his attention to me. "I don't understand what you mean."

"We aren't going back in this circle again. You know exactly what I mean. You know what's in this box. I'm assuming whatever's in the folder has to do with how you won the election."

"Give me the box."

"That won't do you any good," I said and stepped between them.

"Give me the box."

"We know what's in the box and will tell the authorities. The right authorities."

"No one will believe you."

"You're wrong. We have nothing to gain for telling this story. You have everything to lose."

"Give me the damn box!"

Thomas shifted and started to reach down, as if he was going for his gun. I kicked some leaves to distract him, but I had no further plan than that. As he bent down, Abigail kicked him on the side of the head. It wasn't a hard kick but made him lose his balance. He toppled sideways, still reaching for his gun.

A loud pop exploded out of nowhere, and Thomas's hands flew to his left eye. Relief and fear flooded through me at the same time.

He let out a yelp. "What the hell was that?"

"It was me." Jorge approached slowly from the right, carrying a gun in one hand and a phone in the other.

Thomas had clearly been shot. His eye was getting puffy immediately, but there wasn't much blood.

"You shot him!" declared Abigail.

"No, this dumb bastard only got me . . ." Thomas's hand was now pressed to his face.

"Don't do it!" Jorge demanded. "This gun won't stop you, but this phone will. Deputy Baumann will be here in a minute with backup from Kirkasaw County. You can reach for your gun and blow us all away, or you can have some real guts and walk out of here like a man."

Thomas kneeled. "I don't have to listen to you. You can take your bb gun and jump in the river. I'm going—"

"You're not doing anything. Lie down and spread your arms and legs." Deputy Baumann approached from the walking path with his gun drawn. Several squad cars were pulling into the parking lot.

Thomas hung his head and raised his hands, his shoulders slumping. He rolled onto his side and then onto his stomach and did as he was told.

Abigail and I stepped back over the log we had unearthed. Jorge lowered his bb gun and held it out to Deputy Baumann.

The deputy still held his gun on Thomas, so he shook his head. "Put it on the tree stump, step back five feet, and don't leave the area." He waved in the Kirkasaw County sheriff and his two deputies.

When the deputies had taken control of Thomas, Deputy Baumann took the box from me. He gestured with a nod towards the parking lot. "The three of you should wait in the parking lot so someone can take your statements."

We didn't say anything, just walked out in silence, and waited on a bench facing the river—the same bench Abigail and Mayor Carl had sat on the day before. I sat in the middle between Abigail and Jorge, and we stared at the river, not turning to watch as they escorted Thomas to a squad car.

Abigail put her hands together between her knees, shaking slightly despite the warm temperature. Jorge hunched forward with his elbows on his knees. It was a position that showed his adrenaline was dropping but he was ready to spring to action if needed.

I crossed my arms across my chest, looking from one to the other. "A bb gun? What did you expect to do with a bb gun? Why does a grown man even have a bb gun?"

Abigail leaned forward and smirked at us.

Jorge sat back, relaxed, and rested his arm on the bench behind my back. "I don't know why you're complaining. It did the trick. It stopped him."

"It wasn't going to keep him down."

"I know that! It's all I had. I didn't even know if I needed something. It can easily be mistaken for a real gun, and I was hoping the sight of it would be enough."

Abigail gestured towards him. "How did you know we needed help and where we were?"

"I told him," I said.

Abigail looked shocked.

"Don't get all uptight now. Obviously, we needed some help. When I went to say goodbye to him earlier, I mentioned we would be taking a walk to the river, and *hopefully*, we would be back soon."

"Ladies, I don't know what and why everything has been going on, but I know when something is not right. After you left, I was still working in the garage and noticed Thomas driving his personal car past the house. Twice. Slowly. I didn't like it. I figured it couldn't hurt if I wandered down here. I bought the bb gun earlier this spring to take care of the crow situation in our neighborhood. I tried all other means of getting rid of those birds, but I had enough of them. I wasn't going to live with them forever and let them destroy my garden and shit on my car.

"I called my friend, Wyatt—Deputy Baumann—and told him what I had observed. He kept me on the phone in case something else happened. He couldn't go into details but said they'd had suspicions about Thomas and were getting ready to issue a warrant for his arrest."

"Arrest him for what? Wasn't it Jean?" Tears welled up in Abigail's eyes. After everything, she clearly still didn't want Thomas to be guilty.

Jorge shrugged his shoulders. "Wyatt wouldn't give me the details."

I motioned towards the box. "If I had to guess, it was election fraud or blackmail. I only had a glimpse of the envelope in the box, but it doesn't look good for Thomas. I don't think he can deny his involvement or push it all off on Jean."

One squad car left with Thomas, and two

deputies came over to take our statements. While Jorge and Abigail gave theirs, I watched the river.

My mind went back to that night from over twenty years ago. Seeing Teddy at the bonfire, our kiss on the log. I stopped the memory train when I got to the point of stoning the scarecrow that turned out to be Teddy's dad.

A wave of nausea hit me. What I'd done to another human being stung me. Maybe he was already dead, but did that excuse what I did?

Jorge came back first, and I went to speak to the deputy. When I was done, I watched Abigail standing on the riverbank. Crying.

I wasn't sure what she was mourning most. Was it the emotions of hiding Teddy's dad in this river and revealing that secret now, or losing Thomas, who was another connection to Joe? Maybe it was tears of relief that it was all over.

CHAPTER FORTY-NINE

Deputy Baumann offered us a ride, but we declined. Jorge and I waited for Abigail, and the three of us walked back to my house in silence.

When we got there, I said, "Abigail, I'm not sure if you want to be alone or not, but you are welcome to come in and stay for a bit or overnight."

"I appreciate the offer, but I'm good." She stepped back, hesitating, and then stepped forward. "Actually, I would love the company."

"Jorge, please come in too. I think I owe you something for all the wine, Scotch, and heroics. The least I could do is fix you dinner."

Jorge nodded and opened the door for us.

"I think I'm done drinking for the day. My head is spinning enough. How about some tea?" Abigail said.

Jorge got the three of us hot water, and we sat at the table in silence for a moment.

I sat up straighter. "Enough silence and reflection. Let's raise our glass and have a toast to—"

"Wait, toasting with water is bad luck," Abigail said.

Jorge laughed. "I think you ladies are past the bad luck. How many more times are you going to see the police this weekend?"

Abigail raised her mug. "You're right, go ahead, EG."

Jorge and I raised ours, and I said, "Here's to being civil. No more gunshots. And ending this saga!"

"Two out of three isn't bad," Abigail said. "We got civil, and we ended this saga!"

"I think we're three for three. A bb gun? Does that really count for a gunshot?" I said.

"You know, Jorge, I bet EG could get you a scarecrow for your yard. Why resort to violence?" She looked at me and smiled.

We laughed. And laughed. We laughed until we cried for the next several hours. Abigail and I recounted the entire story for Jorge, figuring at this point he was part of the group whether he liked it or not. We laughed at parts that hadn't been funny twenty-four hours ago. We cried when the laughing stopped. It was the best healing session someone could have hoped for in a situation like this.

Claudia came home later that evening. We told her what had happened, and after a few more laughs, tears, and hugs, we declared it was time for bed.

Claudia went upstairs. Abigail took the sofa in the living room, I went to my room, and Jorge was on the porch.

I yelled one last time for all in the house to hear. "A bb gun?"

Jorge's booming voice came from the porch. "Someone in this town had to get rid of those damn crows!"

CROW

-According to EG
As stated earlier by Merriam-Webster Dictionary

-According to Claudia
An annoying bird
To cry for attention

-According to Sherrie
~~Bitch~~, I mean whatever EG and Claudia said.

-According to TJ Makkai
Everyone in the book

BOOK CLUB DISCUSSION QUESTIONS

Could you help bury a body and walk away? Tommy did it to help his friend and Abigail did it to help her family. Is there a reason that would make you do it?

Does that answer change in twenty years?

Does the integrity/character of the dead person affect your answer?

Claudia kept Jackson around for rent money. Did you ever stay with someone (friend or significant other) for the wrong reason.

Did you notice the dead man never had a name? Did you notice Claudia never said Aunt EG or my Aunt? It was always just EG.

Why do you think EG stayed in River Bend? Was she hoping for Teddy to return?

Do you name your car?

Claudia kept her secret to herself (knowing she was adopted) Could you keep that to yourself?

If a movie was made from the book who do you see playing each character.

ACKNOWLEDGMENTS

If you are family or friend you may find your name or some variation of your name in the book. Large or small character, hero or villain, endearing or annoying just know there is no correlation to you and to the character. I needed a name and I choose from what I know and what means something to me. Just know the name was used out of love and familiarity.

Thank you to my editor Starr Waddell. The story and mistakes are mine but Starr helped smooth out the rough edges.

Thank you to Eva Sippel. My biggest cheerleader when there was not much on the pages to cheer about and for the nonstop encouragement.

Thank you to beta readers for the feedback- Alexis, Molly, Sara, Eva, Kelly, Nick.

A special shout out to Mel Renfrow for the detailed feedback. Just know you missed your calling—the publishing world needs you. And to Molly Stretten, a big thank you for answering all my crazy questions and being my sounding board.

Most of all thank you to my husband and son for their love and support.

ABOUT THE AUTHOR

TJ grew up in Wisconsin and graduated from the University of Wisconsin-Stout. Working with national hotel brands took her zig-zagging across the country before ending up in Kansas where she lives with her husband, son and dog Reba.